THE BEST SHORT STORIES EVER

Terry O'Brien is a connoisseur of literature. An academician turned full-time writer, he believes in John Donne's dictum: 'We'll build in sonnets pretty rooms'. His passion is to showcase the gems of timeless classics. He is a man of many parts—language expert, motivational trainer and a versatile bestselling author.

THE BEST SHORT STORIES EVER

EDITED BY
TERRY O'BRIEN

Published by
Rupa Publications India Pvt. Ltd 2022
7/16, Ansari Road, Daryaganj
New Delhi 110002

Sales centres:
Allahabad Bengaluru Chennai
Hyderabad Jaipur Kathmandu
Kolkata Mumbai

Introduction and selection copyright © Terry O'Brien, 2022

Edition copyright © Rupa Publications India Pvt. Ltd 2022

First published by Westland Publications Private Limited in 2021

All rights reserved.
No part of this publication may be reproduced, transmitted,
or stored in a retrieval system, in any form or by any means,
electronic, mechanical, photocopying, recording or otherwise,
without the prior permission of the publisher.

Illustrations by Pratik Bhide

Book design by New Media Line Creations, New Delhi 110 062

ISBN: 978-93-5520-415-8

Third impression 2022

10 9 8 7 6 5 4 3

The moral right of the author has been asserted.

Printed in India

This book is sold subject to the condition that it shall not,
by way of trade or otherwise, be lent, resold, hired out, or otherwise
circulated, without the publisher's prior consent, in any form of binding or
cover other than that in which it is published.

CONTENTS

Introduction   1

1. *Lie Thee Down, Oddity*—T.F. Powys   3
2. *The Rain Horse*—Ted Hughes   13
3. *The Story Of An Hour*—Kate Chopin   24
4. *The Lady Or The Tiger?*—Frank R. Stockton   28
5. *A Tell-Tale Heart*—Edgar Allan Poe   36
6. *Luck*—Mark Twain   42
7. *The Model Millionaire*—Oscar Wilde   47
8. *The Secret Life Of Walter Mitty*—James Thurber   53
9. *The Boarded Window*—Ambrose Bierce   59
10. *The Five Boons Of Life*—Mark Twain   65
11. *The Evil Clergyman*—H.P. Lovecraft   68
12. *The Necklace*—Guy De Maupassant   73
13. *The Fly*—Katherine Mansfield   82
14. *An Occurrence At Owl Creek Bridge*—Ambrose Bierce   89
15. *After Twenty Years*—O. Henry   100
16. *My Financial Career*—Stephen Leacock   104
17. *The Dancing Partner*—Jerome K. Jerome   108
18. *The Gift Of The Magi*—O. Henry   116
19. *The Open Window*—Saki   122
20. *Indian Camp*—Ernest Hemingway   126
21. *A Coward*—Guy de Maupassant   131
22. *Old Man At The Bridge*—Ernest Hemingway   140
23. *Haunted House*—Virginia Woolf   143
24. *The Last Leaf*—O. Henry   146

25.	*The Confession*—Guy de Maupassant	153
26.	*The Cactus*—O. Henry	159
27.	*A School Story*—M.R. James	163
28.	*My Own True Ghost Story*—Rudyard Kipling	171
29.	*The Lottery Ticket*—Anton Chekhov	180
30.	*Salvatore*—Somerset Maugham	186
31.	*The Dream*—O. Henry	191
32.	*A Very Old Man With Enormous Wings* – Gabriel García Márquez	195
33.	*The Bet*—Anton Chekhov	203
34.	*A Retrieved Reformation*—O. Henry	211
35.	*Quality*—John Galsworthy	220
36.	*A Cup Of Tea*—Katherine Mansfield	228
37.	*A Chameleon*—Anton Chekhov	237
38.	*The Outsider*—H.P. Lovecraft	241
39.	*The Picture In The House*—H.P. Lovecraft	249
40.	*The Hand*—Guy De Maupassant	258
41.	*Monday Or Tuesday*—Virginia Woolf	265

INTRODUCTION

Some say a novel is a 'great still book'. This is not true, especially for great novels. A short story is a 'moment's monument,' instead ... a snapshot of life. It leaves the reader desirous for more, at the end! Great art kindles the imagination, it does not satisfy it, and neither does a short story. Lorrie Moore subtly compares a short story and a novel, 'A short story is a love affair; a novel is a marriage. A short story is a photo; a novel is a film.'

The poetics of a short story is to 'carve on an inch of ivory'. Irving Washington's *Rip Van Winkle* is the story of a farmer who goes up to the Catskill Mountains where a group of dwarfs playing ninepins, offer him a drink, and he promptly falls asleep.

When he awakened, he is an old man with a long white beard, and the dwarfs are nowhere in sight. His dog had gone, and his gun had turned rusty. In fact, he had slept for twenty years on the Catskill Mountains and returned home to find his little daughter, now a mother, and his grandchild playing in the village. Had this story been a novel, several events that happened within the span of these twenty years would have been described. Thus a short story is short, not only in length but in content.

The narrative structure of a short story could be three-fold: STORY or 'life in time'; PLOT or 'life in values' and RHYTHM or 'repetition with variations'.

A short story has two basic canons: singleness of aim and singleness of effect. Unlike a novel, it does not have many layers in its narrative. If brevity is the soul of wit, so is it of a short story.

Time is the broad canvas on which a narrative is created. Time hangs from clocks and calendars, yet each individual has their own personal time. A narrative can have 'linear time' or 'progressive time', wherein one is born, grows up, ages and dies.

There is 'cyclic time': what happened in Crete 5000 years ago happened yesterday in Texas. Then there may be 'existential time'. Existentialism is a philosophy that believes that existence comes before essence. One may exist yet not live! There also is 'mind time' or the stream of consciousness: 'Life is not a series of gig lamps symmetrically arranged.' It is indeed 'a semi-transparent halo' from the beginning of our consciousness to the end. Time is broken into atoms in the narrative.

Realism could also be the core of a short story. This deals with a slice of life. There could also be an element of symbolism, which is a special mode of experience. In fact, it is 'the actualising of inarticulate experience is an apprehensible form'.

Finally, language is the main tool. The rhetoric of fiction is best displayed in a good short story. In Beckett's novel *Malone Dies*, the narrator retrogresses in time: he walks and runs and finally crawls. The narrator writes his story with a quarter-inch long pencil, and ironically, the novel ends midsentence when his pencil is finished! Indeed, it is a verbal world.

It exemplifies the nuances of fiction in many subtle ways. A short story has a single mood; 'every sentence must build towards it', wrote Edgar Allan Poe.

This collection of *Best Short Stories Ever* comprises a selection of stories with a variety of all the above characteristics. Don't only enjoy the stories; ponder over them. This collection will provide the reader with the joys of reading. These stories will make you laugh, cry, smile or sulk and indeed make you read each short story again and again.

A classic cannot be re-written; it can be re-read. Indeed a short story is the most interesting form of storytelling. When you read a short story, you become a little more aware of the world around you.

This anthology is now for you to cherish, read and re-read.

HAPPY READING!
Terry O'Brien

1

LIE THEE DOWN, ODDITY

T.F. POWYS

Though the sun shone with summer heat, the damp August warmth giving the rather faded countryside a new glow in her cheeks—for there had been a good all-night's rain—yet Mr Cronch wore his black felt hat, of the cut that used to be worn by evangelical clergymen in the last century.

The Honourable George Bullman, who employed Mr Cronch as head-gardener, had spoken to him some years before about this hat of his, which was the only thing about Mr Cronch that gave a hint of peculiarities. 'Your Methodist hat will be the ruin of you one day, Cronch,' Mr Bullman had observed, while discussing with his gardener the making of a new lawn.

Mr Cronch was mowing the lawn; he had bid the under-gardener work elsewhere. To please and humour Cronch, Mr Bullman used no motor-mowing machine. Cronch did not like them. But the under-gardener had hardly looked at the old-fashioned mower before he complained that such labour was beyond his power. To push all day such an awkward instrument 'that might', the young man said, 'have been used by Adam' was out of the question for anyone who understood the arts and fancies of oil-driven machinery. Mr Cronch did the work himself. 'One has, you know, to pay for one's oddities,' he told his wife Jane.

At Green Gate House the grounds were always in the best order; there was never a weed in the kitchen-garden or a plantain on the lawn, but in one place, bordering the lawn, there were railings, and over these railings there was the heath. A different world, that looked with contempt upon the soft pelt of a smooth lawn, which was indeed like the skin of a tamed beast that did nothing else but lie and bask in the sun while its sleek hide was being curry-combed by Mr Cronch.

The heath was a different matter from the garden. All was nature there, and she is a wild, fierce, untutored mother. Flowers and weeds, unnoticed, lived there, fighting the battle of their lives, careless of man, but living as they were commanded to live at the first moving of the waters. The raven and the falcon nested in the tall trees beyond a desolate swamp, and only a solitary heath-cutter might sometimes be seen with his load, taking a long track towards the waste land. Who, indeed, would view such barrenness when there was the Honourable George Bullman's garden to admire?

Mr Bullman could afford a good gardener. The head-gardener's cottage, where Mr Cronch and his wife lived, had every comfort of a modern well-built house. No servant of Mr Bullman had anything to complain of. No one would leave such service, could they avoid doing so.

Over the heath, even the winds blew differently from the gentle garden ones. Out there the blasts could roar and bellow, wrench the boughs from the trees, and rush along madly, but in the summer-time garden all winds were soft.

Mr Cronch stopped. He took the box from the mower and tipped the cut grass into the wheelbarrow. The wheelbarrow was full of sweet-smelling grass. Mr Cronch then whistled softly, and Robert, the under-gardener, left his weeding and trundled the barrow to the cucumber-frames. He returned with the empty barrow at a slow, even pace—the gait of a well-paid gardener, as learned from Mr Cronch.

Mr Cronch began to mow again. He came near to the railings beyond which was the heath. Then he stopped. He took off his hat and looked into it. He looked at the lawn. Nowhere in the world, out of England, could any lawn have been smoother or more green. There was not the smallest clover leaf there that was not consecrated to the fine taste of a proper gentleman, and ready to be pressed by the elegant foot of a real lady. The smooth banks, the beds of flowers near by, might have been a modern picture in colours; they were so unlike nature. There was nothing rude or untidy there, and every cabbage in the kitchen-garden wore a coronet.

Mr Cronch should, after a little rest, have continued to push the machine, but instead of doing so, he looked over the railings at the heath.

Mr Cronch had not changed, as the garden was changed when it became the heath. He was the same Mr Cronch who had, at one o'clock, cut the finest cucumber in the garden for Mr Bullman's lunch. He waited for another moment or two and then softly put on his hat. After doing so, he spoke aloud. 'Lie thee down, Oddity!' said Mr Cronch. Then Mr Cronch shook his head, as much as to say that if the Oddity would not lie down, it was no fault of his. For such a being it was impossible to control. Had the Oddity lain down, then Mr Cronch would have gone on with his work, as a wise man should, who earns four pounds a week, with a good house and garden, and with leave to sell whatever he likes from his master's.

But Mr Cronch did not start work again. It was no good; whatever happened to him the Oddity must be obeyed. The Oddity knew best. Mr Cronch left the machine where it was, near to the railings. He walked with the same slow gardener's walk—that showed, as much as any walk could, a hatred of all untidiness and disorder—and came to the potting-shed. Then he put on his coat.

The hour was three in the afternoon. Mr Cronch learned that from his watch. Then he listened. What he expected, happened; the church clock, that was just across the way, struck three. Mr Cronch's watch was always right. It was no use mentioning that to the Oddity. He would not lie down the more because Mr Cronch's gold watch—a gift of Mr Bullman's—went with the church time.

Mr Cronch shut the potting-shed door and went home. He remarked, when he saw his wife, as though he said nothing of particular interest, that he had given up work at Green Gate House. He told her to begin to pack, for they were leaving the gardener's cottage as soon as possible.

Jane thought him mad, and when the under-gardener, Robert, heard of it, he blamed the mowing-machine. 'To have to push anything like that would drive any man away,' he said to Mr Bullman.

The Honourable George Bullman was anxious that Mr Cronch should still remain in the gardener's cottage. He would give him a pension, he said, for he did not want to lose so good a neighbour, whose advice he valued so highly. Mr Bullman, of course, blamed the hat for the trouble. Jane wished to stay, but as the Oddity would not lie down, Mr Cronch said they must go.

About two miles away from Green Gate House, upon the heath, there was a wretched cottage that had once been inhabited by a rabbit-catcher. Mr Cronch chose this hut as a residence. About an acre of land went with it. Mr Cronch repaired the cottage with his own hands, and put up new railings round the garden. In order to do this neatly he spent most of the money he had saved in service. Then he began to reclaim the garden that was fallen out of cultivation and had become heath again.

The wild spirit of the wasteland struggled against him. But here the poverty of the soil met its match. Nature is no respecter of persons; she gives alike to the good and to the evil. The potato-blight will ruin a good man's crop as well as a naughty one's. The heath was not a curry-combed creature, tamed with milk and wine. It was a savage animal, now friendly and kind, now cruel and vindictive, then mild. One day smiling like a pretty maid, and the next biting at you with ugly-shaped teeth.

There was no pleasant shelter there, no glass-houses. No high walls, no trimmed box-hedges. The winds of Heaven had free passage, a snake could roam at large and find only its natural enemies to attack it. The wild birds had rest. Mr Cronch bowed his head and laboured. It needed something stronger than nature to cast him down. With the Oddity asleep, he could go on with his work. There was no need for him to rest, he was an obedient servant. He required no telling what to do in the way of work: even the Honourable George Bullman had put himself under Mr Cronch's guidance. While he had hands and tools he could compel the most sour-tempered soil to serve his needs. His broad shoulders were ever bent over the ground as he turned the earthen clod.

It was not long before Mr Cronch compelled the heath to pay him tribute, and soon a pleasant cottage and a large well-cultivated garden arose in the wilderness. There were many who respected Mr Cronch for leaving so much good at Mr Bullman's to do battle with nature upon the heath, but others said he only left his master out of pride. Mr Cronch smiled when he heard that. 'Here was a fine matter, indeed,' he thought, 'that a mortal man should have pride—a nice folly to call a leaf proud that is driven willy-nilly before a November gale. A fine pride that leaf must have when, at the last, it is buried in a dunghill!'

But if Mr Cronch was proud, as some thought, it was only because he had the knowledge that, within him, something slept ...

Mr Cronch was resting contentedly one Sunday, reading a country paper. Even that morning he had been busy in his garden, and was glad now to rest while Jane prepared the dinner. Mr Cronch sat there, a simple, working-class man, respectable—in years too—wearing spectacles, and reading his paper. He found something to read that interested him, for he read the same paragraph three times.

This was a police case. An old woman, who was employed on Saturdays by the Stonebridge town clerk to scrub his floors, had found upon the dining-room floor a blank cheque. This cheque she had filled in herself, and because she was a simple woman, without pride, she had written the town clerk's name instead of her own.

For thirty years Mrs Tibby had kept herself and her husband John—who spent all his time in leaning over the town bridge to watch the water flow under—and now his one wish was to go to London to see the King. His wife wished to give him this treat. 'E do need a holiday,' she said.

When a charwoman picks up money she has a right to it. Mrs Tibby thought the cheque money. Money, after a card-party, which there had been at the clerk's, is often left on the floor for the sweeper—that is the custom of the country.

Mrs Tibby was not greedy; she only wrote 'four pounds' upon the cheque. She supposed that sum to be enough to take her husband to see the King. If the clerk were annoyed, she knew she could work the money out in scrubbing the floors.

When she was taken up, she could get no bail, so she went to prison.

Mr Cronch carefully folded the paper.

The month was November. Over the heath, dark sweeping clouds, like great besoms, were driving. The two ravens, who nested in the high fir tree, enjoyed the wind. The mist from the sea brought memories to their minds; they remembered stories told of men hanged in chains on Blacknoll Mound, whose bones could be pecked clean. The ravens flew off and looked for a lamb to kill.

Mr Cronch laid the paper on the table, beside a smoking dish of fried beef and onions—there were other vegetables to come— and a rice pudding.

Mr Cronch rose slowly and sniffed.

But the Oddity would not lie down. So Mr Cronch told his wife he was going out. The distance to Stonebridge was twelve miles. Mr Cronch put on his overcoat; he went to a drawer and took out twenty-five pounds. He put on his large black hat, opened the cottage-door and went out—the rain greeted him with a lively shower of water-drops. Jane let him go. She supposed him to be in one of his mad fits, that the Giant Despair in the Pilgrim's Progress used to have.

Mr Cronch walked along with his usual slow, steady step—the gait of a careful gardener. When he reached Stonebridge he was not admitted into the jail, and so he took a lodging for the night.

In the morning he visited Mrs Tibby. 'I wish to be your bail,' he said cheerfully.

Mrs Tibby was in a maze. She did not know what she had done wrong. She was happy where she was, she was allowed to gossip with the prison charwoman, who was an old friend of hers. She begged Mr Crouch, if he wished to be good to her, to allow her to stay with her friend, and to take her husband to London to see the King. Mrs Tibby liked the prison. 'Everyone is so kind,' she said, 'and when I complained to the doctor about my headaches, he ordered me gin. I have never been so happy before.'

Mr Cronch found Mr Tibby smoking his pipe and leaning over the town bridge. He told him he was going to take him to see the King, and Mr Tibby agreed to go, but first he knocked out his pipe on the stone coping of the bridge.

When they reached London, the King was out of town. He was soon to return, and Mr Tibby spent the time happily, smoking his pipe and leaning over Waterloo Bridge, although the fog was so dense he could not see the river. When the King came, Mr Cronch took Mr Tibby into the crowd to see the King go by. Mr Tibby sang 'God Save the King', and shouted 'Hurrah!' The King bowed.

'Now I shall die happy,' said Mr Tibby, 'but how shall I get home?'

Mr Cronch paid his fare to Stonebridge, and saw him off at the station.

The weather had improved; a brisk wind from the south-west had driven off the fog. Mr Cronch, to please himself, walked into the city. He had fifteen pounds in his pocket, and he looked into the shop windows. He still wore his large black hat and the beggars avoided him. They thought him a Jewish money-lender, or else a Baptist minister. Beggars are shrewd judges of character. They have to decide quickly. Their income depends upon it. To beg from the wrong man means loss of time—perhaps prison.

Mr Cronch went down a narrow street where some offices were. One of these was the office of a money-lender. A gentleman, who looked worn out by sickness and trouble, came out of the door. A woman, his wife, who carried a baby in her arms, waited for him in the street. The gentleman shook his head. Evidently the security that he had to offer was not good enough.

Then there arose a little conversation between them.

'I could go to mother's,' the woman said.

'If I had money, I could go with you,' the man observed, 'the change would do me good, and I might get work in Bristol'.

'Baby will be easier to manage in a few months,' the woman said. 'Mother will not mind taking us, but you will have to stay here.'

'I can't let you go,' said the man.

He made a curious sound in his throat.

Mr Cronch stood nearby on the pavement. Who would have noticed Mr Cronch? The couple paid no need to him. But presently they turned to where he stood, for Mr Cronch spoke.

'Lie thee down, Oddity!' he said aloud.

The gentleman smiled, he could do nothing else. The baby held out her arms to Mr Cronch; she wanted his hat. Mr Cronch took two five-pound notes from his wallet and gave them to the woman. Then he walked away. For his own pleasure, he walked out of the city into the poor parts of the town. He walked along slowly and looked at the vegetables in the greengrocers' shops. He wondered how people could buy such old stuff. If he offered anything like that at the Weyminster market, he would never find a purchaser. He remembered the lordly freedom of the wild heath. There, nature might be cruel, but life and death joined hands in the dance. The sun could shine, and when darkness came it was the darkness of God. The town was different.

Mr Cronch went down a dingy court. Clothes were hung from house to house, and barefooted children played in the gutter. The air was heavy with human odours and factory stench. Then Mr Cronch came upon something worse than misery.

A man sat leaning against a wall, with half his face eaten away. His eyes were gone; he cried out to everyone whose footstep he heard, to lead him to the river. When Mr Cronch came by, he cried out the more. Mr Cronch stopped.

'Lie thee down, Oddity!' he said angrily.

Lie Thee Down, Oddity

'Lead me to the river,' the man begged.

'Come,' said Mr Cronch, and led the man to the river. A policeman, who knew the man's wish, followed them. At the brink of the river the man said, 'I am afraid; only give me one little push, and I shall die.'

'Certainly,' said Mr Cronch, and pushed him into the river. The man sank like a stone.

The police officer came up to demand Mr Cronch's name and address; he had made a note of what had happened.

'You will appear at court, charged with murder,' he said. 'But now you may go!'

Mr Cronch walked out of the great city. He had enough money to take him home by train, but he liked walking. As he went along he decided to plant a part of his garden with spinach. He had seen a good deal of this green stuff in the London shops, and he thought he could sell it at home.

He walked ten miles out of town, and then took a lodging for the night. Since the Oddity had risen last, Mr Cronch had behaved just as a sober gardener would when out for a holiday.

When he came to an allotment he would look into it to see what was grown. He found the ground good. But he believed that more glass might be used, and the city dung he thought too heating for the soil. He was especially interested in the window-flowers that he saw, but wondered that no hyacinths were seen, the bulbs having been all planted too late to bloom at that season.

Starting his walk again the next morning, Mr Cronch came upon a large crowd watching a high factory chimney. This immense chimney, as high as the clouds and weighing many hundreds of tons, was being brought down. The workmen were busy at its base, and the crowd watched from a safe distance.

All was ready for the fall; the masons and engineers left the chimney. But one of the men remained to give the final stroke that would cause the huge structure to sway and fall. This mason completed his task, and began to walk to safety. When he was a few yards off the chimney, he trod upon a wet plank hidden in the mud, and fell heavily. The spectators expected him to jump up and run off. But he did not do so. An official held his watch in his hand, 'One, two, three,' he counted. When he reached sixty seconds the chimney would fall.

Its direction was known. It would fall directly upon the man. He tried to rise, but his leg was broken. He tried to crawl, but the pain prevented him. He raised himself up, and looked at the huge mass above him; he knew what was coming. None of the onlookers moved. It was too late to save the man; to go to him would mean certain death.

The chimney began to totter, to rock.

Then Mr Cronch said softly, 'Lie thee down, Oddity!' but the Oddity would not listen to him. Mr Cronch spoke in so low a tone that perhaps the Oddity never even heard what he said.

Mr Cronch walked with his slow gardener's step to the man.

'What are you afraid of?' he asked him.

'Of the chimney,' cried the man, 'it's falling.'

'What if it does fall,' observed Mr Cronch, looking up as though he thought the huge mass above him was a small pear tree.

'It's coming,' cried the man.

Mr Cronch took off his hat. The man smiled.

―――

To bring a smile on to the face of a man who faces dreadful death can also be the signature tune for being compassionate. 'Life does not cease to be funny when people die any more than it ceases to be serious when people laugh', wrote George Bernard Shaw. Not everyone reveals his/her fears and trials. 'I always like walking in the rain, so no one can see me crying,' said the greatest actor of all time, Charlie Chaplin.

2

THE RAIN HORSE

TED HUGHES

As the young man came over the hill, the first thin blowing of rain met him. He turned his coat-collar up and stood on top of the shelving rabbit-riddled hedgebank, looking down into the valley.

He had come too far. What had set out as a walk along pleasantly-remembered tarmac lanes had turned dreamily by gate and path and hedge-gap into a cross-ploughland trek, his shoes ruined, the dark mud of the lower fields inching up the trouser legs of his grey suit where they rubbed against each other. And now there was a raw, flapping wetness in the air that would be downpour again at any minute. He shivered, holding himself tense against the cold.

This was the view he had been thinking of. Vaguely, without really directing his walk, he had felt he would get the whole thing from this point. For twelve years, whenever he had recalled this scene, he had imagined it as it looked from here. Now the valley lay sunken in front of him, utterly deserted, shallow, bare fields, black and sodden as the bed of an ancient lake after the weeks of rain.

Nothing happened. Not that he had looked forward to any very transfiguring experience. But he had expected something, some pleasure, some meaningful sensation, he didn't quite know what.

So he waited, trying to nudge the right feelings alive with the details—the surprisingly familiar curve of the hedges, the stone gate-pillar and iron gatehook let into it that he had used as a target, the long bank of the rabbit-warren on which he stood and which had been the first thing he ever noticed about the hill when twenty years ago, from the distance of the village, he had said to himself 'That looks like rabbits.'

Twelve years had changed him. This land no longer recognised him, and he looked back at it coldly, as at a finally visited home-country, known only through the stories of a grandfather; felt nothing but the dullness of feeling nothing. Boredom. Then, suddenly, impatience, with a whole exasperated swarm of little anxieties about his shoes and the spitting rain and his new suit and that sky and the two-mile trudge through the mud back to the road.

It would be quicker to go straight forward to the farm a mile away in the valley and behind which the road looped. But the thought of meeting the farmer—to be embarrassingly remembered or shouted at as a trespasser—deterred him. He saw the rain pulling up out of the distance, dragging its grey broken columns, smudging the trees and the farms.

A wave of anger went over him: anger against himself for blundering into this mud-trap and anger against the land that made him feel so outcast, so old and stiff and stupid. He wanted nothing but to get away from it as quickly as possible. But as he turned, something moved in his eye-corner. All his senses startled alert. He stopped.

Over to his right a thin, black horse was running across the ploughland towards the hill, its head down, neck stretched out. It seemed to be running on its toes like a cat, like a dog up to no good.

From the high point on which he stood the hill dipped slightly and rose to another crested point fringed with the tops of trees, three hundred yards to his right. As he watched it, the horse ran up to that crest, showed against the sky—for a moment like a nightmarish leopard—and disappeared over the other side.

For several seconds he stared at the skyline, stunned by the unpleasantly strange impression the horse had made on him. Then the plastering beat of icy rain on his bare skull brought him to himself. The distance had vanished in a wall of grey. All around him the fields were jumping and streaming.

Holding his collar close and tucking his chin down into it he ran back over the hilltop toward the town-side, the lee-side, his feet sucking and splashing, at every stride plunging to the ankle.

This hill was shaped like a wave, a gently rounded back lifting out of the valley to a sharply crested, almost concave front hanging over the river meadows toward the town. Down this front, from the crest, hung two small woods separated by a fallow field. The near wood was nothing more than a quarry, circular, full of stones and bracken, with a few thorns and non descript saplings, foxholes and rabbit holes. The other was rectangular, mainly a planting of scrub oak trees. Beyond the river smouldered the town like a great heap of blue cinders.

He ran along the top of the first wood and finding no shelter but the thin, leafless thorns of the hedge, dipped below the crest out of the wind and jogged along through thick grass to the wood of oaks. In blinding rain he lunged through the barricade of brambles at the wood's edge. The little crippled trees were small choice in the way of shelter, but at a sudden fierce thickening of the rain he took one at random and crouched down under the leaning trunk.

Still panting from his run, drawing his knees up tightly, he watched the bleak lines of rain, grey as hail, slanting through the boughs into the clumps of bracken and bramble. He felt hidden and safe. The sound of the rain as it rushed and lulled in the wood seemed to seal him in. Soon the chilly sheet lead of his suit became a tight, warm mould, and gradually he sank into a state of comfort that was all but trance, though the rain beat steadily on his exposed shoulders and trickled down the oak trunk on to his neck.

All around him the boughs angled down, glistening, black as iron. From their tips and elbows the drops hurried steadily, and the channels of the bark pulsed and gleamed. For a time he amused himself calculating the variation in the rainfall by the variations in a dribble of water from a trembling twig-end two feet in front of his nose. He studied the twig, bringing dwarfs and continents and animals out of its scurfy bark. Beyond the boughs the blue shoal of the town was rising and falling, and darkening and fading again, in the pale, swaying backdrop of rain.

He wanted this rain to go on for ever. Whenever it seemed to be drawing off he listened anxiously until it closed in again. As long as it lasted he was suspended from life and time. He didn't want to return to his sodden shoes and his possibly ruined suit and the walk back over that land of mud.

All at once he shivered. He hugged his knees to squeeze out the cold and found himself thinking of the horse. The hair on the nape of his neck prickled slightly. He remembered how it had run up to the crest and showed against the sky.

He tried to dismiss the thought. Horses wander about the countryside often enough. But the image of the horse as it had appeared against the sky stuck in his mind. It must have come over the crest just above the wood in which he was now sitting. To clear his mind, he twisted around and looked up the wood between the tree stems, to his left.

At the wood top, with the silvered grey light coming in behind it, the black horse was standing under the oaks, its head high and alert, its ears pricked, watching him.

A horse sheltering from the rain generally goes into a sort of stupor, tilts a hind hoof and hangs its head and lets its eyelids droop, and so it stays as long as the rain lasts. This horse was nothing like that. It was watching him intently, standing perfectly still, its soaked neck and flank shining in the hard light.

He turned back. His scalp went icy and he shivered. What was he to do? Ridiculous to try driving it away. And to leave the wood, with the rain still coming down full pelt, was out of the question.

Meanwhile the idea of being watched became more and more unsettling until at last he had to twist around again, to see if the horse had moved. It stood exactly as before.

This was absurd. He took control of himself and turned back deliberately, determined not to give the horse one more thought. If it wanted to share the wood with him, let it. If it wanted to stare at him, let it. He was nestling firmly into these resolutions when the ground shook and he heard the crash of a heavy body coming down the wood. Like lightning his legs bounded him upright and about face. The horse was almost on top of him, its head stretching forward, ears flattened and lips lifted back from the long yellow teeth. He got one snapshot glimpse of the red-veined eyeball as he flung himself backwards around the tree. Then he was away up the slope, whipped by oak twigs as he leapt the brambles and brushwood, twisting between the close trees till he tripped and sprawled. As he fell the warning flashed through his head that he must at all costs keep his suit out of the leaf-mould, but a more urgent instinct was already rolling him violently sideways. He spun around, sat up and looked back, ready to scramble off in a flash to one side. He was panting from the sudden excitement and effort. The horse had disappeared. The wood was empty except for the drumming, slant grey rain, dancing the bracken and glittering from the branches.

He got up, furious. Knocking the dirt and leaves from his suit as well as he could he looked around for a weapon. The horse was evidently mad, had an abscess on its brain or something of the sort. Or maybe it was just spiteful. Rain sometimes puts creatures into queer states. Whatever it was, he was going to get away from the wood as quickly as possible, rain or no rain.

Since the horse seemed to have gone on down the wood, his way to the farm over the hill was clear. As he went, he broke a yard length of wrist-thick dead branch from one of the oaks, but immediately threw it aside and wiped the slime of rotten wet bark from his hands with his soaked handkerchief. Already he was thinking it incredible that the horse could have meant to attack him. Most likely it was just going down the wood for better shelter and had made a feint at him in passing—as much out of curiosity or playfulness as anything. He recalled the way horses menace each other when they are galloping round in a paddock.

The wood rose to a steep bank topped by the hawthorn hedge that ran along the whole ridge of the hill. He was pulling himself up to a thin place in the hedge by the bare stem of one of the hawthorns when he ducked and shrank down again. The whole swelling gradient of fields lay in front of him, smoking in the slowly crossing rain. Out in the middle of the first field, tall as a statue, and a ghostly silver in the under-cloud light, stood the horse, watching the wood.

He lowered his head slowly, slithered back down the bank and crouched. An awful feeling of helplessness came over him. He felt certain the horse had been looking straight at him. Waiting for him? Was it clairvoyant? Maybe a mad animal can be clairvoyant. At the same time he was ashamed to find himself acting so inanely, ducking and creeping about in this way just to keep out of sight of a horse. He tried to imagine how anybody in their senses would just walk off home. This cooled him a little, and he retreated further down the wood. He would go back the way he had come, along under the hill crest, without any more nonsense.

The wood hummed and the rain was a cold weight, but he observed this rather than felt it. The water ran down inside his clothes and squelched in his shoes as he eased his way carefully over the bedded twigs and leaves. At every instant he expected to see the prick-eared black head looking down at him from the hedge above.

At the woodside he paused, close against a tree. The success of this last manoeuvre was restoring his confidence, but he didn't want to venture out into the open field without making sure that the horse was just where he had left it. The perfect move would be to withdraw quietly and leave the horse standing out there in the rain. He crept up again among the trees to the crest and peeped through the hedge.

The grey field and the whole slope were empty. He searched the distance. The horse was quite likely to have forgotten him altogether and wandered off. Then he raised himself and leaned out to see if it had come in close to the hedge. Before he was aware of anything the ground shook. He twisted around wildly to see how he had been caught. The black shape was above him, right across the light. Its whinnying snort and the spattering whack of its hooves seemed to be actually inside his head as he fell backwards down the bank, and leapt again like a madman, dodging among the oaks, imagining how the buffet would come and how he would be knocked headlong. Halfway down the wood the oaks gave way to bracken and old roots and stony rabbit diggings. He was well out into the middle of this before he realised that he was running alone.

Gasping for breath now and cursing mechanically, without a thought for his suit he sat down on the ground to rest his shaking legs, letting the rain plaster the hair down over his forehead and watching the dense flashing lines disappear abruptly into the soil all around him as if he were watching through thick plate glass. He took deep breaths in the effort to steady his heart and regain control of himself. His right trouser turn-up was ripped at the seam and his suitjacket was splashed with the yellow mud of the top field.

Obviously the horse had been farther along the hedge above the steep field, waiting for him to come out at the woodside just as he had intended. He must have peeped through the hedge— peeping the wrong way—within yards of it.

However, this last attack had cleared up one thing. He need no longer act like a fool out of mere uncertainty as to whether the horse was simply being playful or not. It was definitely after him. He picked up two stones about the size of goose eggs and set off towards the bottom of the wood, striding carelessly.

A loop of the river bordered all this farmland. If he crossed the little meadow at the bottom of the wood, he could follow the three-mile circuit, back to the road. There were deep hollows in the river-bank, shoaled with pebbles, as he remembered, perfect places to defend himself from if the horse followed him out there.

The hawthorns that choked the bottom of the wood—some of them good-sized trees—knitted into an almost impassable barrier. He had found a place where the growth thinned slightly and had begun to lift aside the long spiny stems, pushing himself forward, when he stopped. Through the bluish veil of bare twigs he saw the familiar shape out in the field below the wood.

But it seemed not to have noticed him yet. It was looking out across the field towards the river. Quietly, he released himself from the thorns and climbed back across the clearing towards the one side of the wood he had not yet tried. If the horse would only stay down there he could follow his first and easiest plan, up the wood and over the hilltop to the farm.

Now he noticed that the sky had grown much darker. The rain was heavier every second, pressing down as if the earth had to be flooded before nightfall. The oaks ahead blurred and the ground drummed. He began to run. And as he ran he heard a deeper sound running with him. He whirled around. The horse was in the middle of the clearing. It might have been running to get out of the terrific rain except that it was coming straight for him, scattering clay and stones, with an immensely supple and powerful motion. He let out a tearing roar and threw the stone in his right hand. The result was instantaneous. Whether at the roar or the stone the horse reared as if against a wall and shied to the left. As it dropped back on to its forefeet he flung his second stone, at ten yards' range, and saw a bright mud blotch suddenly appear on the glistening black flank. The horse surged down the wood, splashing the earth like water, tossing its long tail as it plunged out of sight among the hawthorns.

He looked around for stones. The encounter had set the blood beating in his head and given him a savage energy. He could have killed the horse at that moment. That this brute should pick on him and play with him in this malevolent fashion was more than he could bear. Whoever owned it, he thought, deserved to have its neck broken for letting the dangerous thing loose.

He came out at the woodside in open battle now, still searching for the right stones. There were plenty here, piled and scattered where they had been ploughed out of the field . He selected two, then straightened and saw the horse twenty yards off in the middle of the steep field, watching him calmly. They looked at each other.

'Out of it!' he shouted, brandishing his arm. 'Out of it! Go on!' The horse twitched its pricked ears. With all his force he threw. The stone soared and landed beyond with a soft thud. He re-armed and threw again. For several minutes he kept up his bombardment without a single hit, working himself into a despair and throwing more and more wildly, till his arm began to ache with the unaccustomed exercise. Throughout the performance the horse watched him fixedly. Finally he had to stop and ease his shoulder muscles. As if the horse had been waiting for just this, it dipped its head twice and came at him.

He snatched up two stones and roaring with all his strength flung the one in his right hand. He was astonished at the crack of the impact. It was as if he had struck a tile—and the horse actually stumbled. With another roar he jumped forward and hurled his other stone. His aim seemed to be under superior guidance. The stone struck and rebounded straight up into the air, spinning fiercely, as the horse swirled away and went careering down towards the far bottom corner of the field, at first with great, swinging leaps, then at a canter, leaving deep churned holes in the soil.

It turned up the far side of the field, climbing till it was level with him. He felt a little surprise of pity to see it shaking its head, and once it paused to lower its head and paw over its ear with its forehoof as a cat does.

'You stay there!' he shouted. 'Keep your distance and you'll not get hurt.'

And indeed the horse did stop at that moment, almost obediently. It watched him as he climbed to the crest.

The rain swept into his face and he realised that he was freezing, as if his very flesh were sodden. The farm seemed miles away over the dreary fields.

Without another glance at the horse—he felt too exhausted to care now what it did—he loaded the crook of his left arm with stones and plunged out on to the waste of mud.

He was halfway to the first hedge before the horse appeared, silhouetted against the sky at the corner of the wood, head high and attentive, watching his laborious retreat over the three fields.

The ankle-deep clay dragged at him. Every stride was a separate, deliberate effort, forcing him up and out of the sucking earth, burdened as he was by his sogged clothes and load of stones and limbs that seemed themselves to be turning to mud. He fought to keep his breathing even, two strides in, two strides out, the air ripping his lungs. In the middle of the last field he stopped and looked around. The horse, tiny on the skyline, had not moved.

At the corner of the field he unlocked his clasped arms and dumped the stones by the gatepost, then leaned on the gate. The farm was in front of him. He became conscious of the rain again and suddenly longed to stretch out full length under it, to take the cooling, healing drops all over his body and forget himself in the last wretchedness of the mud. Making an effort, he heaved his weight over the gate-top. He leaned again, looking up at the hill.

Rain was dissolving land and sky together like a wet watercolour as the afternoon darkened. He concentrated, raising his head, searching the sky-line from end to end. The horse had vanished. The hill looked lifeless and desolate, an island lifting out of the sea, awash with every tide.

Under the long shed where the tractors, plough, binders and the rest were drawn up, waiting for their seasons, he sat on a sack thrown over a petrol drum, trembling, his lungs heaving. The mingled smell of paraffin, creosote, fertiliser, dust—all was exactly as he had left it twelve years ago. The ragged swallows' nests were still there tucked in the angles of the rafters. He remembered three dead foxes hanging in a row from one of the beams, their teeth bloody.

The ordeal with the horse had already sunk from reality. It hung under the surface of his mind, an obscure confusion of fright and shame, as after a narrowly-escaped street accident. There was a solid pain in his chest, like a spike of bone stabbing, that made him wonder if he had strained his heart on that last stupid burdened run. Piece by piece he began to take off his clothes, wringing the grey water out of them, but soon he stopped that and just sat staring at the ground, as if some important part had been cut out of his brain.

When one waits to reach his destination, he may look around and may be disappointed by what he sees. Indeed living is like travelling; the journey is better than its destination. The unique feature of this short story is the painting of myriad emotions such as struggle, fear and change and much more. Disappointment becomes the core theme. After all, this experience perhaps is 'some important part that had been cut out' of the brain.

3
THE STORY OF AN HOUR

KATE CHOPIN

Knowing that Mrs Mallard was afflicted with a heart trouble, great care was taken to break to her as gently as possible the news of her husband's death.

It was her sister Josephine who told her, in broken sentences; veiled hints that revealed in half concealing. Her husband's friend Richards was there, too, near her. It was he who had been in the newspaper office when intelligence of the railroad disaster was received, with Brently Mallard's name leading the list of 'killed.' He had only taken the time to assure himself of its truth by a second telegram, and had hastened to forestall any less careful, less tender friend in bearing the sad message.

She did not hear the story as many women have heard the same, with a paralyzed inability to accept its significance. She wept at once, with sudden, wild abandonment, in her sister's arms. When the storm of grief had spent itself she went away to her room alone. She would have no one follow her.

There stood, facing the open window, a comfortable, roomy armchair. Into this she sank, pressed down by a physical exhaustion that haunted her body and seemed to reach into her soul.

She could see in the open square before her house the tops of trees that were all aquiver with the new spring life. The delicious breath of rain was in the air. In the street below a peddler was crying his wares. The notes of a distant song which some one was singing reached her faintly, and countless sparrows were twittering in the eaves.

There were patches of blue sky showing here and there through the clouds that had met and piled one above the other in the west facing her window.

She sat with her head thrown back upon the cushion of the chair, quite motionless, except when a sob came up into her throat and shook her, as a child who has cried itself to sleep continues to sob in its dreams.

She was young, with a fair, calm face, whose lines bespoke repression and even a certain strength. But now there was a dull stare in her eyes, whose gaze was fixed away off yonder on one of those patches of blue sky. It was not a glance of reflection, but rather indicated a suspension of intelligent thought.

There was something coming to her and she was waiting for it, fearfully. What was it? She did not know; it was too subtle and elusive to name. But she felt it, creeping out of the sky, reaching toward her through the sounds, the scents, the color that filled the air.

Now her bosom rose and fell tumultuously. She was beginning to recognize this thing that was approaching to possess her, and she was striving to beat it back with her will—as powerless as her two white slender hands would have been. When she abandoned herself a little whispered word escaped her slightly parted lips. She said it over and over under her breath: 'free, free, free!' The vacant stare and the look of terror that had followed it went from her eyes. They stayed keen and bright. Her pulse beat fast, and the coursing blood warmed and relaxed every inch of her body.

She did not stop to ask if it were or were not a monstrous joy that held her. A clear and exalted perception enabled her to dismiss the suggestion as trivial. She knew that she would weep again when she saw the kind, tender hands folded in death; the face that had never looked save with love upon her, fixed and gray and dead. But she saw beyond that bitter moment a long procession of years to come that would belong to her absolutely. And she opened and spread her arms out to them in welcome.

There would be no one to live for during those coming years; she would live for herself. There would be no powerful will bending hers in that blind persistence with which men and women believe they have a right to impose a private will upon a fellow-creature. A kind intention or a cruel intention made the act seem no less a crime as she looked upon it in that brief moment of illumination.

And yet she had loved him—sometimes. Often she had not. What did it matter! What could love, the unsolved mystery, count for in the face of this possession of self-assertion which she suddenly recognized as the strongest impulse of her being!

'Free! Body and soul free!' she kept whispering.

Josephine was kneeling before the closed door with her lips to the keyhole, imploring for admission. 'Louise, open the door! I beg; open the door—you will make yourself ill. What are you doing, Louise? For heaven's sake open the door.'

'Go away. I am not making myself ill.' No; she was drinking in a very elixir of life through that open window.

Her fancy was running riot along those days ahead of her. Spring days and summer days and all sorts of days, that would be her own. She breathed a quick prayer that life might be long. It was only yesterday she had thought with a shudder that life might be long.

She arose at length and opened the door to her sister's importunities. There was a feverish triumph in her eyes, and she carried herself unwittingly like a goddess of Victory. She clasped her sister's waist, and together they descended the stairs. Richards stood waiting for them at the bottom.

Someone was opening the front door with a latchkey. It was Brently Mallard who entered, a little travel-stained, composedly carrying his grip-sack and umbrella. He had been far from the scene of the accident, and did not even know there had been one.

He stood amazed at Josephine's piercing cry; at Richards' quick motion to screen him from the view of his wife.

When the doctors came they said she had died of heart disease—of the joy that kills.

Shakespeare once wrote, 'Better three hours too soon than a minute too late.'

◈

Dying is not easy. One has to die in time. Truth can be explosive. 'Don't wake up a woman in love. Let her dream, so that she does not weep when she returns to her bitter reality.' wrote Mark Twain. And of course Shakespeare once wrote, 'Better three hours too soon than a minute too late.'

4

THE LADY OR THE TIGER?

FRANK R. STOCKTON

In the very olden time there lived a semi-barbaric king, whose ideas, though somewhat polished and sharpened by the progressiveness of distant Latin neighbors, were still large, florid, and untrammeled, as became the half of him which was barbaric. He was a man of exuberant fancy, and, withal, of an authority so irresistible that, at his will, he turned his varied fancies into facts. He was greatly given to self-communing, and, when he and himself agreed upon anything, the thing was done. When every member of his domestic and political systems moved smoothly in its appointed course, his nature was bland and genial; but, whenever there was a little hitch, and some of his orbs got out of their orbits, he was blander and more genial still, for nothing pleased him so much as to make the crooked straight and crush down uneven places.

Among the borrowed notions by which his barbarism had become semified was that of the public arena, in which, by exhibitions of manly and beastly valor, the minds of his subjects were refined and cultured.

But even here the exuberant and barbaric fancy asserted itself. The arena of the king was built, not to give the people an opportunity of hearing the rhapsodies of dying gladiators, nor to enable them to view the inevitable conclusion of a conflict between religious opinions and hungry jaws, but for purposes far better adapted to widen and develop the mental energies of the people. This vast amphitheater, with its encircling galleries, its mysterious vaults, and its unseen passages, was an agent of poetic justice, in which crime was punished, or virtue rewarded, by the decrees of an impartial and incorruptible chance.

When a subject was accused of a crime of sufficient importance to interest the king, public notice was given that on an appointed day the fate of the accused person would be decided in the king's arena, a structure which well deserved its name, for, although its form and plan were borrowed from afar, its purpose emanated solely from the brain of this man, who, every barleycorn a king, knew no tradition to which he owed more allegiance than pleased his fancy, and who ingrafted on every adopted form of human thought and action the rich growth of his barbaric idealism.

When all the people had assembled in the galleries, and the king, surrounded by his court, sat high up on his throne of royal state on one side of the arena, he gave a signal, a door beneath him opened, and the accused subject stepped out into the amphitheater. Directly opposite him, on the other side of the enclosed space, were two doors, exactly alike and side by side. It was the duty and the privilege of the person on trial to walk directly to these doors and open one of them. He could open either door he pleased; he was subject to no guidance or influence but that of the aforementioned impartial and incorruptible chance. If he opened the one, there came out of it a hungry tiger, the fiercest and most cruel that could be procured, which immediately sprang upon him and tore him to pieces as a punishment for his guilt. The moment that the case of the criminal was thus decided, doleful iron bells were clanged, great wails went up from the hired mourners posted on the outer rim of the arena, and the vast audience, with bowed heads and downcast hearts, wended slowly their homeward way, mourning greatly that one so young and fair, or so old and respected, should have merited so dire a fate.

But, if the accused person opened the other door, there came forth from it a lady, the most suitable to his years and station that his majesty could select among his fair subjects, and to this lady he was immediately married, as a reward of his innocence. It mattered not that he might already possess a wife and family, or that his affections might be engaged upon an object of his own selection; the king allowed no such subordinate arrangements to interfere with his great scheme of retribution and reward. The exercises, as in the other instance, took place immediately, and in the arena. Another door opened beneath the king, and a priest, followed by a band of choristers, and dancing maidens blowing joyous airs on golden horns and treading an epithalamic measure, advanced to where the pair stood, side by side, and the wedding was promptly and cheerily solemnized. Then the gay brass bells rang forth their merry peals, the people shouted glad hurrahs, and the innocent man, preceded by children strewing flowers on his path, led his bride to his home.

This was the king's semi-barbaric method of administering justice. Its perfect fairness is obvious. The criminal could not know out of which door would come the lady; he opened either he pleased, without having the slightest idea whether, in the next instant, he was to be devoured or married. On some occasions the tiger came out of one door, and on some out of the other. The decisions of this tribunal were not only fair, they were positively determinate: the accused person was instantly punished if he found himself guilty, and, if innocent, he was rewarded on the spot, whether he liked it or not. There was no escape from the judgments of the king's arena.

The institution was a very popular one. When the people gathered together on one of the great trial days, they never knew whether they were to witness a bloody slaughter or a hilarious wedding. This element of uncertainty lent an interest to the occasion which it could not otherwise have attained. Thus, the masses were entertained and pleased, and the thinking part of the community could bring no charge of unfairness against this plan, for did not the accused person have the whole matter in his own hands?

This semi-barbaric king had a daughter as blooming as his most florid fancies, and with a soul as fervent and imperious as his own. As is usual in such cases, she was the apple of his eye, and was loved by him above all humanity. Among his courtiers was a young man of that fineness of blood and lowness of station common to the conventional heroes of romance who love royal maidens. This royal maiden was well satisfied with her lover, for he was handsome and brave to a degree unsurpassed in all this kingdom, and she loved him with an ardor that had enough of barbarism in it to make it exceedingly warm and strong. This love affair moved on happily for many months, until one day the king happened to discover its existence. He did not hesitate nor waver in regard to his duty in the premises. The youth was immediately cast into prison, and a day was appointed for his trial in the king's arena. This, of course, was an especially important occasion, and his majesty, as well as all the people, was greatly interested in the workings and development of this trial. Never before had such a case occurred; never before had a subject dared to love the daughter of the king. In after years such things became commonplace enough, but then they were in no slight degree novel and startling.

The tiger-cages of the kingdom were searched for the most savage and relentless beasts, from which the fiercest monster might be selected for the arena; and the ranks of maiden youth and beauty throughout the land were carefully surveyed by competent judges in order that the young man might have a fitting bride in case fate did not determine for him a different destiny. Of course, everybody knew that the deed with which the accused was charged had been done. He had loved the princess, and neither he, she, nor any one else, thought of denying the fact; but the king would not think of allowing any fact of this kind to interfere with the workings of the tribunal, in which he took such great delight and satisfaction. No matter how the affair turned out, the youth would be disposed of, and the king would take an aesthetic pleasure in watching the course of events, which would determine whether or not the young man had done wrong in allowing himself to love the princess.

The appointed day arrived. From far and near the people gathered, and thronged the great galleries of the arena, and crowds, unable to gain admittance, massed themselves against its outside walls. The king and his court were in their places, opposite the twin doors, those fateful portals, so terrible in their similarity.

All was ready. The signal was given. A door beneath the royal party opened, and the lover of the princess walked into the arena. Tall, beautiful, fair, his appearance was greeted with a low hum of admiration and anxiety. Half the audience had not known so grand a youth had lived among them. No wonder the princess loved him! What a terrible thing for him to be there!

As the youth advanced into the arena he turned, as the custom was, to bow to the king, but he did not think at all of that royal personage. His eyes were fixed upon the princess, who sat to the right of her father. Had it not been for the moiety of barbarism in her nature it is probable that lady would not have been there, but her intense and fervid soul would not allow her to be absent on an occasion in which she was so terribly interested. From the moment that the decree had gone forth that her lover should decide his fate in the king's arena, she had thought of nothing, night or day, but this great event and the various subjects connected with it. Possessed of more power, influence, and force of character than any one who had ever before been interested in such a case, she had done what no other person had done—she had possessed herself of the secret of the doors. She knew in which of the two rooms that lay behind those doors, stood the cage of the tiger, with its open front, and in which waited the lady. Through these thick doors, heavily curtained with skins on the inside, it was impossible that any noise or suggestion should come from within to the person who should approach to raise the latch of one of them. But gold, and the power of a woman's will, had brought the secret to the princess.

And not only did she know in which room stood the lady ready to emerge, all blushing and radiant, should her door be opened, but she knew who the lady was. It was one of the fairest and loveliest of the damsels of the court who had been selected as the reward of the accused youth, should he be proved innocent of the crime of aspiring to one so far above him; and the princess hated her. Often had she seen, or imagined that she had seen, this fair creature throwing glances of admiration upon the person of her lover, and sometimes she thought these glances were perceived, and even returned. Now and then she had seen them talking together; it was but for a moment or two, but much can be said in a brief space; it may have been on most unimportant topics, but how could she know that? The girl was lovely, but she had dared to raise her eyes to the loved one of the princess; and, with all the intensity of the savage blood transmitted to her through long lines of wholly barbaric ancestors, she hated the woman who blushed and trembled behind that silent door.

When her lover turned and looked at her, and his eye met hers as she sat there, paler and whiter than anyone in the vast ocean of anxious faces about her, he saw, by that power of quick perception which is given to those whose souls are one, that she knew behind which door crouched the tiger, and behind which stood the lady. He had expected her to know it. He understood her nature, and his soul was assured that she would never rest until she had made plain to herself this thing, hidden to all other lookers-on, even to the king. The only hope for the youth in which there was any element of certainty was based upon the success of the princess in discovering this mystery; and the moment he looked upon her, he saw she had succeeded, as in his soul he knew she would succeed.

Then it was that his quick and anxious glance asked the question: 'Which?' It was as plain to her as if he shouted it from where he stood. There was not an instant to be lost. The question was asked in a flash; it must be answered in another.

Her right arm lay on the cushioned parapet before her. She raised her hand, and made a slight, quick movement toward the right. No one but her lover saw her. Every eye but his was fixed on the man in the arena.

He turned, and with a firm and rapid step he walked across the empty space. Every heart stopped beating, every breath was held, every eye was fixed immovably upon that man. Without the slightest hesitation, he went to the door on the right, and opened it.

Now, the point of the story is this: Did the tiger come out of that door, or did the lady?

The more we reflect upon this question, the harder it is to answer. It involves a study of the human heart which leads us through devious mazes of passion, out of which it is difficult to find our way. Think of it, fair reader, not as if the decision of the question depended upon yourself, but upon that hot-blooded, semi-barbaric princess, her soul at a white heat beneath the combined fires of despair and jealousy. She had lost him, but who should have him?

How often, in her waking hours and in her dreams, had she started in wild horror, and covered her face with her hands as she thought of her lover opening the door on the other side of which waited the cruel fangs of the tiger!

But how much oftener had she seen him at the other door! How in her grievous reveries had she gnashed her teeth, and torn her hair, when she saw his start of rapturous delight as he opened the door of the lady! How her soul had burned in agony when she had seen him rush to meet that woman, with her flushing cheek and sparkling eye of triumph; when she had seen him lead her forth, his whole frame kindled with the joy of recovered life; when she had heard the glad shouts from the multitude, and the wild ringing of the happy bells; when she had seen the priest, with his joyous followers, advance to the couple, and make them man and wife before her very eyes; and when she had seen them walk away together upon their path of flowers, followed by the tremendous shouts of the hilarious multitude, in which her one despairing shriek was lost and drowned!

Would it not be better for him to die at once, and go to wait for her in the blessed regions of semi-barbaric futurity?

And yet, that awful tiger, those shrieks, that blood!

Her decision had been indicated in an instant, but it had been made after days and nights of anguished deliberation. She had known she would be asked, she had decided what she would answer, and, without the slightest hesitation, she had moved her hand to the right.

The question of her decision is one not to be lightly considered, and it is not for me to presume to set myself up as the one person able to answer it. And so I leave it with all of you: Which came out of the opened door—the lady, or the tiger?

Ambiguity is the essence of modernism: a story that is liable to more than one interpretation. The narrator does not presume to tell us what decision the princess came to; and for a final time puts the question to us: 'Which came out of the opened door—the lady, or the tiger?' The story is steeped in symbolism. The door symbolises fate; the tiger represents death and punishment, the lady represents innocence and reward: it is not her fault that she is lovely and in turn the princess is jealous. There are diametrical opposite symbols too—the 'Doleful iron bells' represent mourning, while 'gay brass bells' represent life and celebration. This story does not follow the proscenium form... it is left to the reader to take a call.

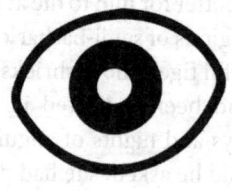

5

A TELL-TALE HEART

EDGAR ALLAN POE

True!—nervous—very, very dreadfully nervous I had been and am; but why will you say that I am mad? The disease had sharpened my senses—not destroyed—not dulled them. Above all was the sense of hearing acute. I heard all things in the heaven and in the earth. I heard many things in hell. How, then, am I mad? Hearken! and observe how healthily—how calmly I can tell you the whole story.

It is impossible to say how first the idea entered my brain; but once conceived, it haunted me day and night. Object there was none. Passion there was none. I loved the old man. He had never wronged me. He had never given me insult. For his gold I had no desire. I think it was his eye! Yes, it was this! He had the eye of a vulture—a pale blue eye, with a film over it. Whenever it fell upon me, my blood ran cold; and so by degrees—very gradually—I made up my mind to take the life of the old man, and thus rid myself of the eye forever.

Now this is the point. You fancy me mad. Madmen know nothing. But you should have seen me. You should have seen how wisely I proceeded—with what caution—with what foresight—

with what dissimulation I went to work! I was never kinder to the old man than during the whole week before I killed him. And every night, about midnight, I turned the latch of his door and opened it—oh so gently! And then, when I had made an opening sufficient for my head, I put in a dark lantern, all closed, closed, that no light shone out, and then I thrust in my head. Oh, you would have laughed to see how cunningly I thrust it in! I moved it slowly—very, very slowly, so that I might not disturb the old man's sleep. It took me an hour to place my whole head within the opening so far that I could see him as he lay upon his bed. Ha! would a madman have been so wise as this? And then, when my head was well in the room, I undid the lantern cautiously—oh, so cautiously—cautiously (for the hinges creaked)—I undid it just so much that a single thin ray fell upon the vulture eye. And this I did for seven long nights—every night just at midnight—but I found the eye always closed; and so it was impossible to do the work; for it was not the old man who vexed me, but his Evil Eye. And every morning, when the day broke, I went boldly into the chamber, and spoke courageously to him, calling him by name in a hearty tone, and inquiring how he has passed the night. So you see he would have been a very profound old man, indeed, to suspect that every night, just at twelve, I looked in upon him while he slept.

Upon the eighth night I was more than usually cautious in opening the door. A watch's minute hand moves more quickly than did mine. Never before that night had I felt the extent of my own powers—of my sagacity. I could scarcely contain my feelings of triumph. To think that there I was, opening the door, little by little, and he not even to dream of my secret deeds or thoughts. I fairly chuckled at the idea; and perhaps he heard me; for he moved on the bed suddenly, as if startled. Now you may think that I drew back—but no. His room was as black as pitch with the thick darkness, (for the shutters were close fastened, through fear of robbers,) and so I knew that he could not see the opening of the door, and I kept pushing it on steadily, steadily.

I had my head in, and was about to open the lantern, when my thumb slipped upon the tin fastening, and the old man sprang up in bed, crying out—'Who's there?'

I kept quite still and said nothing. For a whole hour I did not move a muscle, and in the meantime I did not hear him lie down. He was still sitting up in the bed listening;—just as I have done, night after night, hearkening to the death watches in the wall.

Presently I heard a slight groan, and I knew it was the groan of mortal terror. It was not a groan of pain or of grief—oh, no!—it was the low stifled sound that arises from the bottom of the soul when overcharged with awe. I knew the sound well. Many a night, just at midnight, when all the world slept, it has welled up from my own bosom, deepening, with its dreadful echo, the terrors that distracted me. I say I knew it well. I knew what the old man felt, and pitied him, although I chuckled at heart. I knew that he had been lying awake ever since the first slight noise, when he had turned in the bed. His fears had been ever since growing upon him. He had been trying to fancy them causeless, but could not. He had been saying to himself—'It is nothing but the wind in the chimney—it is only a mouse crossing the floor,' or 'It is merely a cricket which has made a single chirp.' Yes, he had been trying to comfort himself with these suppositions: but he had found all in vain. All in vain; because Death, in approaching him had stalked with his black shadow before him, and enveloped the victim. And it was the mournful influence of the unperceived shadow that caused him to feel—although he neither saw nor heard—to *feel* the presence of my head within the room.

When I had waited a long time, very patiently, without hearing him lie down, I resolved to open a little—a very, very little crevice in the lantern. So I opened it—you cannot imagine how stealthily, stealthily—until, at length a simple dim ray, like the thread of the spider, shot from out the crevice and fell full upon the vulture eye.

It was open—wide, wide open—and I grew furious as I gazed upon it. I saw it with perfect distinctness—all a dull blue, with a hideous veil over it that chilled the very marrow in my bones; but

I could see nothing else of the old man's face or person: for I had directed the ray as if by instinct, precisely upon the damned spot.

And have I not told you that what you mistake for madness is but over-acuteness of the sense?—now, I say, there came to my ears a low, dull, quick sound, such as a watch makes when enveloped in cotton. I knew that sound well, too. It was the beating of the old man's heart. It increased my fury, as the beating of a drum stimulates the soldier into courage.

But even yet I refrained and kept still. I scarcely breathed. I held the lantern motionless. I tried how steadily I could maintain the ray upon the eye. Meantime the hellish tattoo of the heart increased. It grew quicker and quicker, and louder and louder every instant. The old man's terror *must* have been extreme! It grew louder, I say, louder every moment!—do you mark me well I have told you that I am nervous: so I am. And now at the dead hour of the night, amid the dreadful silence of that old house, so strange a noise as this excited me to uncontrollable terror. Yet, for some minutes longer I refrained and stood still. But the beating grew louder, louder! I thought the heart must burst. And now a new anxiety seized me—the sound would be heard by a neighbour! The old man's hour had come! With a loud yell, I threw open the lantern and leaped into the room. He shrieked once—once only. In an instant I dragged him to the floor, and pulled the heavy bed over him. I then smiled gaily, to find the deed so far done. But, for many minutes, the heart beat on with a muffled sound. This, however, did not vex me; it would not be heard through the wall. At length it ceased. The old man was dead. I removed the bed and examined the corpse. Yes, he was stone, stone dead. I placed my hand upon the heart and held it there many minutes. There was no pulsation. He was stone dead. His eye would trouble me no more.

If still you think me mad, you will think so no longer when I describe the wise precautions I took for the concealment of the body. The night waned, and I worked hastily, but in silence. First of all I dismembered the corpse. I cut off the head and the arms and the legs.

I then took up three planks from the flooring of the chamber, and deposited all between the scantlings. I then replaced the boards so cleverly, so cunningly, that no human eye—not even *his*—could have detected any thing wrong. There was nothing to wash out—no stain of any kind—no blood-spot whatever. I had been too wary for that. A tub had caught all—ha! ha!

When I had made an end of these labors, it was four o'clock—still dark as midnight. As the bell sounded the hour, there came a knocking at the street door. I went down to open it with a light heart,—for what had I *now* to fear? There entered three men, who introduced themselves, with perfect suavity, as officers of the police. A shriek had been heard by a neighbour during the night; suspicion of foul play had been aroused; information had been lodged at the police office, and they (the officers) had been deputed to search the premises.

I smiled—for *what* had I to fear? I bade the gentlemen welcome. The shriek, I said, was my own in a dream. The old man, I mentioned, was absent in the country. I took my visitors all over the house. I bade them search—search *well*. I led them, at length, to *his* chamber. I showed them his treasures, secure, undisturbed. In the enthusiasm of my confidence, I brought chairs into the room, and desired them here to rest from their fatigues, while I myself, in the wild audacity of my perfect triumph, placed my own seat upon the very spot beneath which reposed the corpse of the victim.

The officers were satisfied. My *manner* had convinced them. I was singularly at ease. They sat, and while I answered cheerily, they chatted of familiar things. But, ere long, I felt myself getting pale and wished them gone. My head ached, and I fancied a ringing in my ears: but still they sat and still chatted. The ringing became more distinct:—It continued and became more distinct: I talked more freely to get rid of the feeling: but it continued and gained definiteness—until, at length, I found that the noise was *not* within my ears.

No doubt I now grew *very* pale;—but I talked more fluently, and with a heightened voice. Yet the sound increased—and what could I do? It was *a low, dull, quick sound—much such a sound as a watch makes when enveloped in cotton.* I gasped for breath—and yet the officers heard it not. I talked more quickly—more vehemently; but the noise steadily increased. I arose and argued about trifles, in a high key and with violent gesticulations; but the noise steadily increased. Why *would* they not be gone? I paced the floor to and fro with heavy strides, as if excited to fury by the observations of the men—but the noise steadily increased. Oh God! what could I do? I foamed—I raved—I swore! I swung the chair upon which I had been sitting, and grated it upon the boards, but the noise arose over all and continually increased. It grew louder—louder—*louder*! And still the men chatted pleasantly, and smiled. Was it possible they heard not? Almighty God!—no, no! They heard!—they suspected!—they *knew*!—they were making a mockery of my horror!—this I thought, and this I think. But anything was better than this agony! Anything was more tolerable than this derision! I could bear those hypocritical smiles no longer! I felt that I must scream or die!—and now—again!—hark! louder! louder! louder! *louder*!

'Villains!' I shrieked, 'dissemble no more! I admit the deed!—tear up the planks! here, here!—it is the beating of his hideous heart!'

The story is one of conflicts: Man vs. Self. The narrator struggles to resist the awful ticking of the dead man's heart that haunts him. Man vs. Society. The narrator must lie to the police, and cover up the murder. And finally Man vs. Man.

6
LUCK
MARK TWAIN

It was at a banquet in London in honour of one of the two or three conspicuously illustrious English military names of this generation. For reasons which will presently appear, I will withhold his real name and titles, and call him Lieutenant General Lord Arthur Scoresby, V.C., K.C.B., etc., etc., etc. What a fascination there is in a renowned name! There sat the man, in actual flesh, whom I had heard of so many thousands of times since that day, thirty years before, when his name shot suddenly to the zenith from a Crimean battlefield, to remain forever celebrated. It was food and drink to me to look, and look, and look at that demigod; scanning, searching, noting: the quietness, the reserve, the noble gravity of his countenance; the simple honesty that expressed itself all over him; the sweet unconsciousness of his greatness—unconsciousness of the hundreds of admiring eyes fastened upon him, unconsciousness of the deep, loving, sincere worship welling out of the breasts of those people and flowing toward him.

The clergyman at my left was an old acquaintance of mine—clergyman now, but had spent the first half of his life in the camp and field, and as an instructor in the military school at Woolwich. Just at the moment I have been talking about, a veiled and singular light glimmered in his eyes, and he leaned down and muttered confidentially to me—indicating the hero of the banquet with a gesture:

'Privately—he's an absolute fool.'

This verdict was a great surprise to me. If its subject had been Napoleon, or Socrates, or Solomon, my astonishment could not have been greater. Two things I was well aware of: that the Reverend was a man of strict veracity, and that his judgement of men was good. Therefore I knew, beyond doubt or question, that the world was mistaken about this hero: he was a fool. So I meant to find out, at a convenient moment, how the Reverend, all solitary and alone, had discovered the secret.

Some days later the opportunity came, and this is what the Reverend told me.

About forty years ago I was an instructor in the military academy at Woolwich. I was present in one of the sections when young Scoresby underwent his preliminary examination. I was touched to the quick with pity; for the rest of the class answered up brightly and handsomely, while he—why, dear me, he didn't know anything, so to speak. He was evidently good, and sweet, and loveable, and guileless; and so it was exceedingly painful to see him stand there, as serene as a graven image, and deliver himself of answers which were veritably miraculous for stupidity and ignorance. All the compassion in me was aroused in his behalf. I said to myself, when he comes to be examined again, he will be flung over, of course; so it will be simply a harmless act of charity to ease his fall as much as I can. I took him aside, and found that he knew a little of Caesar's history; and as he didn't know anything else, I went to work and drilled him like a galley slave on a certain line of stock questions concerning Caesar which I knew would be used. If you'll believe me, he went through with flying colours on examination day! He went through on that purely superficial 'cram,' and got compliments too, while others, who knew a thousand times more than he, got plucked. By some strangely lucky accident—an accident not likely to happen twice in a century—he was asked no question outside of the narrow limits of his drill.

It was stupefying. Well, all through his course I stood by him, with something of the sentiment which a mother feels for a crippled child; and he always saved himself—just by miracle, apparently.

Now of course the thing that would expose him and kill him at last was mathematics. I resolved to make his death as easy as I could; so I drilled him and crammed him, and crammed him and drilled him, just on the line of questions which the examiners would be most likely to use, and then launching him on his fate. Well, sir, try to conceive of the result: to my consternation, he took the first prize! And with it he got a perfect ovation in the way of compliments.

Sleep? There was no more sleep for me for a week. My conscience tortured me day and night. What I had done I had done purely through charity, and only to ease the poor youth's fall—I never had dreamed of any such preposterous result as the thing that had happened. I felt as guilty and miserable as the creator of Frankenstein. Here was a woodenhead whom I had put in the way of glittering promotions and prodigious responsibilities, and but one thing could happen: he and his responsibilities would all go to ruin together at the first opportunity.

The Crimean war had just broken out. Of course there had to be a war, I said to myself: we couldn't have peace and give this donkey a chance to die before he is found out. I waited for the earthquake. It came. And it made me reel when it did come. He was actually gazetted to a captaincy in a marching regiment! Better men grow old and grey in the service before they climb to a sublimity like that. And who could ever have foreseen that they would go and put such a load of responsibility on such green and inadequate shoulders? I could just barely have stood it if they had made him a cornet; but a captain—think of it! I thought my hair would turn white.

Consider what I did—I who so loved repose and inaction. I said to myself, I am responsible to the country for this, and I must go along with him and protect the country against him as far as I can. So I took my poor little capital that I had saved up through years of work and grinding economy, and went with a sigh and bought a cornetcy in his regiment, and away we went to the field.

And there—oh dear, it was awful. Blunders? Why, he never did anything but blunder. But, you see, nobody was in the fellow's secret—everybody had him focused wrong, and necessarily misinterpreted his performance every time—consequently they took his idiotic blunders for inspirations of genius; they did, honestly! His mildest blunders were enough to make a man in his right mind cry; and they did make me cry—and rage and rave too, privately. And the thing that kept me always in a sweat of apprehension was the fact that every fresh blunder he made increased the lustre of his reputation! I kept saying to myself, he'll get so high, that when discovery does finally come, it will be like the sun falling out of the sky.

He went right along up, from grade to grade, over the dead bodies of his superiors, until at last, in the hottest moment of the battle of—down went our colonel, and my heart jumped into my mouth, for Scoresby was next in rank! Now for it, said I; we'll all land in Sheol in ten minutes, sure.

The battle was awfully hot; the allies were steadily giving way all over the field. Our regiment occupied a position that was vital; a blunder now must be destruction. At this crucial moment, what does this immortal fool do but detach the regiment from its place and order a charge over a neighbouring hill where there wasn't a suggestion of an enemy! 'There you go!' I said to myself; 'this is the end at last.'

And away we did go, and were over the shoulder of the hill before the insane movement could be discovered and stopped. And what did we find? An entire and unsuspected Russian army in reserve! And what happened? We were eaten up? That is necessarily what would have happened in ninety-nine cases out of a hundred. But no, those Russians argued that no single regiment would come browsing around there at such a time. It must be the entire English army, and that the sly Russian game was detected and blocked; so they turned tail, and away they went, pell-mell, over the hill and down into the field, in wild confusion, and we after them; they themselves broke the solid Russian centre in the field, and tore through, and in no time there was the most tremendous rout you ever saw, and the defeat of the allies was turned into a sweeping and splendid victory! Marshal Canrobert looked on, dizzy with astonishment, admiration, and delight; and sent right off for Scoresby, and hugged him, and decorated him on the field, in presence of all the armies!

And what was Scoresby's blunder that time? Merely mistaking his right hand for his left—that was all. An order had come to him to fall back and support our right; and instead, he fell forward and went over the hill to the left. But the name he won that day as a marvelous military genius filled the world with his glory, and that glory will never fade while history books last.

He is just as good and sweet and loveable and unpretending as a man can be, but he doesn't know enough to come in when it rains. Now that is absolutely true. He is the supremest ass in the universe; and until half an hour ago nobody knew it but himself and me. He has been pursued, day by day and year by year, by a most phenomenal and astonishing luckiness. He has been a shining soldier in all our wars for a generation; he has littered his whole military life with blunders, and yet has never committed one that didn't make him a knight or a baronet or a lord or something. Look at his breast; why, he is just clothed in domestic and foreign decorations. Well, sir, every one of them is the record of some shouting stupidity or other; and taken together, they are proof that the very best thing in all this world that can befall a man is to be born lucky. I say again, as I said at the banquet, Scoresby's an absolute fool.

Who says fortune favours the brave! Sometimes morons may be successful in their stupidity due to sheer luck. This is a story written in 1886. This story perhaps preempted Tom Hanks' film, Forest Gump, *which in turn was based on a novel written by Winston Groom in 1986. A moron is a person who frowns when he reads a comic! But Dame Fortune has other plans.*

7

THE MODEL MILLIONAIRE

OSCAR WILDE

Unless one is wealthy there is no use in being a charming fellow. Romance is the privilege of the rich, not the profession of the unemployed. The poor should be practical and prosaic. It is better to have a permanent income than to be fascinating. These are the great truths of modern life which Hughie Erskine never realised. Poor Hughie! Intellectually, we must admit, he was not of much importance. He never said a brilliant or even an ill-natured thing in his life. But then he was wonderfully good-looking, with his crisp brown hair, his clear-cut profile, and his grey eyes. He was as popular with men as he was with women, and he had every accomplishment except that of making money. His father had bequeathed him his cavalry sword, and a *History of the Peninsular War* in fifteen volumes. Hughie hung the first over his looking-glass, put the second on a shelf between Ruff's Guide and Bailey's Magazine, and lived on two hundred a year that an old aunt allowed him. He had tried everything. He had gone on the Stock Exchange for six months; but what was a butterfly to do among bulls and bears? He had been a tea-merchant for a little longer, but had soon tired of pekoe and souchong. Then he had tried selling dry sherry. That did not answer; the sherry was a little too dry. Ultimately he became nothing, a delightful, ineffectual young man with a perfect profile and no profession.

To make matters worse, he was in love. The girl he loved was Laura Merton, the daughter of a retired Colonel who had lost his temper and his digestion in India, and had never found either of them again. Laura adored him, and he was ready to kiss her shoe-strings. They were the handsomest couple in London, and had not a penny-piece between them. The Colonel was very fond of Hughie, but would not hear of any engagement.

'Come to me, my boy, when you have got ten thousand pounds of your own, and we will see about it,' he used to say; and Hughie looked very glum on those days, and had to go to Laura for consolation.

One morning, as he was on his way to Holland Park, where the Mertons lived, he dropped in to see a great friend of his, Alan Trevor. Trevor was a painter. Indeed, few people escape that nowadays. But he was also an artist, and artists are rather rare. Personally he was a strange rough fellow, with a freckled face and a red ragged beard. However, when he took up the brush he was a real master, and his pictures were eagerly sought after. He had been very much attracted by Hughie at first, it must be acknowledged, entirely on account of his personal charm. 'The only people a painter should know,' he used to say, 'are people who are *bete* and beautiful, people who are an artistic pleasure to look at and an intellectual repose to talk to. Men who are dandies and women who are darlings rule the world, at least they should do so.' However, after he got to know Hughie better, he liked him quite as much for his bright buoyant spirits and his generous reckless nature, and had given him the permanent *entree* to his studio.

When Hughie came in he found Trevor putting the finishing touches to a wonderful life-size picture of a beggar-man. The beggar himself was standing on a raised platform in a corner of the studio. He was a wizened old man, with a face like wrinkled parchment, and a most piteous expression. Over his shoulders was flung a coarse brown cloak, all tears and tatters; his thick boots were patched and cobbled, and with one hand he leant on a rough stick, while with the other he held out his battered hat for alms.

'What an amazing model!' whispered Hughie, as he shook hands with his friend.

'An amazing model?' shouted Trevor at the top of his voice, 'I should think so! Such beggars as he are not to be met with every day. A *trouvaille, mort cher*; a living Velasquez! My stars! what an etching Rembrandt would have made of him!'

'Poor old chap!' said Hughie, 'how miserable he looks! But I suppose, to you painters, his face is his fortune?'

'Certainly,' replied Trevor, 'you don't want a beggar to look happy, do you?'

'How much does a model get for sitting?' asked Hughie, as he found himself a comfortable seat on a divan.

'A shilling an hour.'

'And how much do you get for your picture, Alan?'

'Oh, for this I get two thousand!'

'Pounds?'

'Guineas. Painters, poets, and physicians always get guineas.'

'Well, I think the model should have a percentage,' cried Hughie, laughing, 'they work quite as hard as you do.'

'Nonsense, nonsense! Why, look at the trouble of laying on the paint alone, and standing all day long at one's easel! It's all very well, Hughie, for you to talk, but I assure you that there are moments when Art almost attains the dignity of manual labour. But you mustn't chatter; I'm very busy. Smoke a cigarette, and keep quiet.'

After some time the servant came in, and told Trevor that the frame-maker wanted to speak to him.

'Don't run away, Hughie,' he said, as he went out, 'I will be back in a moment.'

The old beggar-man took advantage of Trevor's absence to rest for a moment on a wooden bench that was behind him. He looked so forlorn and wretched that Hughie could not help pitying him, and felt in his pockets to see what money he had. All he could find was a sovereign and some coppers. 'Poor old fellow,' he thought to himself, 'he wants it more than I do, but it means no hansoms for a fortnight,' and he walked across the studio and slipped the sovereign into the beggar's hand.

The old man started, and a faint smile flitted across his withered lips. 'Thank you, sir,' he said, 'thank you.'

Then Trevor arrived, and Hughie took his leave, blushing a little at what he had done. He spent the day with Laura, got a charming scolding for his extravagance, and had to walk home.

That night he strolled into the Palette Club at about eleven o'clock, and found Trevor sitting by himself in the smoking-room drinking hock and seltzer.

'Well, Alan, did you get the picture finished all right?' he said, as he lit his cigarette.

'Finished and framed, my boy!' answered Trevor, 'and, by-the-by, you have made a conquest. That old model you saw is quite devoted to you. I had to tell him all about you—who you are, where you live, what your income is, what prospects you have—'

'My dear Alan,' cried Hughie, 'I shall probably find him waiting for me when I go home. But of course you are only joking. Poor old wretch! I wish I could do something for him. I think it is dreadful that any one should be so miserable. I have got heaps of old clothes at home—do you think he would care for any of them? Why, his rags were falling to bits.'

'But he looks splendid in them,' said Trevor. 'I wouldn't paint him in a frock-coat for anything. What you call rags I call romance. What seems poverty to you is picturesqueness to me. However, I'll tell him of your offer.'

'Alan,' said Hughie seriously, 'you painters are a heartless lot.'

'An artist's heart is his head,' replied Trevor, 'and besides, our business is to realise the world as we see it, not to reform it as we know it. *a chacun son metier*. And now tell me how Laura is. The old model was quite interested in her.'

'You don't mean to say you talked to him about her?' said Hughie.

'Certainly I did. He knows all about the relentless colonel, the lovely Laura, and the £10,000.'

'You told that old beggar all my private affairs?' cried Hughie, looking very red and angry.

'My dear boy,' said Trevor, smiling, 'that old beggar, as you call him, is one of the richest men in Europe. He could buy all London tomorrow without overdrawing his account. He has a house in every capital, dines off gold plates, and can prevent Russia going to war when he chooses.'

'What on earth do you mean?' exclaimed Hughie.

'What I say,' said Trevor. 'The old man you saw today in the studio was Baron Hausberg. He is a great friend of mine, buys all my pictures and that sort of thing, and gave me a commission a month ago to paint him as a beggar. *Que voulez-vous? La fantaisie d'un millionnaire!* And I must say he made a magnificent figure in his rags, or perhaps I should say in my rags; they are an old suit I got in Spain.'

'Baron Hausberg!' cried Hughie. 'Good heavens! I gave him a sovereign!' and he sank into an armchair the picture of dismay.

'Gave him a sovereign!' shouted Trevor, and he burst into a roar of laughter. 'My dear boy, you'll never see it again. *Son affaire c'est l'argent des autres.*'

'I think you might have told me, Alan,' said Hughie sulkily, 'and not have let me make such a fool of myself.'

'Well, to begin with, Hughie,' said Trevor, 'it never entered my mind that you went about distributing alms in that reckless way. I can understand your kissing a pretty model, but your giving a sovereign to an ugly one—by Jove, no! Besides, the fact is that I really was not at home today to any one; and when you came in I didn't know whether Hausberg would like his name mentioned. You know he wasn't in full dress.'

'What a duffer he must think me!' said Hughie.

'Not at all. He was in the highest spirits after you left; kept chuckling to himself and rubbing his old wrinkled hands together. I couldn't make out why he was so interested to know all about you; but I see it all now. He'll invest your sovereign for you, Hughie, pay you the interest every six months, and have a capital story to tell after dinner.'

'I am an unlucky devil,' growled Hughie. 'The best thing I can do is to go to bed; and, my dear Alan, you mustn't tell any one. I shouldn't dare show my face in the Row.'

'Nonsense! It reflects the highest credit on your philanthropic spirit, Hughie. And don't run away. Have another cigarette, and you can talk about Laura as much as you like.'

However, Hughie wouldn't stop, but walked home, feeling very unhappy, and leaving Alan Trevor in fits of laughter.

The next morning, as he was at breakfast, the servant brought him up a card on which was written, 'Monsieur Gustave Naudin, *de la part de* M. le Baron Hausberg.'

'I suppose he has come for an apology,' said Hughie to himself; and he told the servant to show the visitor up.

An old gentleman with gold spectacles and grey hair came into the room, and said, in a slight French accent, 'Have I the honour of addressing Monsieur Erskine?'

Hughie bowed.

'I have come from Baron Hausberg,' he continued. 'The Baron—'

'I beg, sir, that you will offer him my sincerest apologies,' stammered Hughie.

'The Baron,' said the old gentleman, with a smile, 'has commissioned me to bring you this letter,' and he extended a sealed envelope.

On the outside was written, 'A wedding present to Hugh Erskine and Laura Merton, from an old beggar,' and inside was a cheque for £10,000.

When they were married Alan Trevor was the best man, and the Baron made a speech at the wedding breakfast.

'Millionaire models,' remarked Alan, 'are rare enough; but, by Jove, model millionaires are rarer still!'

Oscar Wilde explores the theme on a pun, words that sound alike but have different meanings. He juxtaposes the ideas of 'millionaire models' and 'model millionaires'!

8
THE SECRET LIFE OF WALTER MITTY
JAMES THURBER

'We're going through!' The Commander's voice was like thin ice breaking. He wore his full-dress uniform, with the heavily braided white cap pulled down rakishly over one cold gray eye. 'We can't make it, sir. It's spoiling for a hurricane, if you ask me.' 'I'm not asking you, Lieutenant Berg,' said the Commander. 'Throw on the power lights! Rev her up to 8,500! We're going through!' The pounding of the cylinders increased: ta-pocketa-pocketa-pocketa-*pocketa-pocketa*. The Commander stared at the ice forming on the pilot window. He walked over and twisted a row of complicated dials. 'Switch on No. 8 auxiliary!' he shouted. 'Switch on No. 8 auxiliary!' repeated Lieutenant Berg. 'Full strength in No. 3 turret!' shouted the Commander. 'Full strength in No. 3 turret!' The crew, bending to their various tasks in the huge, hurtling eight-engined Navy hydroplane, looked at each other and grinned. 'The Old Man'll get us through,' they said to one another. 'The Old Man ain't afraid of Hell!' ...

'Not so fast! You're driving too fast!' said Mrs Mitty. 'What are you driving so fast for?'

'Hmm?' said Walter Mitty. He looked at his wife, in the seat beside him, with shocked astonishment. She seemed grossly unfamiliar, like a strange woman who had yelled at him in a crowd. 'You were up to fifty-five,' she said. 'You know I don't like to go more than forty. You were up to fifty-five.' Walter Mitty drove on toward Waterbury in silence, the roaring of the SN202 through the worst storm in twenty years of Navy flying fading in the remote, intimate airways of his mind. 'You're tensed up again,' said Mrs Mitty. 'It's one of your days. I wish you'd let Dr. Renshaw look you over.'

Walter Mitty stopped the car in front of the building where his wife went to have her hair done. 'Remember to get those overshoes while I'm having my hair done,' she said. 'I don't need overshoes,' said Mitty. She put her mirror back into her bag. 'We've been all through that,' she said, getting out of the car. 'You're not a young man any longer.' He raced the engine a little. 'Why don't you wear your gloves? Have you lost your gloves?' Walter Mitty reached in a pocket and brought out the gloves. He put them on, but after she had turned and gone into the building and he had driven on to a red light, he took them off again. 'Pick it up, brother!' snapped a cop as the light changed, and Mitty hastily pulled on his gloves and lurched ahead. He drove around the streets aimlessly for a time, and then he drove past the hospital on his way to the parking lot.

... 'It's the millionaire banker, Wellington McMillan,' said the pretty nurse. 'Yes?' said Walter Mitty, removing his gloves slowly. 'Who has the case?' 'Dr. Renshaw and Dr. Benbow, but there are two specialists here, Dr. Remington from New York and Dr. Pritchard-Mitford from London. He flew over.' A door opened down a long, cool corridor and Dr. Renshaw came out. He looked distraught and haggard. 'Hello, Mitty,' he said. 'We're having the devil's own time with McMillan, the millionaire banker and close personal friend of Roosevelt. Obstreosis of the ductal tract. Tertiary. Wish you'd take a look at him.' 'Glad to,' said Mitty.

In the operating room there were whispered introductions: 'Dr. Remington, Dr. Mitty. Dr. Pritchard-Mitford, Dr. Mitty.' 'I've read your book on streptothricosis,' said Pritchard-Mitford, shaking hands. 'A brilliant performance, sir.' 'Thank you,' said Walter Mitty. 'Didn't know you were in the States, Mitty,' grumbled

Remington. 'Coals to Newcastle, bringing Mitford and me up here for a tertiary.' 'You are very kind,' said Mitty. A huge, complicated machine, connected to the operating table, with many tubes and wires, began at this moment to go pocketa-pocketa-pocketa. 'The new anaesthetizer is giving way!' shouted an interne. 'There is no one in the East who knows how to fix it!' 'Quiet, man!' said Mitty, in a low, cool voice. He sprang to the machine, which was now going pocketa-pocketa-queep-pocketa-queep. He began fingering delicately a row of glistening dials. 'Give me a fountain pen!' he snapped. Someone handed him a fountain pen. He pulled a faulty piston out of the machine and inserted the pen in its place. 'That will hold for ten minutes,' he said. 'Get on with the operation.' A nurse hurried over and whispered to Renshaw, and Mitty saw the man turn pale. 'Coreopsis has set in,' said Renshaw nervously. 'If you would take over, Mitty?' Mitty looked at him and at the craven figure of Benbow, who drank, and at the grave, uncertain faces of the two great specialists. 'If you wish,' he said. They slipped a white gown on him; he adjusted a mask and drew on thin gloves; nurses handed him shining ...

'Back it up, Mac! Look out for that Buick!' Walter Mitty jammed on the brakes. 'Wrong lane, Mac,' said the parking-lot attendant, looking at Mitty closely. 'Gee. Yeh,' muttered Mitty. He began cautiously to back out of the lane marked 'Exit Only.' 'Leave her sit there,' said the attendant. 'I'll put her away.' Mitty got out of the car. 'Hey, better leave the key.' 'Oh,' said Mitty, handing the man the ignition key. The attendant vaulted into the car, backed it up with insolent skill, and put it where it belonged.

They're so damn cocky, thought Walter Mitty, walking along Main Street; they think they know everything. Once he had tried to take his chains off, outside New Milford, and he had got them wound around the axles. A man had had to come out in a wrecking car and unwind them, a young, grinning garageman. Since then Mrs Mitty always made him drive to a garage to have the chains taken off. The next time, he thought, I'll wear my right arm in a sling; they won't grin at me then. I'll have my right arm in a sling and they'll see I couldn't possibly take the chains off myself. He kicked at the slush on the sidewalk. 'Overshoes,' he said to himself, and he began looking for a shoe store.

When he came out into the street again, with the overshoes in a box under his arm, Walter Mitty began to wonder what the other thing was his wife had told him to get. She had told him, twice, before they set out from their house for Waterbury. In a way he hated these weekly trips to town—he was always getting something wrong. Kleenex, he thought, Squibb's, razor blades? No. Toothpaste, toothbrush, bicarbonate, carborundum, initiative and referendum? He gave it up. But she would remember it. 'Where's the what's-its-name?' she would ask. 'Don't tell me you forgot the what's-its-name.' A newsboy went by shouting something about the Waterbury trial.

... 'Perhaps this will refresh your memory.' The District Attorney suddenly thrust a heavy automatic at the quiet figure on the witness stand. 'Have you ever seen this before?' Walter Mitty took the gun and examined it expertly. 'This is my Webley-Vickers 50.80,' he said calmly. An excited buzz ran around the courtroom. The Judge rapped for order. 'You are a crack shot with any sort of firearms, I believe?' said the District Attorney, insinuatingly. 'Objection!' shouted Mitty's attorney. 'We have shown that the defendant could not have fired the shot. We have shown that he wore his right arm in a sling on the night of the fourteenth of July.' Walter Mitty raised his hand briefly and the bickering attorneys were stilled. 'With any known make of gun,' he said evenly, 'I could have killed Gregory Fitzhurst at three hundred feet *with my left hand*.' Pandemonium broke loose in the courtroom. A woman's scream rose above the bedlam and suddenly a lovely, dark-haired girl was in Walter Mitty's arms. The District Attorney struck at her savagely. Without rising from his chair, Mitty let the man have it on the point of the chin. 'You miserable cur!' ...

'Puppy biscuit,' said Walter Mitty. He stopped walking and the buildings of Waterbury rose up out of the misty courtroom and surrounded him again. A woman who was passing laughed. 'He said "Puppy biscuit,"' she said to her companion. 'That man said "Puppy biscuit" to himself.' Walter Mitty hurried on. He went into an A. & P., not the first one he came to but a smaller one farther up the street. 'I want some biscuit for small, young dogs,' he said to the clerk. 'Any special brand, sir?' The greatest pistol shot in the world thought a moment. 'It says 'Puppies Bark for It' on the box,' said Walter Mitty.

His wife would be through at the hairdresser's in fifteen minutes, Mitty saw in looking at his watch, unless they had trouble drying it; sometimes they had trouble drying it. She didn't like to get to the hotel first; she would want him to be there waiting for her as usual. He found a big leather chair in the lobby, facing a window, and he put the overshoes and the puppy biscuit on the floor beside it. He picked up an old copy of *Liberty* and sank down into the chair. "Can Germany Conquer the World Through the Air?" Walter Mitty looked at the pictures of bombing planes and of ruined streets.

... 'The cannonading has got the wind up in young Raleigh, sir,' said the sergeant. Captain Mitty looked up at him through touselled hair. 'Get him to bed,' he said wearily. 'With the others. I'll fly alone.' 'But you can't, sir,' said the sergeant anxiously. 'It takes two men to handle that bomber and the Archies are pounding hell out of the air. Von Richtman's circus is between here and Saulier.' 'Somebody's got to get that ammunition dump,' said Mitty. 'I'm going over. Spot of brandy?' He poured a drink for the sergeant and one for himself. War thundered and whined around the dugout and battered at the door. There was a rending of wood and splinters flew through the room. 'A bit of a near thing,' said Captain Mitty carelessly. 'The box barrage is closing in,' said the sergeant. 'We only live once, Sergeant,' said Mitty, with his faint, fleeting smile. 'Or do we?' He poured another brandy and tossed it off. 'I never see a man could hold his brandy like you, sir,' said the sergeant. 'Begging your pardon, sir.' Captain Mitty stood up and strapped on his huge Webley-Vickers automatic. 'It's forty kilometres through hell, sir,' said the sergeant. Mitty finished one last brandy. 'After all,' he said softly, 'what isn't?' The pounding of the cannon increased; there was the rat-tat-tatting of machine guns, and from somewhere came the menacing pocketa-pocketa-pocketa of the new flame-throwers. Walter Mitty walked to the door of the dugout humming 'Auprès de Ma Blonde.' He turned and waved to the sergeant. 'Cheerio!' he said....

Something struck his shoulder. 'I've been looking all over this hotel for you,' said Mrs Mitty. 'Why do you have to hide in this old chair? How did you expect me to find you?' 'Things close in,' said Walter Mitty vaguely. 'What?' Mrs Mitty said. 'Did you get the what's-its-name? The puppy biscuit? What's in that box?' 'Overshoes,' said Mitty. 'Couldn't you have put them on in the store?' 'I was thinking,' said Walter Mitty. 'Does it ever occur to you that I am sometimes thinking?' She looked at him. 'I'm going to take your temperature when I get you home,' she said.

They went out through the revolving doors that made a faintly derisive whistling sound when you pushed them. It was two blocks to the parking lot. At the drugstore on the corner she said, 'Wait here for me. I forgot something. I won't be a minute.' She was more than a minute. Walter Mitty lighted a cigarette. It began to rain, rain with sleet in it. He stood up against the wall of the drugstore, smoking.... He put his shoulders back and his heels together. 'To hell with the handkerchief,' said Walter Mitty scornfully. He took one last drag on his cigarette and snapped it away. Then, with that faint, fleeting smile playing about his lips, he faced the firing squad; erect and motionless, proud and disdainful, Walter Mitty the Undefeated, inscrutable to the last.

The compliments in the fantasy world counteract Mitty's real life sense of shame. His heroic acts are at times laughable. 'It seemed he faced the firing squad; erect and motionless, proud and disdainful, Walter Mitty the Undefeated, inscrutable to the last.'

9

THE BOARDED WINDOW

AMBROSE BIERCE

In 1830, only a few miles away from what is now the great city of Cincinnati, lay an immense and almost unbroken forest. The whole region was sparsely settled by people of the frontier—restless souls who no sooner had hewn fairly habitable homes out of the wilderness and attained to that degree of prosperity which today we should call indigence, than, impelled by some mysterious impulse of their nature, they abandoned all and pushed farther westward, to encounter new perils and privations in the effort to regain the meagre comforts which they had voluntarily renounced. Many of them had already forsaken that region for the remoter settlements, but among those remaining was one who had been of those first arriving. He lived alone in a house of logs surrounded on all sides by the great forest, of whose gloom and silence he seemed a part, for no one had ever known him to smile nor speak a needless word. His simple wants were supplied by the sale or barter of skins of wild animals in the river town, for not a thing did he grow upon the land which, if needful, he might have claimed by right of undisturbed possession. There were evidences of 'improvement'—a few acres of ground immediately about the house had once been cleared of its trees, the decayed stumps of which were half concealed by the new growth that had been suffered to repair the ravage wrought by the axe. Apparently the man's zeal for agriculture had burned with a failing flame, expiring in penitential ashes.

The little log house, with its chimney of sticks, its roof of warping clapboards weighted with traversing poles and its 'chinking' of clay, had a single door and, directly opposite, a window. The latter, however, was boarded up—nobody could remember a time when it was not. And none knew why it was so closed; certainly not because of the occupant's dislike of light and air, for on those rare occasions when a hunter had passed that lonely spot the recluse had commonly been seen sunning himself on his doorstep if heaven had provided sunshine for his need. I fancy there are few persons living today who ever knew the secret of that window, but I am one, as you shall see.

The man's name was said to be Murlock. He was apparently seventy years old, actually about fifty. Something besides years had had a hand in his ageing. His hair and long, full beard were white, his grey, lustreless eyes sunken, his face singularly seamed with wrinkles which appeared to belong to two intersecting systems. In figure he was tall and spare, with a stoop of the shoulders—a burden bearer. I never saw him; these particulars I learned from my grandfather, from whom also I got the man's story when I was a lad. He had known him when living nearby in that early day.

One day Murlock was found in his cabin, dead. It was not a time and place for coroners and newspapers, and I suppose it was agreed that he had died from natural causes or I should have been told, and should remember. I know only that with what was probably a sense of the fitness of things the body was buried near the cabin, alongside the grave of his wife, who had preceded him by so many years that local tradition had retained hardly a hint of her existence. That closes the final chapter of this true story—excepting, indeed, the circumstance that many years afterward, in company with an equally intrepid spirit, I penetrated to the place and ventured near enough to the ruined cabin to throw a stone against it, and ran away to avoid the ghost which every well-informed boy thereabout knew haunted the spot. But there is an earlier chapter—that supplied by my grandfather.

When Murlock built his cabin and began laying sturdily about with his axe to hew out a farm—the rifle, meanwhile, his means of support—he was young, strong and full of hope. In that eastern country whence he came he had married, as was the fashion, a young woman in all ways worthy of his honest devotion, who shared the dangers and privations of his lot with a willing spirit and light heart. There is no known record of her name; of her charms of mind and person tradition is silent and the doubter is at liberty to entertain his doubt; but God forbid that I should share it! Of their affection and happiness there is abundant assurance in every added day of the man's widowed life; for what but the magnetism of a blessed memory could have chained that venturesome spirit to a lot like that?

One day Murlock returned from gunning in a distant part of the forest to find his wife prostrate with fever, and delirious. There was no physician within miles, no neighbour; nor was she in a condition to be left, to summon help. So he set about the task of nursing her back to health, but at the end of the third day she fell into unconsciousness and so passed away, apparently, with never a gleam of returning reason.

From what we know of a nature like his we may venture to sketch in some of the details of the outline picture drawn by my grandfather. When convinced that she was dead, Murlock had sense enough to remember that the dead must be prepared for burial. In performance of this sacred duty he blundered now and again, did certain things incorrectly, and others which he did correctly were done over and over. His occasional failures to accomplish some simple and ordinary act filled him with astonishment, like that of a drunken man who wonders at the suspension of familiar natural laws. He was surprised, too, that he did not weep—surprised and a little ashamed; surely it is unkind not to weep for the dead. 'Tomorrow,' he said aloud, 'I shall have to make the coffin and dig the grave; and then I shall miss her, when she is no longer in sight; but now—she is dead, of course, but it is all right—it must be all right, somehow. Things cannot be so bad as they seem.'

He stood over the body in the fading light, adjusting the hair and putting the finishing touches to the simple toilet, doing all mechanically, with soulless care. And still through his consciousness ran an undersense of conviction that all was right—that he should have her again as before, and everything explained. He had had no experience in grief; his capacity had not been enlarged by use. His heart could not contain it all, nor his imagination rightly conceive it. He did not know he was so hard struck; that knowledge would come later, and never go. Grief is an artist of powers as various as the instruments upon which he plays his dirges for the dead, evoking from some the sharpest, shrillest notes, from others the low, grave chords that throb recurrent like the slow beating of a distant drum. Some natures it startles; some it stupefies. To one it comes like the stroke of an arrow, stinging all the sensibilities to a keener life; to another as the blow of a bludgeon, which in crushing benumbs. We may conceive Murlock to have been that way affected, for (and here we are upon surer ground than that of conjecture) no sooner had he finished his pious work than, sinking into a chair by the side of the table upon which the body lay, and noting how white the profile showed in the deepening gloom, he laid his arms upon the table's edge, and dropped his face into them, tearless yet and unutterably weary. At that moment came in through the open window a long, wailing sound like the cry of a lost child in the far deeps of the darkening woods! But the man did not move. Again, and nearer than before, sounded that unearthly cry upon his failing sense. Perhaps it was a wild beast; perhaps it was a dream. For Murlock was asleep.

Some hours later, as it afterward appeared, this unfaithful watcher awoke and lifting his head from his arms intently listened—he knew not why. There in the black darkness by the side of the dead, recalling all without a shock, he strained his eyes to see—he knew not what. His senses were all alert, his breath was suspended, his blood had stilled its tides as if to assist the silence. Who—what had waked him, and where was it?

Suddenly the table shook beneath his arms, and at the same moment he heard, or fancied that he heard, a light, soft step—another—sounds as of bare feet upon the floor!

He was terrified beyond the power to cry out or move. Perforce he waited—waited there in the darkness through seeming centuries of such dread as one may know, yet live to tell. He tried vainly to speak the dead woman's name, vainly to stretch forth his hand across the table to learn if she were there. His throat was powerless, his arms and hands were like lead. Then occurred something most frightful. Some heavy body seemed hurled against the table with an impetus that pushed it against his breast so sharply as nearly to overthrow him, and at the same instant he heard and felt the fall of something upon the floor with so violent a thump that the whole house was shaken by the impact. A scuffling ensued, and a confusion of sounds impossible to describe. Murlock had risen to his feet. Fear had by excess forfeited control of his faculties. He flung his hands upon the table. Nothing was there!

There is a point at which terror may turn to madness; and madness incites to action. With no definite intent, from no motive but the wayward impulse of a madman, Murlock sprang to the wall, with a little groping seized his loaded rifle, and without aim discharged it. By the flash which lit up the room with a vivid illumination, he saw an enormous panther dragging the dead woman toward the window, its teeth fixed in her throat! Then there was darkness blacker than before, and silence; and when he returned to consciousness the sun was high and the wood vocal with songs of birds.

The body lay near the window, where the beast had left it when frightened away by the flash and report of the rifle. The clothing was deranged, the long hair in disorder, the limbs lay anyhow. From the throat, dreadfully lacerated, had issued a pool of blood not yet entirely coagulated. The ribbon with which he had bound the wrists was broken; the hands were tightly clenched. Between the teeth was a fragment of the animal's ear.

Irony is the essential element of the story. In fact, what appeals most is situational irony: when the outcome is different from the expectation. It is at the end of the story, when the reader finds out the true fate of Murlock's wife. The story end with a macabre image: 'Between the teeth was a fragment of the animal's ear'.

10

THE FIVE BOONS OF LIFE

MARK TWAIN

CHAPTER I

In the morning of life came a good fairy with her basket, and said:

'Here are gifts. Take one, leave the others. And be wary, chose wisely; oh, choose wisely! for only one of them is valuable.'

The gifts were five: Fame, Love, Riches, Pleasure, Death. The youth said, eagerly:

'There is no need to consider'; and he chose Pleasure.

He went out into the world and sought out the pleasures that youth delights in. But each in its turn was short-lived and disappointing, vain and empty; and each, departing, mocked him. In the end he said: 'These years I have wasted. If I could but choose again, I would choose wisely.

CHAPTER II

The fairy appeared, and said:

'Four of the gifts remain. Choose once more; and oh, remember—time is flying, and only one of them is precious.'

The man considered long, then chose Love; and did not mark the tears that rose in the fairy's eyes.

After many, many years the man sat by a coffin, in an empty home. And he communed with himself, saying: 'One by one they have gone away and left me; and now she lies here, the dearest and the last. Desolation after desolation has swept over me; for each hour of happiness the treacherous trader, Love, has sold me I have paid a thousand hours of grief. Out of my heart of hearts I curse him.'

CHAPTER III

'Choose again.' It was the fairy speaking.

'The years have taught you wisdom—surely it must be so. Three gifts remain. Only one of them has any worth—remember it, and choose warily.'

The man reflected long, then chose Fame; and the fairy, sighing, went her way.

Years went by and she came again, and stood behind the man where he sat solitary in the fading day, thinking. And she knew his thought:

'My name filled the world, and its praises were on every tongue, and it seemed well with me for a little while. How little a while it was! Then came envy; then detraction; then calumny; then hate; then persecution. Then derision, which is the beginning of the end. And last of all came pity, which is the funeral of fame. Oh, the bitterness and misery of renown! Target for mud in its prime, for contempt and compassion in its decay.'

CHAPTER IV

'Choose yet again.' It was the fairy's voice.

'Two gifts remain. And do not despair. In the beginning there was but one that was precious, and it is still here.'

'Wealth—which is power! How blind I was!' said the man. 'Now, at last, life will be worth the living. I will spend, squander, dazzle. These mockers and despisers will crawl in the dirt before me, and I will feed my hungry heart with their envy. I will have all luxuries, all joys, all enchantments of the spirit, all contentments of the body that man holds dear. I will buy, buy, buy! deference, respect, esteem, worship—every pinchbeck grace of life the market of a trivial world can furnish forth. I have lost much time, and chosen badly heretofore, but let that pass; I was ignorant then, and could but take for best what seemed so.'

Three short years went by, and a day came when the man sat shivering in a mean garret; and he was gaunt and wan and hollow-eyed, and clothed in rags; and he was gnawing a dry crust and mumbling:

'Curse all the world's gifts, for mockeries and gilded lies! And miscalled, every one. They are not gifts, but merely lendings. Pleasure, Love, Fame, Riches: they are but temporary disguises for lasting realities—Pain, Grief, Shame, Poverty. The fairy said true; in all her store there was but one gift which was precious, only one that was not valueless. How poor and cheap and mean I know those others now to be, compared with that inestimable one, that dear and sweet and kindly one, that steeps in dreamless and enduring sleep the pains that persecute the body, and the shames and griefs that eat the mind and heart. Bring it! I am weary, I would rest.'

CHAPTER V

The fairy came, bringing again four of the gifts, but Death was wanting. She said:

'I gave it to a mother's pet, a little child. It was ignorant, but trusted me, asking me to choose for it. You did not ask me to choose.'

'Oh, miserable me! What is left for me?'

'What not even you have deserved: the wanton insult of Old Age.'

A fable is one of 'fixities and definites' unlike imagination that 'dissolves, diffuses and dissipates' in order to recreate. This parabolic short story however ends with a sadistic twist.

11

THE EVIL CLERGYMAN

H.P. LOVECRAFT

I was shewn into the attic chamber by a grave, intelligent-looking man with quiet clothes and an iron-grey beard, who spoke to me in this fashion: 'Yes, *he* lived here—but I don't advise your doing anything. Your curiosity makes you irresponsible. *We* never come here at night, and it's only because of *his* will that we keep it this way. You know what *he* did. That abominable society took charge at last, and we don't know where *he* is buried. There was no way the law or anything else could reach the society.

'I hope you won't stay till after dark. And I beg of you to let that thing on the table—the thing that looks like a match box—alone. We don't know what it is, but we suspect it has something to do with what *he* did. We even avoid looking at it very steadily.'

After a time the man left me alone in the attic room. It was very dingy and dusty, and only primitively furnished, but it had a neatness which shewed it was not a slum-denizen's quarters. There were shelves full of theological and classical books, and another bookcase containing treatises on magic—Paracelsus, Albertus Magnus, Trithemius, Hermes Trismegistus, Borellus, and others in strange alphabets whose titles I could not decipher.

The furniture was very plain. There was a door, but it led only into a closet. The only egress was the aperture in the floor up to which the crude, steep staircase led. The windows were of bull's-eye pattern, and the black oak beams bespoke unbelievable antiquity. Plainly, this house was of the old world. I seemed to know where I was, but cannot recall what I then knew. Certainly the town was *not* London. My impression is of a small seaport.

The small object on the table fascinated me intensely. I seemed to know what to do with it, for I drew a pocket electric light—or what looked like one—out of my pocket and nervously tested its flashes. The light was not white but violet, and seemed less like true light than like some radio-active bombardment. I recall that I did not regard it as a common flashlight—indeed, I *had* a common flashlight in another pocket.

It was getting dark, and the ancient roofs and chimney-pots outside looked very queer through the bull's-eye window-panes. Finally I summoned up courage and propped the small object up on the table against a book—then turned the rays of the peculiar violet light upon it. The light seemed now to be more like a rain or hail of small violet particles than like a continuous beam. As the particles struck the glassy surface at the centre of the strange device, they seemed to produce a crackling noise like the sputtering of a vacuum tube through which sparks are passed. The dark glassy surface displayed a pinkish glow, and a vague white shape seemed to be taking form at its centre. Then I noticed that I was not alone in the room—and put the ray-projector back in my pocket.

But the newcomer did not speak—nor did I hear any sound whatever during all the immediately following moments. Everything was shadowy pantomime, as if seen at a vast distance through some intervening haze—although on the other hand the newcomer and all subsequent comers loomed large and close, as if both near and distant, according to some abnormal geometry.

The newcomer was a thin, dark man of medium height attired in the clerical garb of the Anglican church. He was apparently about thirty years old, with a sallow, olive complexion and fairly good features, but an abnormally high forehead. His black hair was well cut and neatly brushed, and he was clean-shaven though blue-chinned with a heavy growth of beard. He wore rimless spectacles with steel bows. His build and lower facial features were like other clergymen I had seen, but he had a vastly higher forehead, and was darker and more intelligent-looking—also more subtly and concealedly *evil*-looking. At the present moment—having just lighted a faint oil lamp—he looked nervous, and before I knew it he was casting all his magical books into a fireplace on the window side of the room (where the wall slanted sharply) which I had not noticed before. The flames devoured the volumes greedily—leaping up in strange colours and emitting indescribably hideous odours as the strangely hieroglyphed leaves and wormy bindings succumbed to the devastating element. All at once I saw there were others in the room—grave-looking men in clerical costume, one of whom wore the bands and knee-breeches of a bishop. Though I could hear nothing, I could see that they were bringing a decision of vast import to the first-comer. They seemed to hate and fear him at the same time, and he seemed to return these sentiments. His face set itself into a grim expression, but I could see his right hand shaking as he tried to grip the back of a chair. The bishop pointed to the empty case and to the fireplace (where the flames had died down amidst a charred, non-committal mass), and seemed filled with a peculiar loathing. The first-comer then gave a wry smile and reached out with his left hand toward the small object on the table. Everyone then seemed frightened. The procession of clerics began filing down the steep stairs through the trap-door in the floor, turning and making menacing gestures as they left. The bishop was last to go.

The first-comer now went to a cupboard on the inner side of the room and extracted a coil of rope. Mounting a chair, he attached one end of the rope to a hook in the great exposed central beam of black oak, and began making a noose with the other end. Realising he was about to hang himself, I started forward to dissuade or save him. He saw me and ceased his preparations, looking at me with a kind of *triumph* which puzzled and disturbed me. He slowly stepped down from the chair and began gliding toward me with a positively wolfish grin on his dark, thin-lipped face.

I felt somehow in deadly peril, and drew out the peculiar ray-projector as a weapon of defence. Why I thought it could help me, I do not know. I turned it on—full in his face, and saw the sallow features glow first with violet and then with pinkish light. His expression of wolfish exultation began to be crowded aside by a look of profound fear—which did not, however, wholly displace the exultation. He stopped in his tracks—then, flailing his arms wildly in the air, began to stagger backward. I saw he was edging toward the open stair-well in the floor, and tried to shout a warning, but he did not hear me. In another instant he had lurched backward through the opening and was lost to view.

I found difficulty in moving toward the stair-well, but when I did get there I found no crushed body on the floor below. Instead there was a clatter of people coming up with lanterns, for the spell of phantasmal silence had broken, and I once more heard sounds and saw figures as normally tridimensional. Something had evidently drawn a crowd to this place. Had there been a noise I had not heard? Presently the two people (simply villagers, apparently) farthest in the lead saw me—and stood paralysed. One of them shrieked loudly and reverberently:

'Ahrrh! ... It be 'ee, zur? Again?'

Then they all turned and fled frantically. All, that is, but one. When the crowd was gone I saw the grave-bearded man who had brought me to this place—standing alone with a lantern. He was gazing at me gaspingly and fascinatedly, but did not seem afraid. Then he began to ascend the stairs, and joined me in the attic. He spoke:

'So you *didn't* let it alone! I'm sorry. I know what has happened. It happened once before, but the man got frightened and shot himself. You ought not to have made *him* come back. You know what *he* wants. But you mustn't get frightened like the other man he got. Something very strange and terrible has happened to you, but it didn't get far enough to hurt your mind and personality. If you'll keep cool, and accept the need for making certain radical readjustments in your life, you can keep right on enjoying the world, and the fruits of your scholarship. But you can't live here—and I don't think you'll wish to go back to London. I'd advise America.

'You mustn't try anything more with that—thing. Nothing can be put back now. It would only make matters worse to do—or summon—anything. You are not as badly off as you might be—but you must get out of here at once and stay away. You'd better thank heaven it didn't go further....

'I'm going to prepare you as bluntly as I can. There's been a certain change—in your personal appearance. *He* always causes that. But in a new country you can get used to it. There's a mirror up at the other end of the room, and I'm going to take you to it. You'll get a shock—though you will see nothing repulsive.'

I was now shaking with a deadly fear, and the bearded man almost had to hold me up as he walked me across the room to the mirror, the faint lamp (i.e., that formerly on the table, not the still fainter lantern he had brought) in his free hand. This is what I saw in the glass:

A thin, dark man of medium stature attired in the clerical garb of the Anglican church, apparently about thirty, and with rimless, steel-bowed glasses glistening beneath a sallow, olive forehead of abnormal height.

It was the silent first-comer who had burned his books.

For all the rest of my life, in outward form, I was to be that man!

∞

'The Evil Clergyman' is an excerpt from a letter written by American horror fiction writer H. P. Lovecraft in 1933. After his death, it was published in the April 1939 issue of Weird Tales as a short story.

12
THE NECKLACE

GUY DE MAUPASSANT

She was one of those pretty and charming girls born, as if by an error of fate, into a family of clerks. She had no dowry, no expectations, no means of becoming known, understood, loved or wedded by a man of wealth and distinction; and so she let herself be married to a minor official at the Ministry of Education.

She dressed plainly because she had never been able to afford anything better, but she was as unhappy as if she had once been wealthy. Women don't belong to a caste or class; their beauty, grace, and natural charm take the place of birth and family. Natural delicacy, instinctive elegance and a quick wit determine their place in society, and make the daughters of commoners the equals of the very finest ladies.

She suffered endlessly, feeling she was entitled to all the delicacies and luxuries of life. She suffered because of the poorness of her house as she looked at the dirty walls, the worn-out chairs and the ugly curtains. All these things that another woman of her class would not even have noticed, tormented her and made her resentful. The sight of the little Brenton girl who did her housework filled her with terrible regrets and hopeless fantasies. She dreamed of silent antechambers hung with Oriental tapestries, lit from above by torches in bronze holders, while two tall footmen in knee-length breeches napped in huge armchairs, sleepy from the stove's oppressive warmth. She dreamed of vast living rooms furnished in rare old silks, elegant furniture loaded with priceless ornaments, and inviting smaller rooms, perfumed, made for afternoon chats with close friends—famous, sought after men, who all women envy and desire.

When she sat down to dinner at a round table covered with a three-day-old cloth opposite her husband who, lifting the lid off the soup, shouted excitedly, 'Ah! Beef stew! What could be better,' she dreamed of fine dinners, of shining silverware, of tapestries which peopled the walls with figures from another time and strange birds in fairy forests; she dreamed of delicious dishes served on wonderful plates, of whispered gallantries listened to with an inscrutable smile as one ate the pink flesh of a trout or the wings of a quail.

She had no dresses, no jewels, nothing; and these were the only things she loved. She felt she was made for them alone. She wanted so much to charm, to be envied, to be desired and sought after.

She had a rich friend, a former schoolmate at the convent, whom she no longer wanted to visit because she suffered so much when she came home. For whole days afterwards she would weep with sorrow, regret, despair and misery.

One evening her husband came home with an air of triumph, holding a large envelope in his hand.

'Look,' he said, 'here's something for you.'

She tore open the paper and drew out a card, on which was printed the words:

'The Minister of Education and Mme Georges Rampouneau request the pleasure of M. and Mme. Loisel's company at the Ministry, on the evening of Monday January 18th.'

Instead of being delighted, as her husband had hoped, she threw the invitation on the table resentfully, and muttered:

'What do you want me to do with that?'

'But, my dear, I thought you would be pleased. You never go out, and it will be such a lovely occasion! I had awful trouble getting it. Every one wants to go; it is very exclusive, and they're not giving many invitations to clerks. The whole ministry will be there.'

She stared at him angrily, and said, impatiently: 'And what do you expect me to wear if I go?' He hadn't thought of that. He stammered: 'Why, the dress you go to the theatre in. It seems very nice to me ...'

He stopped, stunned, distressed to see his wife crying. Two large tears ran slowly from the corners of her eyes towards the corners of her mouth. He stuttered: 'What's the matter? What's the matter?'

With great effort she overcame her grief and replied in a calm voice, as she wiped her wet cheeks: 'Nothing. Only I have no dress and so I can't go to this party. Give your invitation to a friend whose wife has better clothes than I do.'

He was distraught, but tried again: 'Let's see, Mathilde. How much would a suitable dress cost, one which you could use again on other occasions, something very simple?'

She thought for a moment, computing the cost, and also wondering what amount she could ask for without an immediate refusal and an alarmed exclamation from the thrifty clerk. At last she answered hesitantly: 'I don't know exactly, but I think I could do it with four hundred francs.'

He turned a little pale, because he had been saving that exact amount to buy a gun and treat himself to a hunting trip the following summer, in the country near Nanterre, with a few friends who went lark-shooting there on Sundays.

However, he said: 'Very well, I can give you four hundred francs. But try and get a really beautiful dress.'

The day of the party drew near, and Madame Loisel seemed sad, restless, anxious. Her dress was ready, however. One evening her husband said to her: 'What's the matter? You've been acting strange these last three days.'

She replied: 'I'm upset that I have no jewels, not a single stone to wear. I will look cheap. I would almost rather not go to the party.'

'You could wear flowers,' he said. 'They are very fashionable at this time of year. For ten francs you could get two or three magnificent roses.'

She was not convinced.

'No, there is nothing more humiliating than looking poor in the middle of a lot of rich women.'

'How stupid you are!' her husband cried. 'Go and see your friend Madame Forestier and ask her to lend you some jewels. You know her well enough for that.'

She uttered a cry of joy. 'Of course. I had not thought of that.'

The next day she went to her friend's house and told her of her distress.

Madame Forestier went to her mirrored wardrobe, took out a large box, brought it back, opened it, and said to Madame Loisel: 'Choose, my dear.'

First she saw some bracelets, then a pearl necklace, then a gold Venetian cross set with precious stones, of exquisite craftsmanship. She tried on the jewelry in the mirror, hesitated, could not bear to part with them, to give them back. She kept asking: 'You have nothing else?'

'Why, yes. But I don't know what you like.'

Suddenly she discovered, in a black satin box, a superb diamond necklace, and her heart began to beat with uncontrolled desire. Her hands trembled as she took it. She fastened it around her neck, over her high-necked dress, and stood lost in ecstasy as she looked at herself.

Then she asked anxiously, hesitating: 'Would you lend me this, just this?'

'Why, yes, of course.'

She threw her arms around her friend's neck, embraced her rapturously, then fled with her treasure.

The day of the party arrived. Madame Loisel was a success. She was prettier than all the other women, elegant, gracious, smiling, and full of joy. All the men stared at her, asked her name, tried to be introduced. All the cabinet officials wanted to waltz with her. The minister noticed her.

She danced wildly, with passion, drunk on pleasure, forgetting everything in the triumph of her beauty, in the glory of her success, in a sort of cloud of happiness, made up of all this respect, all this admiration, all these awakened desires, of that sense of triumph that is so sweet to a woman's heart.

She left at about four o'clock in the morning. Her husband had been dozing since midnight in a little deserted anteroom with three other gentlemen whose wives were having a good time.

He threw over her shoulders the clothes he had brought for her to go outside in, the modest clothes of an ordinary life, whose poverty contrasted sharply with the elegance of the ball dress. She felt this and wanted to run away, so she wouldn't be noticed by the other women who were wrapping themselves in expensive furs.

Loisel held her back.

'Wait a moment, you'll catch a cold outside. I'll go and find a cab.'

But she would not listen to him, and ran down the stairs. When they were finally in the street, they could not find a cab, and began to look for one, shouting at the cabmen they saw passing in the distance.

They walked down toward the Seine in despair, shivering with cold. At last they found on the quay one of those old night cabs that one sees in Paris only after dark, as if they were ashamed to show their shabbiness during the day.

They were dropped off at their door in the Rue des Martyrs, and sadly walked up the steps to their apartment. It was all over, for her. And he was remembering that he had to be back at his office at ten o'clock.

In front of the mirror, she took off the clothes around her shoulders, taking a final look at herself in all her glory. But suddenly she uttered a cry. She no longer had the necklace round her neck!

'What is the matter?' asked her husband, already half undressed.

She turned towards him, panic-stricken.

'I have ... I have ... I no longer have Madame Forestier's necklace.'

He stood up, distraught.

'What! ... how? ... That's impossible!'

They looked in the folds of her dress, in the folds of her cloak, in her pockets, everywhere. But they could not find it.

'Are you sure you still had it on when you left the ball?' he asked.

'Yes. I touched it in the hall at the Ministry.'

'But if you had lost it in the street we would have heard it fall. It must be in the cab.'

'Yes. That's probably it. Did you take his number?'

'No. And you, didn't you notice it?'

'No.'

They stared at each other, stunned. At last Loisel put his clothes on again.

'I'm going back,' he said, 'over the whole route we walked, see if I can find it.'

He left. She remained in her ball dress all evening, without the strength to go to bed, sitting on a chair, with no fire, her mind blank.

Her husband returned at about seven o'clock. He had found nothing.

He went to the police, to the newspapers to offer a reward, to the cab companies, everywhere the tiniest glimmer of hope led him.

She waited all day, in the same state of blank despair from before this frightful disaster. Loisel returned in the evening, a hollow, pale figure; he had found nothing.

'You must write to your friend,' he said, 'tell her you have broken the clasp of her necklace and that you are having it mended. It will give us time to look some more.'

She wrote as he dictated.

At the end of one week they had lost all hope.

And Loisel, who had aged five years, declared: 'We must consider how to replace the jewel.'

The next day they took the box which had held it, and went to the jeweler whose name they found inside. He consulted his books.

'It was not I, madame, who sold the necklace; I must simply have supplied the case.'

And so they went from jeweler to jeweler, looking for a necklace like the other one, consulting their memories, both sick with grief and anguish.

In a shop at the Palais Royal, they found a string of diamonds which seemed to be exactly what they were looking for. It was worth forty thousand francs. They could have it for thirty-six thousand.

So they begged the jeweler not to sell it for three days. And they made an arrangement that he would take it back for thirty-four thousand francs if the other necklace was found before the end of February.

Loisel had eighteen thousand francs which his father had left him. He would borrow the rest. And he did borrow, asking for a thousand francs from one man, five hundred from another, five louis here, three louis there. He gave notes, made ruinous agreements, dealt with usurers, with every type of money-lender. He compromised the rest of his life, risked signing notes without knowing if he could ever honor them, and, terrified by the anguish still to come, by the black misery about to fall on him, by the prospect of every physical privation and every moral torture he was about to suffer, he went to get the new necklace, and laid down on the jeweler's counter thirty-six thousand francs.

When Madame Loisel took the necklace back, Madame Forestier said coldly:

'You should have returned it sooner, I might have needed it.'

To the relief of her friend, she did not open the case. If she had detected the substitution, what would she have thought? What would she have said? Would she have taken her friend for a thief?

From then on, Madame Loisel knew the horrible life of the very poor. But she played her part heroically. The dreadful debt must be paid. She would pay it. They dismissed their maid; they changed their lodgings; they rented a garret under the roof.

She came to know the drudgery of housework, the odious labors of the kitchen. She washed the dishes, staining her rosy nails on greasy pots and the bottoms of pans. She washed the dirty linen, the shirts and the dishcloths, which she hung to dry on a line; she carried the garbage down to the street every morning, and carried up the water, stopping at each landing to catch her breath. And, dressed like a commoner, she went to the fruiterer's, the grocer's, the butcher's, her basket on her arm, bargaining, insulted, fighting over every miserable sou.

Each month they had to pay some notes, renew others, get more time.

Her husband worked every evening, doing accounts for a tradesman, and often, late into the night, he sat copying a manuscript at five sous a page.

And this life lasted ten years.

At the end of ten years they had paid off everything, everything, at usurer's rates and with the accumulations of compound interest.

Madame Loisel looked old now. She had become strong, hard and rough like all women of impoverished households. With hair half combed, with skirts awry, and reddened hands, she talked loudly as she washed the floor with great swishes of water. But sometimes, when her husband was at the office, she sat down near the window and thought of that evening at the ball so long ago, when she had been so beautiful and so admired.

What would have happened if she had not lost that necklace? Who knows, who knows? How strange life is, how fickle! How little is needed for one to be ruined or saved!

One Sunday, as she was walking in the Champs Élysées to refresh herself after the week's work, suddenly she saw a woman walking with a child. It was Madame Forestier, still young, still beautiful, still charming.

Madame Loisel felt emotional. Should she speak to her? Yes, of course. And now that she had paid, she would tell her all. Why not?

She went up to her.

'Good morning, Jeanne.'

The other, astonished to be addressed so familiarly by this common woman, did not recognize her. She stammered: 'But madame—I don't know. You must have made a mistake.'

'No, I am Mathilde Loisel.'

Her friend uttered a cry.

'Oh! ... my poor Mathilde, how you've changed! ...'

'Yes, I have had some hard times since I last saw you, and many miseries ... and all because of you! ...'

'Me? How can that be?'

'You remember that diamond necklace that you lent me to wear to the Ministry party?'

'Yes. Well?'

'Well, I lost it.'

'What do you mean? You brought it back.'

'I brought you back another exactly like it. And it has taken us ten years to pay for it. It wasn't easy for us, we had very little. But at last it is over, and I am very glad.'

Madame Forestier was stunned.

'You say that you bought a diamond necklace to replace mine?'

'Yes; you didn't notice then? They were very similar.'

And she smiled with proud and innocent pleasure.

Madame Forestier, deeply moved, took both her hands.

'Oh, my poor Mathilde! Mine was an imitation! It was worth five hundred francs at most! ...'

The story is cleverly planned and superbly executed. The theme is a commentary on greed, deceptive appearances, and beauty and vanity. There is an underlying message: 'Cut your coat according to your cloth.'

13

THE FLY

KATHERINE MANSFIELD

'Y'are very snug in here,' piped old Mr Woodifield, and he peered out of the great, green-leather armchair by his friend the boss's desk as a baby peers out of its pram. His talk was over; it was time for him to be off. But he did not want to go. Since he had retired, since his ... stroke, the wife and the girls kept him boxed up in the house every day of the week except Tuesday. On Tuesday he was dressed and brushed and allowed to cut back to the City for the day. Though what he did there the wife and girls couldn't imagine. Made a nuisance of himself to his friends, they supposed.... Well, perhaps so. All the same, we cling to our last pleasures as the tree clings to its last leaves. So there sat old Woodifield, smoking a cigar and staring almost greedily at the boss, who rolled in his office chair, stout, rosy, five years older than he, and still going strong, still at the helm. It did one good to see him.

Wistfully, admiringly, the old voice added, 'It's snug in here, upon my word!'

'Yes, it's comfortable enough,' agreed the boss, and he flipped the *Financial Times* with a paper-knife. As a matter of fact he was proud of his room; he liked to have it admired, especially by old Woodifield. It gave him a feeling of deep, solid satisfaction to be planted there in the midst of it in full view of that frail old figure in the muffler.

'I've had it done up lately,' he explained, as he had explained for the past—how many—weeks.

'New carpet,' and he pointed to the bright red carpet with a pattern of large white rings. 'New furniture,' and he nodded towards the massive bookcase and the table with legs like twisted treacle. 'Electric heating!' He waved almost exultantly towards the five transparent, pearly sausages glowing so softly in the tilted copper pan.

But he did not draw old Woodifield's attention to the photograph over the table of a grave-looking boy in uniform standing in one of those spectral photographers' parks with photographers' storm-clouds behind him. It was not new. It had been there for over six years.

'There was something I wanted to tell you,' said old Woodifield, and his eyes grew dim remembering. 'Now what was it? I had it in my mind when I started out this morning.' His hands began to tremble, and patches of red showed above his beard.

Poor old chap, he's on his last pins, thought the boss. And, feeling kindly, he winked at the old man, and said jokingly, 'I tell you what. I've got a little drop of something here that'll do you good before you go out into the cold again. It's beautiful stuff. It wouldn't hurt a child.' He took a key off his watch-chain, unlocked a cupboard below his desk, and drew forth a dark, squat bottle. 'That's the medicine,' said he. 'And the man from whom I got it told me on the strict Q.T. it came from the cellars at Windsor Castle.'

Old Woodifield's mouth fell open at the sight. He couldn't have looked more surprised if the boss had produced a rabbit.

'It's whisky, ain't it?' he piped feebly.

The boss turned the bottle and lovingly showed him the label. Whisky it was.

'D'you know,' said he, peering up at the boss wonderingly, 'they won't let me touch it at home.' And he looked as though he was going to cry.

'Ah, that's where we know a bit more than the ladies,' cried the boss, swooping across for two tumblers that stood on the table with the water-bottle, and pouring a generous finger into each. 'Drink it down. It'll do you good. And don't put any water with it. It's sacrilege to tamper with stuff like this. Ah!' He tossed off his, pulled out his handkerchief, hastily wiped his moustaches, and cocked an eye at old Woodifield, who was rolling his in his chaps.

The old man swallowed, was silent a moment, and then said faintly, 'It's nutty!'

But it warmed him; it crept into his chill old brain—he remembered.

'That was it,' he said, heaving himself out of his chair. 'I thought you'd like to know. The girls were in Belgium last week having a look at poor Reggie's grave, and they happened to come across your boy's. They're quite near each other, it seems.'

Old Woodifield paused, but the boss made no reply. Only a quiver in his eyelids showed that he heard.

'The girls were delighted with the way the place is kept,' piped the old voice. 'Beautifully looked after. Couldn't be better if they were at home. You've not been across, have yer?'

'No, no!' For various reasons the boss had not been across.

'There's miles of it,' quavered old Woodifield, 'and it's all as neat as a garden. Flowers growing on all the graves. Nice broad paths.' It was plain from his voice how much he liked a nice broad path.

The pause came again. Then the old man brightened wonderfully.

'D'you know what the hotel made the girls pay for a pot of jam?' he piped. 'Ten francs! Robbery, I call it. It was a little pot, so Gertrude says, no bigger than a half-crown. And she hadn't taken more than a spoonful when they charged her ten francs. Gertrude brought the pot away with her to teach 'em a lesson. Quite right, too; it's trading on our feelings. They think because we're over there having a look round we're ready to pay anything. That's what it is.' And he turned towards the door.

'Quite right, quite right!' cried the boss, though what was quite right he hadn't the least idea. He came round by his desk, followed the shuffling footsteps to the door, and saw the old fellow out. Woodifield was gone.

For a long moment the boss stayed, staring at nothing, while the grey-haired office messenger, watching him, dodged in and out of his cubby-hole like a dog that expects to be taken for a run. Then: 'I'll see nobody for half an hour, Macey,' said the boss. 'Understand! Nobody at all.'

'Very good, sir.'

The door shut, the firm heavy steps recrossed the bright carpet, the fat body plumped down in the spring chair, and leaning forward, the boss covered his face with his hands. He wanted, he intended, he had arranged to weep....

It had been a terrible shock to him when old Woodifield sprang that remark upon him about the boy's grave. It was exactly as though the earth had opened and he had seen the boy lying there with Woodifield's girls staring down at him. For it was strange. Although over six years had passed away, the boss never thought of the boy except as lying unchanged, unblemished in his uniform, asleep for ever. 'My son!' groaned the boss. But no tears came yet. In the past, in the first months and even years after the boy's death, he had only to say those words to be overcome by such grief that nothing short of a violent fit of weeping could relieve him. Time, he had declared then, he had told everybody, could make no difference. Other men perhaps might recover, might live their loss down, but not he. How was it possible! His boy was an only son. Ever since his birth the boss had worked at building up this business for him; it had no other meaning if it was not for the boy. Life itself had come to have no other meaning. How on earth could he have slaved, denied himself, kept going all those years without the promise for ever before him of the boy's stepping into his shoes and carrying on where he left off?

And that promise had been so near being fulfilled. The boy had been in the office learning the ropes for a year before the war. Every morning they had started off together; they had come back by the same train. And what congratulations he had received as the boy's father! No wonder; he had taken to it marvellously. As to his popularity with the staff, every man jack of them down to old Macey couldn't make enough of the boy. And he wasn't in the least spoilt. No, he was just his bright natural self, with the right word for everybody, with that boyish look and his habit of saying, 'Simply splendid!'

But all that was over and done with as though it never had been. The day had come when Macey had handed him the telegram that brought the whole place crashing about his head. 'Deeply regret to inform you ...' And he had left the office a broken man, with his life in ruins.

Six years ago, six years.... How quickly time passed! It might have happened yesterday. The boss took his hands from his face; he was puzzled. Something seemed to be wrong with him. He wasn't feeling as he wanted to feel. He decided to get up and have a look at the boy's photograph. But it wasn't a favourite photograph of his; the expression was unnatural. It was cold, even stern-looking. The boy had never looked like that.

At that moment the boss noticed that a fly had fallen into his broad inkpot, and was trying feebly but desperately to clamber out again. Help! Help! said those struggling legs. But the sides of the inkpot were wet and slippery; it fell back again and began to swim. The boss took up a pen, picked the fly out of the ink, and shook it on to a piece of blotting-paper. For a fraction of a second it lay still on the dark patch that oozed round it. Then the front legs waved, took hold, and, pulling its small, sodden body up, it began the immense task of cleaning the ink from its wings. Over and under, over and under, went a leg along a wing as the stone goes over and under the scythe. Then there was a pause, while the fly, seeming to stand on the tips of its toes, tried to expand first one wing and then the other. It succeeded at last, and, sitting down, it began, like a minute cat, to clean its face. Now one could imagine that the little front legs rubbed against each other lightly, joyfully. The horrible danger was over; it had escaped; it was ready for life again.

But just then the boss had an idea. He plunged his pen back into the ink, leaned his thick wrist on the blotting-paper, and as the fly tried its wings down came a great heavy blot. What would it make of that! What indeed! the little beggar seemed absolutely cowed, stunned, and afraid to move because of what would happen next. But then, as if painfully, it dragged itself forward. The front legs waved, caught hold, and, more slowly this time, the task began from the beginning.

He's a plucky little devil, thought the boss, and he felt a real admiration for the fly's courage. That was the way to tackle things; that was the right spirit. Never say die; it was only a question of... But the fly had again finished its laborious task, and the boss had just time to refill his pen, to shake fair and square on the new-cleaned body yet another dark drop. What about it this time? A painful moment of suspense followed. But behold, the front legs were again waving; the boss felt a rush of relief. He leaned over the fly and said to it tenderly, 'You artful little b...' And he actually had the brilliant notion of breathing on it to help the drying process. All the same, there was something timid and weak about its efforts now, and the boss decided that this time should be the last, as he dipped the pen deep into the inkpot.

It was. The last blot fell on the soaked blotting-paper, and the draggled fly lay in it and did not stir. The back legs were stuck to the body; the front legs were not to be seen.

'Come on,' said the boss. 'Look sharp!' And he stirred it with his pen in vain. Nothing happened or was likely to happen. The fly was dead.

The boss lifted the corpse on the end of the paper-knife and flung it into the waste-paper basket. But such a grinding feeling of wretchedness seized him that he felt positively frightened. He started forward and pressed the bell for Macey.

'Bring me some fresh blotting-paper,' he said sternly, 'and look sharp about it.' And while the old dog padded away he fell to wondering what it was he had been thinking about before. What was it? It was ... He took out his handkerchief and passed it inside his collar. For the life of him he could not remember.

∽

Control, ignorance, sacrifice, responsibility, and war form the epicenter of the story. It depicts the conquest of time over grief. The Fly is the symbol; it symbolises the human unwillingness to accept death. It also reveals the experience of grief and loss. The fly that is drowning in the ink must work to rid itself of the burden. This graphic detail is what makes the story unique.

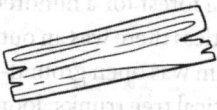

14

AN OCCURRENCE AT OWL CREEK BRIDGE

AMBROSE BIERCE

A man stood upon a railroad bridge in northern Alabama, looking down into the swift water twenty feet below. The man's hands were behind his back, the wrists bound with a cord. A rope closely encircled his neck. It was attached to a stout crosstimber above his head and the slack fell to the level of his knees. Some loose boards laid upon the ties supporting the rails of the railway supplied a footing for him and his executioners—two private soldiers of the Federal army, directed by a sergeant who in civil life may have been a deputy sheriff. At a short remove upon the same temporary platform was an officer in the uniform of his rank, armed. He was a captain. A sentinel at each end of the bridge stood with his rifle in the position known as 'support,' that is to say, vertical in front of the left shoulder, the hammer resting on the forearm thrown straight across the chest—a formal and unnatural position, enforcing an erect carriage of the body. It did not appear to be the duty of these two men to know what was occurring at the center of the bridge; they merely blockaded the two ends of the foot planking that traversed it.

Beyond one of the sentinels nobody was in sight; the railroad ran straight away into a forest for a hundred yards, then, curving, was lost to view. Doubtless there was an outpost farther along. The other bank of the stream was open ground—a gentle slope topped with a stockade of vertical tree trunks, loopholed for rifles, with a single embrasure through which protruded the muzzle of a brass cannon commanding the bridge. Midway up the slope between the bridge and fort were the spectators—a single company of infantry in line, at 'parade rest,' the butts of their rifles on the ground, the barrels inclining slightly backward against the right shoulder, the hands crossed upon the stock. A lieutenant stood at the right of the line, the point of his sword upon the ground, his left hand resting upon his right. Excepting the group of four at the center of the bridge, not a man moved. The company faced the bridge, staring stonily, motionless.

The sentinels, facing the banks of the stream, might have been statues to adorn the bridge. The captain stood with folded arms, silent, observing the work of his subordinates, but making no sign. Death is a dignitary who when he comes announced is to be received with formal manifestations of respect, even by those most familiar with him. In the code of military etiquette silence and fixity are forms of deference.

The man who was engaged in being hanged was apparently about thirty-five years of age. He was a civilian, if one might judge from his habit, which was that of a planter. His features were good—a straight nose, firm mouth, broad forehead, from which his long, dark hair was combed straight back, falling behind his ears to the collar of his well-fitting frock coat. He wore a moustache and pointed beard, but no whiskers; his eyes were large and dark gray, and had a kindly expression which one would hardly have expected in one whose neck was in the hemp. Evidently this was no vulgar assassin. The liberal military code makes provision for hanging many kinds of persons, and gentlemen are not excluded.

The preparations being complete, the two private soldiers stepped aside and each drew away the plank upon which he had been standing. The sergeant turned to the captain, saluted and placed himself immediately behind that officer, who in turn moved apart one pace.

These movements left the condemned man and the sergeant standing on the two ends of the same plank, which spanned three of the cross-ties of the bridge. The end upon which the civilian stood almost, but not quite, reached a fourth. This plank had been held in place by the weight of the captain; it was now held by that of the sergeant. At a signal from the former the latter would step aside, the plank would tilt and the condemned man go down between two ties. The arrangement commended itself to his judgement as simple and effective. His face had not been covered nor his eyes bandaged. He looked a moment at his 'unsteadfast footing,' then let his gaze wander to the swirling water of the stream racing madly beneath his feet. A piece of dancing driftwood caught his attention and his eyes followed it down the current. How slowly it appeared to move! What a sluggish stream!

He closed his eyes in order to fix his last thoughts upon his wife and children. The water, touched to gold by the early sun, the brooding mists under the banks at some distance down the stream, the fort, the soldiers, the piece of drift—all had distracted him. And now he became conscious of a new disturbance. Striking through the thought of his dear ones was a sound which he could neither ignore nor understand, a sharp, distinct, metallic percussion like the stroke of a blacksmith's hammer upon the anvil; it had the same ringing quality.

He wondered what it was, and whether immeasurably distant or near by—it seemed both. Its recurrence was regular, but as slow as the tolling of a death knell. He awaited each new stroke with impatience and—he knew not why—apprehension. The intervals of silence grew progressively longer; the delays became maddening. With their greater infrequency the sounds increased in strength and sharpness. They hurt his ear like the thrust of a knife; he feared he would shriek. What he heard was the ticking of his watch.

He unclosed his eyes and saw again the water below him. 'If I could free my hands,' he thought, 'I might throw off the noose and spring into the stream. By diving I could evade the bullets and, swimming vigorously, reach the bank, take to the woods and get away home. My home, thank God, is as yet outside their lines; my wife and little ones are still beyond the invader's farthest advance.'

As these thoughts, which have here to be set down in words, were flashed into the doomed man's brain rather than evolved from it the captain nodded to the sergeant. The sergeant stepped aside.

***

Peyton Farquhar was a well-to-do planter, of an old and highly respected Alabama family. Being a slave owner and like other slave owners a politician, he was naturally an original secessionist and ardently devoted to the Southern cause. Circumstances of an imperious nature, which it is unnecessary to relate here, had prevented him from taking service with that gallant army which had fought the disastrous campaigns ending with the fall of Corinth, and he chafed under the inglorious restraint, longing for the release of his energies, the larger life of the soldier, the opportunity for distinction. That opportunity, he felt, would come, as it comes to all in wartime.

Meanwhile he did what he could. No service was too humble for him to perform in the aid of the South, no adventure too perilous for him to undertake if consistent with the character of a civilian who was at heart a soldier, and who in good faith and without too much qualification assented to at least a part of the frankly villainous dictum that all is fair in love and war.

One evening while Farquhar and his wife were sitting on a rustic bench near the entrance to his grounds, a gray-clad soldier rode up to the gate and asked for a drink of water. Mrs Farquhar was only too happy to serve him with her own white hands. While she was fetching the water her husband approached the dusty horseman and inquired eagerly for news from the front.

'The Yanks are repairing the railroads,' said the man, 'and are getting ready for another advance. They have reached the Owl

Creek bridge, put it in order and built a stockade on the north bank. The commandant has issued an order, which is posted everywhere, declaring that any civilian caught interfering with the railroad, its bridges, tunnels, or trains will be summarily hanged. I saw the order.'

'How far is it to the Owl Creek bridge?' Farquhar asked.

'About thirty miles.'

'Is there no force on this side of the creek?'

'Only a picket post half a mile out, on the railroad, and a single sentinel at this end of the bridge.'

'Suppose a man—a civilian and student of hanging—should elude the picket post and perhaps get the better of the sentinel,' said Farquhar, smiling, 'what could he accomplish?'

The soldier reflected. 'I was there a month ago,' he replied. 'I observed that the flood of last winter had lodged a great quantity of driftwood against the wooden pier at this end of the bridge. It is now dry and would burn like tinder.'

The lady had now brought the water, which the soldier drank. He thanked her ceremoniously, bowed to her husband and rode away. An hour later, after nightfall, he repassed the plantation, going northward in the direction from which he had come. He was a Federal scout.

***

As Peyton Farquhar fell straight downward through the bridge he lost consciousness and was as one already dead. From this state he was awakened—ages later, it seemed to him—by the pain of a sharp pressure upon his throat, followed by a sense of suffocation. Keen, poignant agonies seemed to shoot from his neck downward through every fiber of his body and limbs. These pains appeared to flash along well defined lines of ramification and to beat with an inconceivably rapid periodicity. They seemed like streams of pulsating fire heating him to an intolerable temperature. As to his head, he was conscious of nothing but a feeling of fullness—of congestion. These sensations were unaccompanied by thought. The intellectual part of his nature was already effaced; he had power only to feel, and feeling was torment. He was conscious of motion. Encompassed in a luminous cloud, of which he was now merely the fiery heart, without material substance, he swung through unthinkable arcs of oscillation, like a vast pendulum. Then all at once, with terrible suddenness, the light about him shot upward with the noise of a loud splash; a frightful roaring was in his ears, and all was cold and dark. The power of thought was restored; he knew that the rope had broken and he had fallen into the stream. There was no additional strangulation; the noose about his neck was already suffocating him and kept the water from his lungs. To die of hanging at the bottom of a river!—the idea seemed to him ludicrous. He opened his eyes in the darkness and saw above him a gleam of light, but how distant, how inaccessible! He was still sinking, for the light became fainter and fainter until it was a mere glimmer. Then it began to grow and brighten, and he knew that he was rising toward the surface—knew it with reluctance, for he was now very comfortable. 'To be hanged and drowned,' he thought, 'that is not so bad; but I do not wish to be shot. No; I will not be shot; that is not fair.'

He was not conscious of an effort, but a sharp pain in his wrist apprised him that he was trying to free his hands. He gave the struggle his attention, as an idler might observe the feat of a juggler, without interest in the outcome. What splendid effort!—what magnificent, what superhuman strength! Ah, that was a fine endeavor!

Bravo! The cord fell away; his arms parted and floated upward, the hands dimly seen on each side in the growing light. He watched them with a new interest as first one and then the other pounced upon the noose at his neck. They tore it away and thrust it fiercely aside, its undulations resembling those of a water snake. 'Put it back, put it back!' He thought he shouted these words to his hands, for the undoing of the noose had been succeeded by the direst pang that he had yet experienced. His neck ached horribly; his brain was on fire, his heart, which had been fluttering faintly, gave a great leap, trying to force itself out at his mouth. His whole body was racked and wrenched with an insupportable anguish! But his disobedient hands gave no heed to the command. They beat the water vigorously with quick, downward strokes, forcing him to the surface. He felt his head emerge; his eyes were blinded by the sunlight; his chest expanded convulsively, and with a supreme and crowning agony his lungs engulfed a great draught of air, which instantly he expelled in a shriek!

He was now in full possession of his physical senses. They were, indeed, preternaturally keen and alert. Something in the awful disturbance of his organic system had so exalted and refined them that they made record of things never before perceived. He felt the ripples upon his face and heard their separate sounds as they struck.

He looked at the forest on the bank of the stream, saw the individual trees, the leaves and the veining of each leaf—he saw the very insects upon them: the locusts, the brilliant bodied flies, the gray spiders stretching their webs from twig to twig. He noted the prismatic colors in all the dewdrops upon a million blades of grass. The humming of the gnats that danced above the eddies of the stream, the beating of the dragonflies' wings, the strokes of the water spiders' legs, like oars which had lifted their boat—all these made audible music. A fish slid along beneath his eyes and he heard the rush of its body parting the water.

He had come to the surface facing down the stream; in a moment the visible world seemed to wheel slowly round, himself the pivotal point, and he saw the bridge, the fort, the soldiers upon the bridge, the captain, the sergeant, the two privates, his executioners. They were in silhouette against the blue sky. They shouted and gesticulated, pointing at him. The captain had drawn his pistol, but did not fire; the others were unarmed. Their movements were grotesque and horrible, their forms gigantic.

Suddenly he heard a sharp report and something struck the water smartly within a few inches of his head, spattering his face with spray. He heard a second report, and saw one of the sentinels with his rifle at his shoulder, a light cloud of blue smoke rising from the muzzle. The man in the water saw the eye of the man on the bridge gazing into his own through the sights of the rifle. He observed that it was a gray eye and remembered having read that gray eyes were keenest, and that all famous marksmen had them. Nevertheless, this one had missed.

A counter-swirl had caught Farquhar and turned him half round; he was again looking at the forest on the bank opposite the fort. The sound of a clear, high voice in a monotonous singsong now rang out behind him and came across the water with a distinctness that pierced and subdued all other sounds, even the beating of the ripples in his ears.

Although no soldier, he had frequented camps enough to know the dread significance of that deliberate, drawling, aspirated chant; the lieutenant on shore was taking a part in the morning's work. How coldly and pitilessly—with what an even, calm intonation, presaging, and enforcing tranquility in the men—with what accurately measured interval fell those cruel words:

'Company! ... Attention! ... Shoulder arms! ... Ready! ... Aim! ... Fire!'

Farquhar dived—dived as deeply as he could. The water roared in his ears like the voice of Niagara, yet he heard the dull thunder of the volley and, rising again toward the surface, met shining bits of metal, singularly flattened, oscillating slowly downward. Some of them touched him on the face and hands, then fell away, continuing their descent. One lodged between his collar and neck; it was uncomfortably warm and he snatched it out. As he rose to the surface, gasping for breath, he saw that he had been a long time under water; he was perceptibly farther downstream—nearer to safety. The soldiers had almost finished reloading; the metal ramrods flashed all at once in the sunshine as they were drawn from the barrels, turned in the air, and thrust into their sockets. The two sentinels fired again, independently and ineffectually.

The hunted man saw all this over his shoulder; he was now swimming vigorously with the current. His brain was as energetic as his arms and legs; he thought with the rapidity of lightning:

'The officer,' he reasoned, 'will not make that martinet's error a second time. It is as easy to dodge a volley as a single shot. He has probably already given the command to fire at will. God help me, I cannot dodge them all!'

An appalling splash within two yards of him was followed by a loud, rushing sound, *diminuendo*, which seemed to travel back through the air to the fort and died in an explosion which stirred the very river to its deeps! A rising sheet of water curved over him, fell down upon him, blinded him, strangled him! The cannon had taken an hand in the game. As he shook his head free from the commotion of the smitten water he heard the deflected shot humming through the air ahead, and in an instant it was cracking and smashing the branches in the forest beyond.

'They will not do that again,' he thought; 'the next time they will use a charge of grape. I must keep my eye upon the gun; the smoke will apprise me—the report arrives too late; it lags behind the missile. That is a good gun.' Suddenly he felt himself whirled round and round—spinning like a top. The water, the banks, the forests, the now distant bridge, fort and men, all were commingled and blurred. Objects were represented by their colors only; circular horizontal streaks of color—that was all he saw. He had been caught in a vortex and was being whirled on with a velocity of advance and gyration that made him giddy and sick. In a few moments he was flung upon the gravel at the foot of the left bank of the stream—the southern bank—and behind a projecting point which concealed him from his enemies. The sudden arrest of his motion, the abrasion of one of his hands on the gravel, restored him, and he wept with delight. He dug his fingers into the sand, threw it over himself in handfuls and audibly blessed it. It looked like diamonds, rubies, emeralds; he could think of nothing beautiful which it did not resemble. The trees upon the bank were giant garden plants; he noted a definite order in their arrangement, inhaled the fragrance of their blooms. A strange roseate light shone through the spaces among their trunks and the wind made in their branches the music of æolian harps.

He had no wish to perfect his escape—he was content to remain in that enchanting spot until retaken. A whiz and a rattle of grapeshot among the branches high above his head roused him from his dream. The baffled cannoneer had fired him a random farewell. He sprang to his feet, rushed up the sloping bank, and plunged into the forest.

All that day he traveled, laying his course by the rounding sun. The forest seemed interminable; nowhere did he discover a break in it, not even a woodman's road. He had not known that he lived in so wild a region. There was something uncanny in the revelation.

By nightfall he was fatigued, footsore, famished. The thought of his wife and children urged him on. At last he found a road which led him in what he knew to be the right direction. It was as wide and straight as a city street, yet it seemed untraveled. No fields bordered it, no dwelling anywhere. Not so much as the barking of a dog suggested human habitation. The black bodies of the trees formed a straight wall on both sides, terminating on the horizon in a point, like a diagram in a lesson in perspective. Overhead, as he looked up through this rift in the wood, shone great golden stars looking unfamiliar and grouped in strange constellations. He was sure they were arranged in some order which had a secret and malign significance. The wood on either side was full of singular noises, among which—once, twice, and again—he distinctly heard whispers in an unknown tongue.

His neck was in pain and lifting his hand to it found it horribly swollen. He knew that it had a circle of black where the rope had bruised it. His eyes felt congested; he could no longer close them.

His tongue was swollen with thirst; he relieved its fever by thrusting it forward from between his teeth into the cold air. How softly the turf had carpeted the untraveled avenue—he could no longer feel the roadway beneath his feet!

Doubtless, despite his suffering, he had fallen asleep while walking, for now he sees another scene—perhaps he has merely recovered from a delirium. He stands at the gate of his own home.

All is as he left it, and all bright and beautiful in the morning sunshine. He must have traveled the entire night. As he pushes open the gate and passes up the wide white walk, he sees a flutter of female garments; his wife, looking fresh and cool and sweet, steps down from the veranda to meet him. At the bottom of the steps she stands waiting, with a smile of ineffable joy, an attitude of matchless grace and dignity. Ah, how beautiful she is! He springs forwards with extended arms. As he is about to clasp her he feels a stunning blow upon the back of the neck; a blinding white light blazes all about him with a sound like the shock of a cannon—then all is darkness and silence!

Peyton Farquhar was dead; his body, with a broken neck, swung gently from side to side beneath the timbers of the Owl Creek bridge.

What appeals most in the story is not linear time; it deals with mind time or the stream of consciousness: Mind time is infinitely greater than actual time. In this story, we find time broken into atoms. The 'here' is diametrically opposite to the contours of what goes within the mind.

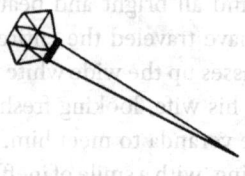

15
AFTER TWENTY YEARS
O. HENRY

The policeman on the beat moved up the avenue impressively. The impressiveness was habitual and not for show, for spectators were few. The time was barely ten o'clock at night, but chilly gusts of wind with a taste of rain in them had well nigh depeopled the streets.

Trying doors as he went, twirling his club with many intricate and artful movements, turning now and then to cast his watchful eye adown the pacific thoroughfare, the officer, with his stalwart form and slight swagger, made a fine picture of a guardian of the peace. The vicinity was one that kept early hours. Now and then you might see the lights of a cigar store or of an all-night lunch counter; but the majority of the doors belonged to business places that had long since been closed.

When about midway of a certain block the policeman suddenly slowed his walk. In the doorway of a darkened hardware store a man leaned, with an unlighted cigar in his mouth. As the policeman walked up to him the man spoke up quickly.

'It's all right, officer,' he said, reassuringly. 'I'm just waiting for a friend. It's an appointment made twenty years ago. Sounds a little funny to you, doesn't it? Well, I'll explain if you'd like to make certain it's all straight. About that long ago there used to be a restaurant where this store stands—'Big Joe' Brady's restaurant.'

'Until five years ago,' said the policeman. 'It was torn down then.'

The man in the doorway struck a match and lit his cigar. The light showed a pale, square-jawed face with keen eyes, and a little white scar near his right eyebrow. His scarf pin was a large diamond, oddly set.

'Twenty years ago tonight,' said the man, 'I dined here at 'Big Joe' Brady's with Jimmy Wells, my best chum, and the finest chap in the world. He and I were raised here in New York, just like two brothers, together. I was eighteen and Jimmy was twenty. The next morning I was to start for the West to make my fortune. You couldn't have dragged Jimmy out of New York; he thought it was the only place on earth. Well, we agreed that night that we would meet here again exactly twenty years from that date and time, no matter what our conditions might be or from what distance we might have to come. We figured that in twenty years each of us ought to have our destiny worked out and our fortunes made, whatever they were going to be.'

'It sounds pretty interesting,' said the policeman. 'Rather a long time between meets, though, it seems to me. Haven't you heard from your friend since you left?'

'Well, yes, for a time we corresponded,' said the other. 'But after a year or two we lost track of each other. You see, the West is a pretty big proposition, and I kept hustling around over it pretty lively. But I know Jimmy will meet me here if he's alive, for he always was the truest, staunchest old chap in the world. He'll never forget. I came a thousand miles to stand in this door tonight, and it's worth it if my old partner turns up.'

The waiting man pulled out a handsome watch, the lids of it set with small diamonds.

'Three minutes to ten,' he announced. 'It was exactly ten o'clock when we parted here at the restaurant door.'

'Did pretty well out West, didn't you?' asked the policeman.

'You bet! I hope Jimmy has done half as well. He was a kind of plodder, though, good fellow as he was. I've had to compete with some of the sharpest wits going to get my pile. A man gets in a groove in New York. It takes the West to put a razor-edge on him.'

The policeman twirled his club and took a step or two.

'I'll be on my way. Hope your friend comes around all right. Going to call time on him sharp?'

'I should say not!' said the other. 'I'll give him half an hour at least. If Jimmy is alive on earth he'll be here by that time. So long, officer.'

'Good-night, sir,' said the policeman, passing on along his beat, trying doors as he went.

There was now a fine, cold drizzle falling, and the wind had risen from its uncertain puffs into a steady blow. The few foot passengers astir in that quarter hurried dismally and silently along with coat collars turned high and pocketed hands. And in the door of the hardware store the man who had come a thousand miles to fill an appointment, uncertain almost to absurdity, with the friend of his youth, smoked his cigar and waited.

About twenty minutes he waited, and then a tall man in a long overcoat, with collar turned up to his ears, hurried across from the opposite side of the street. He went directly to the waiting man.

'Is that you, Bob?' he asked, doubtfully.

'Is that you, Jimmy Wells?' cried the man in the door.

'Bless my heart!' exclaimed the new arrival, grasping both the other's hands with his own. 'It's Bob, sure as fate. I was certain I'd find you here if you were still in existence. Well, well, well!— twenty years is a long time. The old restaurant's gone, Bob; I wish it had lasted, so we could have had another dinner there. How has the West treated you, old man?'

'Bully; it has given me everything I asked it for. You've changed lots, Jimmy. I never thought you were so tall by two or three inches.'

'Oh, I grew a bit after I was twenty.'

'Doing well in New York, Jimmy?'

'Moderately. I have a position in one of the city departments. Come on, Bob; we'll go around to a place I know of, and have a good long talk about old times.'

The two men started up the street, arm in arm. The man from the West, his egotism enlarged by success, was beginning to outline the history of his career. The other, submerged in his overcoat, listened with interest.

At the corner stood a drug store, brilliant with electric lights. When they came into this glare each of them turned simultaneously to gaze upon the other's face.

The man from the West stopped suddenly and released his arm.

'You're not Jimmy Wells,' he snapped. 'Twenty years is a long time, but not long enough to change a man's nose from a Roman to a pug.'

'It sometimes changes a good man into a bad one,' said the tall man. 'You've been under arrest for ten minutes, "Silky" Bob. Chicago thinks you may have dropped over our way and wires us she wants to have a chat with you. Going quietly, are you? That's sensible. Now, before we go on to the station here's a note I was asked to hand you. You may read it here at the window. It's from Patrolman Wells.'

The man from the West unfolded the little piece of paper handed him. His hand was steady when he began to read, but it trembled a little by the time he had finished. The note was rather short.

Bob: I was at the appointed place on time. When you struck the match to light your cigar I saw it was the face of the man wanted in Chicago. Somehow I couldn't do it myself, so I went around and got a plainclothesman to do the job. Jimmy.

∞

Time can take its toll. Each man has his own time. The story appeals because of its twisted plot and surprise ending. Days run like rabbits and there happens to be only one permanent thing: Change.

16
MY FINANCIAL CAREER
STEPHEN LEACOCK

When I go into a bank I get rattled. The clerks rattle me; the wickets rattle me; the sight of the money rattles me; everything rattles me.

The moment I cross the threshold of a bank and attempt to transact business there, I become an irresponsible idiot.

I knew this beforehand, but my salary had been raised to fifty dollars a month and I felt that the bank was the only place for it.

So I shambled in and looked timidly round at the clerks. I had an idea that a person about to open an account must needs consult the manager.

I went up to a wicket marked 'Accountant.' The accountant was a tall, cool devil. The very sight of him rattled me. My voice was sepulchral.

'Can I see the manager?' I said, and added solemnly, 'alone.' I don't know why I said 'alone.'

'Certainly,' said the accountant, and fetched him.

The manager was a grave, calm man. I held my fifty-six dollars clutched in a crumpled ball in my pocket.

'Are you the manager?' I said. God knows I didn't doubt it.

'Yes,' he said.

'Can I see you,' I asked, 'alone?' I didn't want to say 'alone' again, but without it the thing seemed self-evident.

The manager looked at me in some alarm. He felt that I had an awful secret to reveal.

'Come in here,' he said, and led the way to a private room. He turned the key in the lock.

'We are safe from interruption here,' he said; 'sit down.'

We both sat down and looked at each other. I found no voice to speak.

'You are one of Pinkerton's men, I presume,' he said.

He had gathered from my mysterious manner that I was a detective. I knew what he was thinking, and it made me worse.

'No, not from Pinkerton's,' I said, seeming to imply that I came from a rival agency. 'To tell the truth,' I went on, as if I had been prompted to lie about it, 'I am not a detective at all. I have come to open an account. I intend to keep all my money in this bank.'

The manager looked relieved but still serious; he concluded now that I was a son of Baron Rothschild or a young Gould.

'A large account, I suppose,' he said.

'Fairly large,' I whispered. 'I propose to deposit fifty-six dollars now and fifty dollars a month regularly.'

The manager got up and opened the door. He called to the accountant.

'Mr Montgomery,' he said unkindly loud, 'this gentleman is opening an account, he will deposit fifty-six dollars. Good morning.'

I rose. A big iron door stood open at the side of the room.

'Good morning,' I said, and stepped into the safe.

'Come out,' said the manager coldly, and showed me the other way.

I went up to the accountant's wicket and poked the ball of money at him with a quick convulsive movement as if I were doing a conjuring trick.

My face was ghastly pale.

'Here,' I said, 'deposit it.' The tone of the words seemed to mean, 'Let us do this painful thing while the fit is on us.'

He took the money and gave it to another clerk.

He made me write the sum on a slip and sign my name in a book. I no longer knew what I was doing. The bank swam before my eyes.

'Is it deposited?' I asked in a hollow, vibrating voice.

'It is,' said the accountant.

'Then I want to draw a cheque.'

My idea was to draw out six dollars of it for present use. Someone gave me a chequebook through a wicket and someone else began telling me how to write it out. The people in the bank had the impression that I was an invalid millionaire. I wrote something on the cheque and thrust it in at the clerk. He looked at it.

'What! Are you drawing it all out again?' he asked in surprise. Then I realized that I had written fifty-six instead of six. I was too far gone to reason now. I had a feeling that it was impossible to explain the thing. All the clerks had stopped writing to look at me.

Reckless with misery, I made a plunge.

'Yes, the whole thing.'

'You withdraw your money from the bank?'

'Every cent of it.'

'Are you not going to deposit anymore?' said the clerk, astonished.

'Never.'

An idiot hope struck me that they might think something had insulted me while I was writing the cheque and that I had changed my mind. I made a wretched attempt to look like a man with a fearfully quick temper.

The clerk prepared to pay the money.

'How will you have it?' he said.

'What?'

'How will you have it?'

'Oh'—I caught his meaning and answered without even trying to think—'in fifties.'

He gave me a fifty-dollar bill.

'And the six?' he asked dryly.

'In sixes,' I said.

He gave it me and I rushed out.

As the big door swung behind me I caught the echo of a roar of laughter that went up to the ceiling of the bank. Since then I bank no more. I keep my money in cash in my trousers pocket and my savings in silver dollars in a sock.

Stephen Leacock was a humorist who excelled in depiction. Money talks, but interestingly, it is not the narrator's mother tongue. Cold cash is not everyone's cup of tea!

17
THE DANCING PARTNER

JEROME K. JEROME

'This story,' commenced MacShaugnassy, 'comes from Furtwangen, a small town in the Black Forest. There lived there a very wonderful old fellow named Nicholau Geibel. His business was the making of mechanical toys, at which work he had acquired an almost European reputation. He made rabbits that would emerge from the heart of a cabbage, flop their ears, smooth their whiskers, and disappear again; cats that would wash their faces, and mew so naturally that dogs would mistake them for real cats, and fly at them; dolls, with phonographs concealed within them, that would raise their hats and say, 'Good morning; how do you do?' and some that would even sing a song.

'But he was something more than a mere mechanic; he was an artist. His work was with him a hobby, almost a passion. His shop was filled with all manner of strange things that never would, or could, be sold—things he had made for the pure love of making them. He had contrived a mechanical donkey that would trot for two hours by means of stored electricity, and trot, too, much faster than the live article, and with less need for exertion on the part of the driver; a bird that would shoot up into the air, fly around and around in a circle, and drop to earth at the exact spot from where it started; a skeleton that, supported by an upright iron bar, would dance a hornpipe; a life-size lady doll that could play the fiddle; and a gentleman with a hollow inside who could smoke a pipe and drink more lager beer than any three average German students put together, which is saying much.

'Indeed, it was the belief of the town that old Geibel could make a man capable of doing everything that a respectable man need want to do. One day he made a man who did too much, and it came about in this way:

'Young Doctor Follen had a baby, and the baby had a birthday. Its first birthday put Doctor Follen's household into somewhat of a flurry, but on the occasion of its second birhday, Mrs Doctor Follen gave a ball in honor of the event. Old Geibel and his daughter Olga were among the guests.

'During the afternoon of the next day some three or four of Olga's bosom friends, who had also been present at the ball, dropped in to have a chat about it. They naturally fell to discussing the men, and to citicising their dancing. Old Geibel was in the room, but he appeared to be absorbed in his newspaper, and the girls took no notice of him.

'"There seem to be fewer men who can dance at every ball you go to," said one of the girls.

'"Yes, and don't the ones who can, give themselves airs," said another; "they make quite a favor of asking you."

'"And how stupidly they talk," added a third. "They always say exactly the same things, "How charming you are looking tonight." "Do you often go to Vienna? Oh, you should, it's delightful." "What a charming dress you have on." "What a warm day it has been." "Do you like Wagner?" "I do wish they'd think of something new."

'"Oh, I never mind how they talk," said a fourth. "If a man dances well he may be a fool for all I care."

'"He generally is," slipped in a thin girl, rather spitefully.

'"I go to a ball to dance," continued the previous speaker, not noticing the interruption. "All I ask of a partner is that he shall hold me firmly, take me round steadily, and not get tired before I do."

"'A clockwork figure would be the thing for you,' said the girl who had interrupted.

"'Bravo!' cried one of the others, clapping her hands, 'what a capital idea!'

"'What's a capital idea?' they asked.

"'Why, a clockwork dancer, or, better still, one that would go by electricity and never run down.'

"'The girls took up the idea with enthusiasm.

"'Oh, what a lovely partner he would make,' said one; 'he would never kick you, or tread on your toes.'

"'Or tear your dress,' said another.

"'Or get out of step.'

"'Or get giddy and lean on you.'

"'And he would never want to mop his face with his handkerchief. I do hate to see a man do that after every dance.'

"'And wouldn't want to spend the whole evening in the supper room.'

"'Why, with a phonograph inside him to grind out all the stock remarks, you would not be able to tell him from a real man,' said the girl who had first suggested the idea.

"'Oh, yes, you would,' said the thin girl, 'he would be so much nicer.'

'Old Geibel had laid down his paper, and was listening with both his ears. On one of the girls glancing in his direction, however, he hurriedly hid himself again behind it.

'After the girls were gone, he went into his workshop, where Olga heard him walking up and down, and every now and then chuckling to himself; and that night he talked to her a good deal about dancing and dancing men—asked what they usually said and did—what dances were most popular—what steps were gone through, with many other questions bearing on the subject.

'Then for a couple of weeks he kept much to his factory, and was very thoughtful and busy, though prone at unexpected moments to break into a quiet low laugh, as if enjoying a joke that nobody else knew of.

'A month later another ball took place in Furtwangen. On this occasion it was given by old Wetzel, the wealthy timber merchant, to celebrate his niece's betrothal, and Geibel and his daughter were again among the invited.

'When the hour arrived to set out, Olga sought her father. Not finding him in the house, she tapped at the door of his workshop. He appeared in his shirt-sleeves, looking hot but radiant.

'"Don't wait for me," he said, "you go on, I'll follow you. I've got something to finish."

'As she turned to obey he called after her, "Tell them I'm going to bring a young man with me—such a nice young man, and an excellent dancer. All the girls will like him." Then he laughed and closed the door.

'Herr father generally kept his doings secret from everybody, but she had a pretty shrewd suspicion of what he had been planning, and so, to a certain extent, was able to prepare the guests for what was coming. Anticipation ran high, and the arrival of the famous mechanist was eagerly awaited.

'At length the sound of wheels was heard outside, followed by a great commotion in the passage, and old Wenzel himself, his jolly face red with excitement and suppressed laughter, burst into the room and announced in stentorian tones: '"Herr Geibel—and a friend."

'Herr Geibel and his "friend" entered, greeted with shouts of laughter and applause, and advanced to the centre of the room.

'"Allow me, ladies and gentlemen," said Herr Geibel, "to introduce you to my friend, Lieutenant Fritz. Fritz, my dear fellow, bow to the ladies and gentlemen."

'Geibel placed his hand encouragingly on Fritz's shoulder, and the Lieutenant bowed low, accompanying the action with a harsh clicking noise in his throat, unpleasantly suggestive of a death-rattle. But that was only a detail.

'"He walks a little stiffly" (old Geibel took his arm and walked him forward a few steps. He certainly did walk stiffly), "but then, walking is not his forte. He is essentially a dancing man. I have only been able to teach him the waltz as yet, but at that he is faultless. Come, which of you ladies may I introduce him to as a partner? He keeps perfect time; he never gets tired; he won't kick you or tread on your dress; he will hold you as firmly as you like, and go as quickly or a slowly as you please; he never gets giddy; and he is full of conversation. Come, speak up for yourself, my boy."

'The old gentleman twisted one of the buttons at the back of his coat, and immediately Fritz opened his mouth, and in thin tones that appeared to proceed from the back of his head, remarked suddenly, "May I have the pleasure?" and then shut his mouth again with a snap.

'That Lieutenant Fritz had made a strong impression on the company was undoubted, yet none of the girls seemed inclined to dance with him. They looked askance at his waxen face, with its staring eyes and fixed smile, and shuddered. At last old Geibel came to the girl who had conceived the idea.

'"It is your own suggestion, carried out to the letter," said Geibel, "an electric dancer. You owe it to the gentleman to give him a trial."

'She was a bright, saucy little girl, fond of a frolic. Her host added his entreaties, and she consented.

'Her Geibel fixed the figure to her. Its right arm was screwed round her waist, and held her firmly; its delicately jointed left hand was made to fasten upon her right. The old toymaker showed her how to regulate its speed, and how to stop it, and release herself.

'"It will take you round in a complete circle," he explained; "be careful that no one knocks against you, and alters its course."

'The music struck up. Old Geibel put the current in motion, and Annette and her strange partner began to dance.

'For a while everyone stood watching them. The figure performed its purpose admirably. Keeping perfect time and step, and holding its little partner tight clasped in an unyielding embrace, it revolved steadily, pouring forth at the same time a constant flow of squeaky conversation, broken by brief intervals of grinding silence.

The Dancing Partner

'"How charming you are looking tonight," it remarked in its thin, far-away voice. "What a lovely day it has been. Do you like dancing? How well our steps agree. You will give me another, won't you? Oh, don't be so cruel. What a charming gown you have on. Isn't waltzing delightful? I could go on dancing for ever—with you. Have you had supper?"

'As she grew more familiar with the uncanny creature, the girl's nervousness wore off, and she entered into the fun of the thing.

'"Oh, he's just lovely," she cried, laughing; "I could go on dancing with him all my life."

'Couple after couple now joined them, and soon all the dancers in the room were whirling round behind them. Nicholaus Geibel stood looking on, beaming with childish delight at his success.

'Old Wenzel approached him, and whispered something in his ear. Geibel laughed and nodded, and the two worked their way quietly towards the door.

'"This is the young people's house to-night," said Wenzel, as soon as they were outside; "you and I will have a quiet pipe and glass of hock, over in the counting-house."

'Meanwhile the dancing grew more fast and furious. Little Annette loosened the screw regulating her partner's rate of progress, and the figure flew round with her swifter and swifter. Couple after couple dropped out exhausted, but they only went the faster, till at length they remained dancing alone.

'Madder and madder became the waltz. The music lagged behind: the musicians, unable to keep pace, ceased, and sat staring. The younger guests applauded, but the older faces began to grow anxious.

'"Hadn't you better stop, dear," said one of the women, "you'll make yourself so tired."

'But Annette did not answer.

'"I believe she's fainted," cried out a girl who had caught sight of her face as it was swept by.

'One of the men sprang forward and clutched at the figure, but its impetus threw him down on to the floor, where its steel-cased feet laid bare his cheek. The thing evidently did not intend to part with its prize so easily.

'Had any one retained a cool head, the figure, one cannot help thinking, might easily have been stopped. Two or three men acting in concert might have lifted it bodily off the floor, or have jammed it into a corner. But few human heads are capable of remaining cool under excitement. Those who are not present think how stupid must have been those who were; those who are reflect afterwards how simple it would have been to do this, that, or the other, if only they had thought of it at the time.

'The women grew hysterical. The men shouted contradictory directions to one another. Two of them made a bungling rush at the figure, which had the end result of forcing it out of its orbit at the centre of the room, and sending it crashing against the walls and furniture. A stream of blood showed itself down the girl's white frock, and followed her along the floor. The affair was becoming horrible. The women rushed screaming from the room. The men followed them.

'One sensible suggestion was made: "Find Geibel—fetch Geibel."

'No one had noticed him leave the room, no one knew where he was. A party went in search of him. The others, too unnerved to go back into the ballroom, crowded outside the door and listened. They could hear the steady whir of the wheels upon the polished floor as the thing spun round and round; the dull thud as every now and again it dashed itself and its burden against some opposing object and ricocheted off in a new direction.

'And everlastingly it talked in that thin ghostly voice, repeating over and over the same formula: "How charming you look tonight. What a lovely day it has been. Oh, don't be so cruel. I could go on dancing for ever—with you. Have you had supper?"

'Of course they sought Geibel everywhere but where he was. They looked in every room in the house, then they rushed off in a body to his own place, and spent precious minutes waking up his deaf old housekeeper. At last it occurred to one of the party that

Wenzel was missing also, and then the idea of the counting-house across the yard presented itself to them, and there they found him.

'He rose up, very pale, and followed them; and he and old Wenzel forced their way through the crowd of guests gathered outside, and entered the room, and locked the door behind them.

'From within there came the muffled sound of low voices and quick steps, followed by a confused scuffling noise, then silence, then the low voices again.

'After a time the door opened, and those near it pressed forward to enter, but old Wenzel's broad head and shoulders barred the way.

'"I want you—and you, Bekler," he said, addressing a couple of the field er men. His voice was calm, but his face was deadly white. "The rest of you, please go—get the women away as quickly as you can."

'From that day old Nicholaus Geibel confined himself to the making of mechanical rabbits, and cats that mewed and washed their faces.'

'Multum in Parvo': *Much in less. This is an effective horror story but at the same time a commentary regarding the advances of science also.*

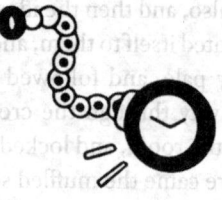

18

THE GIFT OF THE MAGI

O. HENRY

One dollar and eighty-seven cents. That was all. And sixty cents of it was in pennies. Pennies saved one and two at a time by bulldozing the grocer and the vegetable man and the butcher until one's cheeks burned with the silent imputation of parsimony that such close dealing implied. Three times Della counted it. One dollar and eighty-seven cents. And the next day would be Christmas.

There was clearly nothing left to do but flop down on the shabby little couch and howl. So Della did it. Which instigates the moral reflection that life is made up of sobs, sniffles, and smiles, with sniffles predominating.

While the mistress of the home is gradually subsiding from the first stage to the second, take a look at the home. A furnished flat at $8 per week. It did not exactly beggar description, but it certainly had that word on the look-out for the mendicancy squad.

In the vestibule below was a letter-box into which no letter would go, and an electric button from which no mortal finger could coax a ring. Also appertaining thereunto was a card bearing the name 'Mr James Dillingham Young.'

The 'Dillingham' had been flung to the breeze during a former period of prosperity when its possessor was being paid $30 per week. Now, when the income was shrunk to $20, the letters of 'Dillingham' looked blurred, as though they were thinking seriously of contracting to a modest and unassuming D. But whenever Mr James Dillingham Young came home and reached his flat above he was called 'Jim' and greatly hugged by Mrs James Dillingham Young, already introduced to you as Della. Which is all very good.

Della finished her cry and attended to her cheeks with the powder rag. She stood by the window and looked out dully at a grey cat walking a grey fence in a grey backyard. Tomorrow would be Christmas Day, and she had only $1.87 with which to buy Jim a present. She had been saving every penny she could for months, with this result. Twenty dollars a week doesn't go far. Expenses had been greater than she had calculated. They always are. Only $1.87 to buy a present for Jim. Her Jim. Many a happy hour she had spent planning for something nice for him. Something fine and rare and sterling—something just a little bit near to being worthy of the honour of being owned by Jim.

There was a pier-glass between the windows of the room. Perhaps you have seen a pier-glass in an $8 flat. A very thin and very agile person may, by observing his reflection in a rapid sequence of longitudinal strips, obtain a fairly accurate conception of his looks. Della, being slender, had mastered the art.

Suddenly she whirled from the window and stood before the glass. Her eyes were shining brilliantly, but her face had lost its colour within twenty seconds. Rapidly she pulled down her hair and let it fall to its full length.

Now, there were two possessions of the James Dillingham Youngs in which they both took a mighty pride. One was Jim's gold watch that had been his father's and his grandfather's. The other was Della's hair. Had the Queen of Sheba lived in the flat across the airshaft, Della would have let her hair hang out of the window some day to dry just to depreciate Her Majesty's jewels and gifts. Had King Solomon been the janitor, with all his treasures piled up in the basement, Jim would have pulled out his watch every time he passed, just to see him pluck at his beard from envy.

So now Della's beautiful hair fell about her, rippling and shining like a cascade of brown waters. It reached below her knee and made itself almost a garment for her. And then she did it up again nervously and quickly. Once she faltered for a minute and stood still while a tear or two splashed on the worn red carpet.

On went her old brown jacket; on went her old brown hat. With a whirl of skirts and with the brilliant sparkle still in her eyes, she cluttered out of the door and down the stairs to the street.

Where she stopped the sign read: 'Mme Sofronie. Hair Goods of All Kinds.' One flight up Della ran, and collected herself, panting. Madame, large, too white, chilly, hardly looked the 'Sofronie.'

'Will you buy my hair?' asked Della.

'I buy hair,' said Madame. 'Take yer hat off and let's have a sight at the looks of it.'

Down rippled the brown cascade.

'Twenty dollars,' said Madame, lifting the mass with a practised hand.

'Give it to me quick' said Della.

Oh, and the next two hours tripped by on rosy wings. Forget the hashed metaphor. She was ransacking the stores for Jim's present.

She found it at last. It surely had been made for Jim and no one else. There was no other like it in any of the stores, and she had turned all of them inside out. It was a platinum fob chain simple and chaste in design, properly proclaiming its value by substance alone and not by meretricious ornamentation—as all good things should do. It was even worthy of The Watch. As soon as she saw it she knew that it must be Jim's. It was like him. Quietness and value—the description applied to both. Twenty-one dollars they took from her for it, and she hurried home with the eighty-seven cents. With that chain on his watch Jim might be properly anxious about the time in any company. Grand as the watch was, he sometimes looked at it on the sly on account of the old leather strap that he used in place of a chain.

When Della reached home her intoxication gave way a little to prudence and reason. She got out her curling irons and lighted the gas and went to work repairing the ravages made by generosity added to love. Which is always a tremendous task dear friends—a mammoth task.

Within forty minutes her head was covered with tiny, close-lying curls that made her look wonderfully like a truant schoolboy. She looked at her reflection in the mirror long, carefully, and critically.

'If Jim doesn't kill me,' she said to herself, 'before he takes a second look at me, he'll say I look like a Coney Island chorus girl. But what could I do—oh! what could I do with a dollar and eighty-seven cents?'

At seven o'clock the coffee was made and the frying-pan was on the back of the stove hot and ready to cook the chops.

Jim was never late. Della doubled the fob chain in her hand and sat on the corner of the table near the door that he always entered. Then she heard his step on the stair away down on the first flight, and she turned white for just a moment. She had a habit of saying little silent prayers about the simplest everyday things, and now she whispered: 'Please, God, make him think I am still pretty.'

The door opened and Jim stepped in and closed it. He looked thin and very serious. Poor fellow, he was only twenty-two—and to be burdened with a family! He needed a new overcoat and he was without gloves.

Jim stepped inside the door, as immovable as a setter at the scent of quail. His eyes were fixed upon Della, and there was an expression in them that she could not read, and it terrified her. It was not anger, nor surprise, nor disapproval, nor horror, nor any of the sentiments that she had been prepared for. He simply stared at her fixedly with that peculiar expression on his face.

Della wriggled off the table and went for him.

'Jim, darling,' she cried, 'don't look at me that way. I had my hair cut off and sold it because I couldn't have lived through Christmas without giving you a present. It'll grow out again—you won't mind, will you? I just had to do it. My hair grows awfully fast. Say 'Merry Christmas!' Jim, and let's be happy. You don't know what a nice—what a beautiful, nice gift I've got for you.'

'You've cut off your hair?' asked Jim, laboriously, as if he had not arrived at that patent fact yet, even after the hardest mental labour.

'Cut it off and sold it,' said Della. 'Don't you like me just as well, anyhow? I'm me without my hair, ain't I?'

Jim looked about the room curiously. 'You say your hair is gone?' he said, with an air almost of idiocy.

'You needn't look for it,' said Della. 'It's sold, I tell you—sold and gone, too. It's Christmas Eve, boy. Be good to me, for it went for you. Maybe the hairs of my head were numbered,' she went on with a sudden serious sweetness, 'but nobody could ever count my love for you. Shall I put the chops on, Jim?'

Out of his trance Jim seemed quickly to wake. He enfolded his Della. For ten seconds let us regard with discreet scrutiny some inconsequential object in the other direction. Eight dollars a week or a million a year—what is the difference? A mathematician or a wit would give you the wrong answer. The magi brought valuable gifts, but that was not among them. This dark assertion will be illuminated later on.

Jim drew a package from his overcoat pocket and threw it upon the table.

'Don't make any mistake, Dell,' he said, 'about me. I don't think there's anything in the way of a haircut or a shave or a shampoo that could make me like my girl any less. But if you'll unwrap that package you may see why you had me going a while at first.'

White fingers and nimble tore at the string and paper. And then an ecstatic scream of joy; and then, alas! a quick feminine change to hysterical tears and wails, necessitating the immediate employment of all the comforting powers of the lord of the flat.

For there lay The Combs—the set of combs, side and back, that Della had worshipped for long in a Broadway window. Beautiful combs, pure tortoise-shell, with jewelled rims—just the shade to wear in the beautiful vanished hair. They were expensive combs, she knew, and her heart had simply craved and yearned over them without the least hope of possession. And now, they were hers, but the tresses that should have adorned the coveted adornments were gone.

But she hugged them to her bosom, and at length she was able to look up with dim eyes and a smile and say: 'My hair grows so fast, Jim!'

And then Della leaped up like a little singed cat and cried, 'Oh, oh!'

Jim had not yet seen his beautiful present. She held it out to him eagerly upon her open palm. The dull precious metal seemed to flash with a reflection of her bright and ardent spirit.

'Isn't it a dandy, Jim? I hunted all over town to find it. You'll have to look at the time a hundred times a day now. Give me your watch. I want to see how it looks on it.'

Instead of obeying, Jim tumbled down on the couch and put his hands under the back of his head and smiled.

'Dell,' said he, 'let's put our Christmas presents away and keep 'em a while. They're too nice to use just at present. I sold the watch to get the money to buy your combs. And now suppose you put the chops on.'

The magi, as you know, were wise men—wonderfully wise men—who brought gifts to the Babe in the manger. They invented the art of giving Christmas presents. Being wise, their gifts were no doubt wise ones, possibly bearing the privilege of exchange in case of duplication. And here I have lamely related to you the uneventful chronicle of two foolish children in a flat who most unwisely sacrificed for each other the greatest treasures of their house. But in a last word to the wise of these days let it be said that of all who give gifts these two were the wisest. Of all who give and receive gifts, such as they are wisest. Everywhere they are wisest. They are the magi.

'Love is built on sacrifice. Give it till it hurts,' said Mother Teresa.

THE OPEN WINDOW

SAKI

'My aunt will be down presently, Mr Nuttel,' said a very self-possessed young lady of fifteen; 'in the meantime you must try and put up with me.'

Framton Nuttel endeavoured to say the correct something which should duly flatter the niece of the moment without unduly discounting the aunt that was to come. Privately he doubted more than ever whether these formal visits on a succession of total strangers would do much towards helping the nerve cure which he was supposed to be undergoing.

'I know how it will be,' his sister had said when he was preparing to migrate to this rural retreat; 'you will bury yourself down there and not speak to a living soul, and your nerves will be worse than ever from moping. I shall just give you letters of introduction to all the people I know there. Some of them, as far as I can remember, were quite nice.'

Framton wondered whether Mrs Sappleton, the lady to whom he was presenting one of the letters of introduction, came into the nice division.

'Do you know many of the people round here?' asked the niece, when she judged that they had had sufficient silent communion.

'Hardly a soul,' said Framton. 'My sister was staying here, at the rectory, you know, some four years ago, and she gave me letters of introduction to some of the people here.'

He made the last statement in a tone of distinct regret. 'Then you know practically nothing about my aunt?' pursued the self-possessed young lady.

'Only her name and address,' admitted the caller. He was wondering whether Mrs Sappleton was in the married or widowed state. An undefinable something about the room seemed to suggest masculine habitation.

'Her great tragedy happened just three years ago,' said the child; 'that would be since your sister's time.'

'Her tragedy?' asked Framton; somehow in this restful country spot tragedies seemed out of place.

'You may wonder why we keep that window wide open on an October afternoon,' said the niece, indicating a large French window that opened on to a lawn.

'It is quite warm for the time of the year,' said Framton; 'but has that window got anything to do with the tragedy?'

'Out through that window, three years ago to a day, her husband and her two young brothers went off for their day's shooting. They never came back. In crossing the moor to their favourite snipeshooting ground they were all three engulfed in a treacherous piece of bog. It had been that dreadful wet summer, you know, and places that were safe in other years gave way suddenly without warning. Their bodies were never recovered. That was the dreadful part of it.' Here the child's voice lost its self-possessed note and became falteringly human. 'Poor aunt always thinks that they will come back some day, they and the little brown spaniel that was lost with them, and walk in at that window just as they used to do. That is why the window is kept open every evening till it is quite dusk. Poor dear aunt, she has often told me how they went out, her husband with his white waterproof coat over his arm, and Ronnie, her youngest brother, singing 'Bertie, why do you bound?' as he always did to tease her, because she said it got on her nerves. Do you know, sometimes on still, quiet evenings like this, I almost get a creepy feeling that they will all walk in through that window—'

She broke off with a little shudder. It was a relief to Framton when the aunt bustled into the room with a whirl of apologies for being late in making her appearance.

'I hope Vera has been amusing you?' she said. 'She has been very interesting,' said Framton. 'I hope you don't mind the open window,' said Mrs Sappleton briskly; 'my husband and brothers will be home directly from shooting, and they always come in this way. They've been out for snipe in the marshes today, so they'll make a fine mess over my poor carpets. So like you men-folk, isn't it?'

She rattled on cheerfully about the shooting and the scarcity of birds, and the prospects for duck in the winter. To Framton it was all purely horrible. He made a desperate but only partially successful effort to turn the talk on to a less ghastly topic; he was conscious that his hostess was giving him only a fragment of her attention, and her eyes were constantly straying past him to the open window and the lawn beyond. It was certainly an unfortunate coincidence that he should have paid his visit on this tragic anniversary.

'The doctors agree in ordering me complete rest, an absence of mental excitement, and avoidance of anything in the nature of violent physical exercise,' announced Framton, who laboured under the tolerably wide-spread delusion that total strangers and chance acquaintances are hungry for the least detail of one's ailments and infirmities, their cause and cure. 'On the matter of diet they are not so much in agreement,' he continued.

'No?' said Mrs Sappleton, in a voice which only replaced a yawn at the last moment. Then she suddenly brightened into alert attention—but not to what Framton was saying.

'Here they are at last!' she cried. 'Just in time for tea, and don't they look as if they were muddy up to the eyes!'

Framton shivered slightly and turned towards the niece with a look intended to convey sympathetic comprehension. The child was staring out through the open window with dazed horror in her eyes. In a chill shock of nameless fear Framton swung round in his seat and looked in the same direction.

In the deepening twilight three figures were walking across the lawn towards the window; they all carried guns under their arms, and one of them was additionally burdened with a white coat hung over his shoulders. A tired brown spaniel kept close at their heels. Noiselessly they neared the house, and then a hoarse young voice chanted out of the dusk: 'I said, Bertie, why do you bound?'

Framton grabbed wildly at his stick and hat; the hall-door, the gravel-drive, and the front gate were dimly-noted stages in his headlong retreat. A cyclist coming along the road had to run into the hedge to avoid an imminent collision.

'Here we are, my dear,' said the bearer of the white mackintosh, coming in through the window; 'fairly muddy, but most of it's dry. Who was that who bolted out as we came up?'

'A most extraordinary man, a Mr Nuttel,' said Mrs Sappleton; 'could only talk about his illnesses, and dashed off without a word of good-bye or apology when you arrived. One would think he had seen a ghost.'

'I expect it was the spaniel,' said the niece calmly; 'he told me he had a horror of dogs. He was once hunted into a cemetery somewhere on the banks of the Ganges by a pack of pariah dogs, and had to spend the night in a newly dug grave with the creatures snarling and grinning and foaming just above him. Enough to make anyone lose their nerve.'

Romance at short notice was her specialty.

The subtle difference between appearance and reality is effectively portrayed in this short story: 'what is' and 'what may have been'. To draw a line between the two is often hazardous and nerve-racking. The story pits imagination or, 'romance at short notice' against 'reality.' The structure of this story is a frame within a frame.

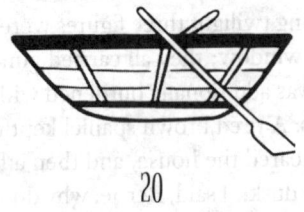

20

INDIAN CAMP

ERNEST HEMINGWAY

At the lake shore there was another rowboat drawn up. The two Indians stood waiting. Nick and his father got in the stern of the boat and the Indians shoved it off and one of them got in to row. Uncle George sat in the stern of the camp rowboat. The young Indian shoved the camp boat off and got in to row Uncle George.

The two boats started off in the dark. Nick heard the oarlocks of the other boat quite a way ahead of them in the mist. The Indians rowed with quick choppy strokes. Nick lay back with his father's arm around him. It was cold on the water.

The Indian who was rowing them was working very hard, but the other boat moved farther ahead in the mist all the time.

'Where are we going, Dad?' Nick asked.

'Over to the Indian camp. There is an Indian lady very sick.'

'Oh', said Nick.

Across the bay they found the other boat beached. Uncle George was smoking a cigar in the dark. The young Indian pulled the boat way up on the beach. Uncle George gave both the Indians cigars.

They walked up from the beach through a meadow that was soaking wet with dew, following the young Indian who carried a lantern. Then they went into the woods and followed a trail that led to the logging road that ran back into the hills. It was much lighter on the logging road as the timber was cut away on both sides. The young Indian stopped and blew out his lantern and they all walked on along the road. They came around a bend and a dog came out barking. Ahead were the lights of the shanties where the Indian bark-peelers lived. More dogs rushed out at them. The two Indians sent them back to the shanties. In the shanty nearest the road there was a light in the window. An old woman stood in the doorway holding a lamp. Inside on a wooden bunk lay a young Indian woman. She had been trying to have her baby for two days. All the old women in the camp had been helping her. The men had moved off up the road to sit in the dark and smoke out of range of the noise she made. She screamed just as Nick and the two Indians followed his father and Uncle George into the shanty. She lay in the lower bunk, very big under a quilt. Her head was turned to one side. In the upper bunk was her husband. He had cut his foot very badly with an axe three days before. He was smoking a pipe. The room smelled very bad.

Nick's father ordered some water to be put on the stove, and while it was heating he spoke to Nick. 'This lady is going to have a baby, Nick,' he said. 'I know,' said Nick.

'You don't know,' said his father. 'Listen to me. What she is going through is called being in labour. The baby wants to be born and she wants it to be born. All her muscles are trying to get the baby born. That is what is happening when she screams.'

'I see,' Nick said. Just then the woman cried out. 'Oh, Daddy, can't you give her something to make her stop screaming?' asked Nick.

'No. I haven't any anaesthetic,' his father said. 'But her screams are not important. I don't hear them because they are not important.'

The husband in the upper bunk rolled over against the wall. The woman in the kitchen motioned to the doctor that the water was hot. Nick's father went into the kitchen and poured about half of the water out of the big kettle into a basin. Into the water left in the kettle he put several things he unwrapped from a handkerchief.

'Those must boil,' he said, and began to scrub his hands in the basin of hot water with a cake of soap he had brought from the camp. Nick watched his father's hands scrubbing each other with the soap. While his father washed his hands very carefully and thoroughly, he talked. 'You see, Nick, babies are supposed to be born head first, but sometimes they're not. When they're not they make a lot of trouble for everybody. Maybe I'll have to operate on this lady. We'll know in a little while.'

When he was satisfied with his hands he went in and went to work.

'Pull back that quilt, will you, George?' he said. 'I'd rather not touch it.'

Later when he started to operate Uncle George and three Indian men held the woman still. She bit Uncle George on the arm and Uncle George said, 'Damn squaw bitch!' and the young Indian who had rowed Uncle George over laughed at him. Nick held the basin for his father. It all took a long time.

His father picked the baby up and slapped it to make it breathe and handed it to the old woman. 'See, it's a boy, Nick,' he said. 'How do you like being an interne?' Nick said, 'All right'. He was looking away so as not to see what his father was doing. 'There. That gets it,' said his father and put something in to the basin.

Nick didn't look at it. 'Now,' his father said, 'there's some stitches to put in. You can watch this or not, Nick, just as you like. I'm going to sew up the incision I made.'

Nick did not watch. His curiosity had been gone for a long time. His father finished and stood up. Uncle George and the three Indian men stood up. Nick put the basin out in the kitchen. Uncle George looked at his arm. The young Indian smiled reminiscently.

'I'll put some peroxide on that, George,' the doctor said. He bent over the Indian woman. She was quiet now and her eyes were closed. She looked very pale. She did not know what had become of the baby or anything. 'I'll be back in the morning,' the doctor said, standing up. 'The nurse should be here from St. Ignace by noon and she'll bring everything we need.'

He was feeling exalted and talkative as football players are in the dressing room after a game. 'That's one for the medical journal, George,' he said. 'Doing a Caesarian with a jack-knife and sewing it up with nine-foot, tapered gut leaders.'

Uncle George was standing against the wall, looking at his arm.

'Oh, you're a great man, all right,' he said. 'Ought to have a look at the proud father. They're usually the worst sufferers in these little affairs,' the doctor said. 'I must say he took it all pretty quietly.' He pulled back the blanket from the Indian's head. His hand came away wet. He mounted on the edge of the lower bunk with the lamp in one hand and looked in. The Indian lay with his face toward the wall. His throat had been cut from ear to ear. The blood had flowed down into a pool where his body sagged the bunk. His head rested on his left arm. The open razor lay, edge up, in the blankets.

'Take Nick out of the shanty, George,' the doctor said. There was no need of that. Nick, standing in the door of the kitchen, had a good view of the upper bunk when his father, the lamp in one hand, tipped the Indian's head back.

It was just beginning to be daylight when they walked along the logging road back toward the lake.

'I'm terribly sorry I brought you along, Nickie,' said his father, all his post-operative exhilaration gone. 'It was an awful mess to put you through.'

'Do ladies always have such a hard time having babies?' Nick asked.

'No, that was very, very exceptional.'

'Why did he kill himself, Daddy?'

'I don't know, Nick. He couldn't stand things, I guess.'

'Do many men kill themselves, Daddy?'

'Not very many, Nick.'

'Do many women?'

'Hardly ever.'

'Don't they ever?'
'Oh, yes. They do sometimes.'
'Daddy?'
'Yes.'
'Where did Uncle George go?'
'He'll turn up all right.'
'Is dying hard, Daddy?'
'No, I think it's pretty easy, Nick. It all depends.'

They were seated in the boat, Nick in the stern, his father rowing. The sun was coming up over the hills. A bass jumped, making a circle in the water. Nick trailed his hand in the water. It felt warm in the sharp chill of the morning.

In the early morning on the lake sitting in the stern of the boat with his father rowing, he felt quite sure that he would never die.

The story draws the reader into polarities—between the effects of the pangs of birth and the consequences of death. This is a story of men who can stand things and men who cannot. It primarily focusses on the relationship of a father and son. It also portrays the initiation into the world of adult experience: childbirth, loss of innocence and even gory suicide.

21

A COWARD

GUY DE MAUPASSANT

Society called him Handsome Signoles. His name was Viscount Gontran-Joseph de Signoles. An orphan, and possessed of an adequate income, he cut a dash, as the saying is. He had a good figure and a good carriage, a sufficient flow of words to pass for wit, a certain natural grace, an air of nobility and pride, a gallant moustache and an eloquent eye, attributes which women like.

He was in demand in drawing-rooms, sought after for *valses*, and in men he inspired that smiling hostility which is reserved for vital and attractive rivals. He had been suspected of several love-affairs of a sort calculated to create a good opinion of a youngster. He lived a happy, care-free life, in the most complete well-being of body and mind. He was known to be a fine swordsman and a still finer shot with the pistol.

'When I come to fight a duel,' he would say, 'I shall choose pistols. With that weapon, I'm sure of killing my man.'

One evening, he went to the theatre with two ladies, quite young, friends of his, whose husbands were also of the party, and after the performance he invited them to take ices at Tortoni's.

They had been sitting there for a few minutes when he noticed a gentleman at a neighbouring table staring obstinately at one of the ladies of the party. She seemed embarrassed and ill at ease, and bent her head. At last she said to her husband:

'There's a man staring at me. I don't know him; do you?'

The husband, who had seen nothing, raised his eyes, but declared:

'No, not in the least.'

Half smiling, half in anger, she replied: 'It's very annoying; the creature's spoiling my ice.'

Her husband shrugged his shoulders.

'Deuce take him, don't appear to notice it. If we had to deal with all the discourteous people one meets, we'd never have done with them.'

But the Viscount had risen abruptly. He could not permit this stranger to spoil an ice of his giving. It was to him that the insult was addressed, since it was at his invitation and on his account that his friends had come to the cafe. The affair was no business of anyone but himself.

He went up to the man and said: 'You have a way of looking at those ladies, sir, which I cannot stomach. Please be so good as to set a limit to your persistence.'

'You hold your tongue,' replied the other.

'Take care, sir,' retorted the Viscount, clenching his teeth; 'you'll force me to overstep the bounds of common politeness.'

The gentleman replied with a single word, a vile word which rang across the cafe from one end to the other, and, like the release of a spring, jerked every person present into an abrupt movement. All those with their backs towards him turned round, all the rest raised their heads; three waiters spun round on their heels like tops; the two ladies behind the counter started, then the whole upper half of their bodies twisted round, as though they were a couple of automata worked by the same handle.

There was a profound silence. Then suddenly a sharp noise resounded in the air. The Viscount had boxed his adversary's ears. Every one rose to intervene. Cards were exchanged.

Back in his home, the Viscount walked for several minutes up and down his room with long quick strides. He was too excited to think. A solitary idea dominated his mind: 'a duel'; but as yet the idea stirred in him no emotion of any kind. He had done what he was compelled to do; he had shown himself to be what he ought to be. People would talk of it, would approve of him, congratulate him. He repeated aloud, speaking as a man speaks in severe mental distress:

'What a hound the fellow is!'

Then he sat down and began to reflect. In the morning he must find seconds. Whom should he choose? He searched his mind for the most important and celebrated names of his acquaintance. At last he decided on the Marquis de la Tour-Noire and Colonel Bourdin, an aristocrat and a soldier; they would do excellently. Their names would look well in the papers. He realised that he was thirsty, and drank three glasses of water one after the other; then he began to walk up and down again. He felt full of energy. If he played the gallant, showed himself determined, insisted on the most strict and dangerous arrangements, demanded a serious duel, a thoroughly serious duel, a positively terrible duel, his adversary would probably retire an apologist.

He took up once more the card which he had taken from his pocket and thrown down upon the table, and read it again as he had read it before, in the cafe, at a glance, and in the cab, by the light of each gas-lamp, on his way home.

'Georges Lamil, 51 rue Moncey.' Nothing more.

He examined the grouped letters; they seemed to him mysterious, full of confused meaning. Georges Lamil? Who was this man? What did he do? Why had he looked at the woman in that way? Was it not revolting that a stranger, an unknown man, could thus disturb a man's life, without warning, just because he chose to fix his insolent eyes upon a woman? Again the Viscount repeated aloud: 'What a hound!'

Then he remained standing stock-still, lost in thought, his eyes still fixed upon the card. A fury against this scrap of paper awoke in him, a fury of hatred in which was mingled a queer sensation of uneasiness. This sort of thing was so stupid! He took up an open knife which lay close at hand and thrust it through the middle of the printed name, as though he had stabbed a man.

So he must fight. Should he choose swords or pistols?—for he regarded himself as the insulted party. With swords there would be less risk, but with pistols there was a chance that his adversary might withdraw. It is very rare that a duel with swords is fatal, for mutual prudence is apt to restrain combatants from engaging at sufficiently close quarters for a point to penetrate deeply. With pistols he ran a grave risk of death; but he might also extricate himself from the affair with all the honours of the situation and without actually coming to a meeting.

'I must be firm,' he said. 'He will take fright.'

The sound of his voice set him trembling, and he looked round. He felt very nervous. He drank another glass of water, then began to undress for bed.

As soon as he was in bed, he blew out the light and closed his eyes.

'I've the whole of tomorrow,' he thought, 'in which to set my affairs in order. I'd better sleep now, so that I shall be quite calm.'

He was very warm in the blankets, but he could not manage to compose himself to sleep. He turned this way and that, lay for five minutes upon his back, turned on to his left side, then rolled over on to his right.

He was still thirsty. He got up to get a drink. A feeling of uneasiness crept over him:

'Is it possible that I'm afraid?'

Why did his heart beat madly at each familiar sound in his room? When the clock was about to strike, the faint squeak of the rising spring made him start; so shaken he was that for several seconds afterwards he had to open his mouth to get his breath.

He began to reason with himself on the possibility of his being afraid.

'Shall I be afraid?'

No, of course he would not be afraid, since he was resolved to see the matter through, and had duly made up his mind to fight and not to tremble. But he felt so profoundly distressed that he wondered:

'Can a man be afraid in spite of himself?'

He was attacked by this doubt, this uneasiness, this terror; suppose a force more powerful than himself, masterful, irresistible, overcame him, what would happen? Yes, what might not happen? Assuredly he would go to the place of the meeting, since he was quite ready to go. But supposing he trembled? Supposing he fainted? He thought of the scene, of his reputation, his good name.

There came upon him a strange need to get up and look at himself in the mirror. He relit his candle. When he saw his face reflected in the polished glass, he scarcely recognised it, it seemed to him as though he had never yet seen himself. His eyes looked to him enormous; and he was pale; yes, without doubt he was pale, very pale.

He remained standing in front of the mirror. He put out his tongue, as though to ascertain the state of his health, and abruptly the thought struck him like a bullet:

'The day after tomorrow, at this very hour, I may be dead.'

His heart began again its furious beating.

'The day after tomorrow, at this very hour, I may be dead. This person facing me, this me I see in the mirror, will be no more. Why, here I am, I look at myself, I feel myself alive, and in twenty-four hours I shall be lying in that bed, dead, my eyes closed, cold, inanimate, vanished.'

He turned back towards the bed, and distinctly saw himself lying on his back in the very sheets he had just left. He had the hollow face of a corpse, his hands had the slackness of hands that will never make another movement.

At that he was afraid of his bed, and, to get rid of the sight of it, went into the smoking-room. Mechanically he picked up a cigar, lit it, and began to walk up and down again. He was cold; he went to the bell to wake his valet; but he stopped, even as he raised his hand to the rope.

'He will see that I am afraid.'

He did not ring; he lit the fire. His hands shook a little, with a nervous tremor, whenever they touched anything. His brain whirled, his troubled thoughts became elusive, transitory, and gloomy; his mind suffered all the effects of intoxication, as though he were actually drunk.

Over and over again he thought: 'What shall I do? What is to become of me?'

His whole body trembled, seized with a jerky shuddering; he got up and, going to the window, drew back the curtains.

Dawn was at hand, a summer dawn. The rosy sky touched the town, its roofs and walls, with its own hue. A broad descending ray, like the caress of the rising sun, enveloped the awakened world; and with the light, hope—a gay, swift, fierce hope—filled the Viscount's heart! Was he mad, that he had allowed himself to be struck down by fear, before anything was settled even, before his seconds had seen those of this Georges Lamil, before he knew whether he was going to fight?

He washed, dressed, and walked out with a firm step. He repeated to himself, as he walked: 'I must be energetic, very energetic. I must prove that I am not afraid.'

His seconds, the Marquis and the Colonel, placed themselves at his disposal, and after hearty handshakes discussed the conditions.

'You are anxious for a serious duel?' asked the Colonel.

'Yes, a very serious one,' replied the Viscount.

'You still insist on pistols?' said the Marquis.

'Yes.'

'You will leave us free to arrange the rest?'

In a dry, jerky voice the Viscount stated: 'Twenty paces; at the signal, raising the arm, and not lowering it. Exchange of shots till one is seriously wounded.'

'They are excellent conditions,' declared the Colonel in a tone of satisfaction. 'You shoot well, you have every chance.'

They departed. The Viscount went home to wait for them. His agitation, momentarily quietened, was now growing minute by minute. He felt a strange shivering, a ceaseless vibration, down his arms, down his legs, in his chest; he could not keep still in one place, neither seated nor standing. There was not the least moistening of saliva in his mouth, and at every instant he made a violent movement of his tongue, as though to prevent it sticking to his palate.

He was eager to have breakfast, but could not eat. Then the idea came to him to drink in order to give himself courage, and he sent for a decanter of rum, of which he swallowed six liqueur glasses full one after the other.

A burning warmth flooded through his body, followed immediately by a sudden dizziness of the mind and spirit.

'Now I know what to do,' he thought. 'Now it is all right.'

But by the end of an hour he had emptied the decanter, and his state of agitation had once more become intolerable. He was conscious of a wild need to roll on the ground, to scream, to bite. Night was falling.

The ringing of a bell gave him such a shock that he had not the strength to rise and welcome his seconds.

He did not even dare to speak to them, to say 'Good evening' to them, to utter a single word, for fear they guessed the whole thing by the alteration in his voice.

'Everything is arranged in accordance with the conditions you fixed,' observed the Colonel. 'At first your adversary claimed the privileges of the insulted party, but he yielded almost at once, and has accepted everything. His seconds are two military men.'

'Thank you,' said the Viscount.

'Pardon us,' interposed the Marquis, 'if we merely come in and leave again immediately, but we have a thousand things to see to. We must have a good doctor, since the combat is not to end until a serious wound is inflicted, and you know that pistol bullets are no laughing-matter. We must appoint the ground, near a house to which we may carry the wounded man if necessary, etc. In fact, we shall be occupied for two or three hours arranging all that there is to arrange.'

'Thank you,' said the Viscount a second time.

'You are all right?' asked the Colonel. 'You are calm?'

'Yes, quite calm, thank you.'

The two men retired.

When he realised that he was once more alone, he thought that he was going mad. His servant had lit the lamps, and he sat down at the table to write letters. After tracing, at the head of a sheet: 'This is my will,' he rose shivering and walked away, feeling incapable of connecting two ideas, of taking a resolution, of making any decision whatever.

So he was going to fight! He could no longer avoid it. Then what was the matter with him? He wished to fight, he had absolutely decided upon this plan of action and taken his resolve, and he now felt clearly, in spite of every effort of mind and forcing of will, that he could not retain even the strength necessary to get him to the place of meeting. He tried to picture the duel, his own attitude and the bearing of his adversary.

From time to time his teeth chattered in his mouth with a slight clicking noise. He tried to read, and took down Chateauvillard's code of duelling. Then he wondered:

'Does my adversary go to shooting-galleries? Is he well known? Is he classified anywhere? How can I find out?'

He bethought himself of Baron Vaux's book on marksmen with the pistol, and ran through it from end to end. Georges Lamil was not mentioned in it. Yet if the man were not a good shot, he would surely not have promptly agreed to that dangerous weapon and those fatal conditions?

He opened, in passing, a case by Gastinne Renette standing on a small table, and took out one of the pistols, then placed himself as though to shoot and raised his arm. But he was trembling from head to foot and the barrel moved in every direction.

At that, he said to himself: 'It's impossible. I cannot fight in this state.'

He looked at the end of the barrel, at the little, black, deep hole that spits death; he thought of the disgrace, of the whispers at the club, of the laughter in drawing-rooms, of the contempt of women, of the allusions in the papers, of the insults which cowards would fling at him.

He was still looking at the weapon, and, raising the hammer, caught a glimpse of a cap gleaming beneath it like a tiny red flame. By good fortune or forgetfulness, the pistol had been left loaded. At the knowledge, he was filled with a confused inexplicable sense of joy.

If, when face to face with the other man, he did not show a proper gallantry and calm, he would be lost for ever. He would be sullied, branded with a mark of infamy, hounded out of society. And he would not be able to achieve that calm, that swaggering poise; he knew it, he felt it. Yet he was brave, since he wanted to fight me ... He was brave, since....

The thought which hovered in him did not even fulfil itself in his mind; but, opening his mouth wide, he thrust in the barrel of his pistol with savage gesture until it reached his throat, and pressed on the trigger.

When his valet ran in, at the sound of the report, he found him lying dead upon his back. A shower of blood had splashed the white paper on the table, and made a great red mark beneath these four words:

'This is my will.'

༄

The story is a pictorial depiction of raw emotions—honour, fear, doubt, appearance, pride, conflict and insecurity. This leads to the disintegration and self-destruction of a coward. 'A coward dies a thousand times ...' wrote Shakespeare.

22

OLD MAN AT THE BRIDGE

ERNEST HEMINGWAY

An old man with steel rimmed spectacles and very dusty clothes sat by the side of the road. There was a pontoon bridge across the river and carts, trucks, and men, women and children were crossing it. The mule-drawn carts staggered up the steep bank from the bridge with soldiers helping push against the spokes of the wheels. The trucks ground up and away heading out of it all and the peasants plodded along in the ankle deep dust. But the old man sat there without moving. He was too tired to go any farther.

It was my business to cross the bridge, explore the bridgehead beyond and find out to what point the enemy had advanced. I did this and returned over the bridge. There were not so many carts now and very few people on foot, but the old man was still there.

'Where do you come from?' I asked him.

'From San Carlos,' he said, and smiled.

That was his native town and so it gave him pleasure to mention it and he smiled.

'I was taking care of animals,' he explained.

'Oh,' I said, not quite understanding.

'Yes,' he said, 'I stayed, you see, taking care of animals. I was the last one to leave the town of San Carlos.'

He did not look like a shepherd nor a herdsman and I looked at his black dusty clothes and his gray dusty face and his steel rimmed spectacles and said, 'What animals were they?'

'Various animals,' he said, and shook his head. 'I had to leave them.'

I was watching the bridge and the African looking country of the Ebro Delta and wondering how long now it would be before we would see the enemy, and listening all the while for the first noises that would signal that ever mysterious event called contact, and the old man still sat there.

'What animals were they?' I asked.

'There were three animals altogether,' he explained. 'There were two goats and a cat and then there were four pairs of pigeons.'

'And you had to leave them?' I asked.

'Yes. Because of the artillery. The captain told me to go because of the artillery.'

'And you have no family?' I asked, watching the far end of the bridge where a few last carts were hurrying down the slope of the bank.

'No,' he said, 'only the animals I stated. The cat, of course, will be all right. A cat can look out for itself, but I cannot think what will become of the others.'

'What politics have you?' I asked.

'I am without politics,' he said. 'I am seventy-six years old. I have come twelve kilometers now and I think now I can go no further.'

'This is not a good place to stop,' I said. 'If you can make it, there are trucks up the road where it forks for Tortosa.'

'I will wait a while,' he said, ' and then I will go. Where do the trucks go?'

'Towards Barcelona,' I told him.

'I know no one in that direction,' he said, 'but thank you very much. Thank you again very much.'

He looked at me very blankly and tiredly, and then said, having to share his worry with someone, 'The cat will be all right, I am sure. There is no need to be unquiet about the cat. But the others. Now what do you think about the others?'

'Why they'll probably come through it all right.'

'You think so?'

'Why not,' I said, watching the far bank where now there were no carts.

'But what will they do under the artillery when I was told to leave because of the artillery?'

'Did you leave the dove cage unlocked?' I asked.

'Yes.'

'Then they'll fly.'

'Yes, certainly they'll fly. But the others. It's better not to think about the others,' he said.

'If you are rested I would go,' I urged. 'Get up and try to walk now.'

'Thank you,' he said and got to his feet, swayed from side to side and then sat down backwards in the dust.

'I was taking care of animals,' he said dully, but no longer to me. 'I was only taking care of animals.'

There was nothing to do about him. It was Easter Sunday and the Fascists were advancing toward the Ebro. It was a gray overcast day with a low ceiling so their planes were not up. That and the fact that cats know how to look after themselves was all the good luck that old man would ever have.

The backdrop is the Spanish civil war. The seventy-six-year-old man had no one, but he was a 'pet parent'—his pets being two goats, a cat and eight pigeons. He had to abandon his unique family. The war's destructive impact has left the family members to fend for themselves. A reference to the old man's town gives him pleasure, the longing for a home during the hazards of war. The bridge is a symbol of communication and union. However, the story reflects the theme of depression and impending death.

23

HAUNTED HOUSE

VIRGINIA WOOLF

Whatever hour you woke there was a door shunting. From room to room they went, hand in hand, lifting here, opening there, making sure—a ghostly couple.

'Here we left it,' she said. And he added, 'Oh, but here too!' 'It's upstairs,' she murmured. 'And in the garden,' he whispered 'Quietly,' they said, 'or we shall wake them.'

But it wasn't that you woke us. Oh, no. 'They're looking for it; they're drawing the curtain,' one might say, and so read on a page or two. 'Now they've found it,' one would be certain, stopping the pencil on the margin. And then, tired of reading, one might rise and see for oneself, the house all empty, the doors standing open, only the wood pigeons bubbling with content and the hum of the threshing machine sounding from the farm. 'What did I come in here for? What did I want to find?' My hands were empty. 'Perhaps it's upstairs then?' The apples were in the loft. And so down again, the garden still as ever, only the book had slipped into the grass. But they had found it in the drawing room. Not that one could ever see them. The window panes reflected apples, reflected roses; all the leaves were green in the glass. If they moved in the drawing room, the apple only turned its yellow side. Yet, the moment after, if the door was opened, spread about the floor, hung upon the walls, pendant from the ceiling—what? My hands were empty. The shadow of a thrush crossed the carpet; from the deepest wells of silence the wood pigeon drew its bubble of sound. 'Safe, safe, safe,' the pulse of the house beat softly. 'The treasure buried; the room...' the pulse stopped short. Oh, was that the buried treasure?

A moment later the light had faded. Out in the garden then? But the trees spun darkness for a wandering beam of sun. So fine, so rare, coolly sunk beneath the surface the beam I sought always burnt behind the glass. Death was the glass; death was between us; coming to the woman first, hundreds of years ago, leaving the house, sealing all the windows; the rooms were darkened. He left it, left her, went North, went East, saw the stars turned in the Southern sky; sought the house, found it dropped beneath the Downs. 'Safe, safe, safe,' the pulse of the house beat gladly. 'The Treasure yours.'

The wind roars up the avenue. Trees stoop and bend this way and that. Moonbeams splash and spill wildly in the rain. But the beam of the lamp falls straight from the window. The candle burns stiff and still. Wandering through the house, opening the windows, whispering not to wake us, the ghostly couple seek their joy.

'Here we slept,' she says. And he adds, 'Kisses without number.' 'Waking in the morning—' 'Silver between the trees—' 'Upstairs—' 'In the garden—' 'When summer came—' 'In winter snowtime—' The doors go shutting far in the distance, gently knocking like the pulse of a heart.

Nearer they come; cease at the doorway. The wind falls, the rain slides silver down the glass. Our eyes darken; we hear no steps beside us; we see no lady spread her ghostly cloak. His hands shield the lantern. 'Look,' he breathes. 'Sound asleep. Love upon their lips.'

Stooping, holding their silver lamp above us, long they look and deeply. Long they pause. The wind drives straightly; the flame stoops slightly. Wild beams of moonlight cross both floor and wall, and, meeting, stain the faces bent; the faces pondering; the faces that search the sleepers and seek their hidden joy.

'Safe, safe, safe,' the heart of the house beats proudly. 'Long years—' he sighs. 'Again you found me.' 'Here,' she murmurs, 'sleeping; in the garden reading; laughing, rolling apples in the loft. Here we left our treasure—' Stooping, their light lifts the lids upon my eyes. 'Safe! safe! safe!' the pulse of the house beats wildly. Waking, I cry 'Oh, is this your buried treasure? The light in the heart.'

∞

Virginia Woolf could 'carve on an inch of ivory'. In a couple of pages only, she touches up on ghost stories with the sensibility of a modern writer. The house itself seems to be speaking. The style is that of a prose-poem: 'Safe safe safe'; the tense shifts from the past to the present.

24

THE LAST LEAF

O. HENRY

In a little district west of Washington Square the streets have run crazy and broken themselves into small strips called 'places.' These 'places' make strange angles and curves. One street crosses itself a time or two. An artist once discovered a valuable possibility in this street. Suppose a collector with a bill for paints, paper and canvas should, in traversing this route, suddenly meet himself coming back, without a cent having been paid on account!

So, to quaint old Greenwich Village the art people soon came prowling, hunting for north windows and eighteenth-century gables and Dutch attics and low rents. Then they imported some pewter mugs and a chafing dish or two from Sixth Avenue, and became a 'colony.'

At the top of a squatty, three story brick Sue and Johnsy had their studio. 'Johnsy' was familiar for Joanna. One was from Maine; the other from California. They had met at the *table d'hote* of an Eighth street 'Delmonico's,' and found their tastes in art, chicory salad and bishop sleeves so congenial that the studio resulted.

That was in May. In November a cold, unseen stranger, whom the doctors called Pneumonia, stalked about the colony, touching one here and there with his icy fingers. Over on the east side this ravager strode boldly, smiting his victims by scores, but his feet trod slowly through the maze of the narrow and moss-grown 'places.'

Mr Pneumonia was not what you would call a chivalric old gentleman. A mite of a little woman with blood thinned by California zephyrs was hardly fair game for the red-fisted, short breathed old duffer. But Johnsy he smote; and she lay scarcely moving, on her painted iron bedstead, looking through the small Dutch window-panes at the blank side of the next brick house.

One morning the busy doctor invited Sue into the hallway with a shaggy, gray eyebrow.

'She has one chance in—let us say, ten,' he said, as he shook down the mercury in his clinical thermometer. 'And that chance is for her to want to live. This way people have of lining-up on the side of the undertaker makes the entire pharmacopoeia look silly. Your little lady has made up her mind that she's not going to get well. Has she anything on her mind?'

'She, she wanted to paint the Bay of Naples some day,' said Sue.

'Paint?—bosh! Has she anything on her mind worth thinking about twice—a man, for instance?'

'A man?' said Sue, with a jew's-harp twang in her voice. 'Is a man worth—but, no, doctor; there is nothing of the kind.'

'Well, it is the weakness, then,' said the doctor. 'I will do all that science, so far as it may filter through my efforts, can accomplish. But whenever my patient begins to count the carriages in her funeral procession I subtract fifty per cent from the curative power of medicines. If you will get her to ask one question about the new winter styles in cloak sleeves I will promise you a one-in-five chance for her, instead of ten.'

After the doctor had gone Sue went into the workroom and cried a Japanese napkin to a pulp. Then she swaggered into Johnsy's room with her drawing board, whistling ragtime.

Johnsy lay, scarcely making a ripple under the bedclothes, with her face toward the window. Sue stopped whistling, thinking she was asleep.

She arranged her board and began a pen and ink drawing to illustrate a magazine story. Young artists must pave their way to Art by drawing pictures for magazine stories that young authors write to pave their way to Literature.

As Sue was sketching a pair of elegant horseshow riding trousers and a monocle on the figure of the hero, an Idaho cowboy, she heard a low sound, several times repeated. She went quickly to the bedside. Johnsy's eyes were open wide. She was looking out the window and counting—counting backward.

'Twelve,' she said, and a little later 'eleven' and then 'ten,' and 'nine' and then 'eight' and 'seven,' almost together.

Sue looked solicitously out the window. What was there to count? There was only a bare, dreary yard to be seen, and the blank side of the brick house twenty feet away. An old, old ivy vine, gnarled and decayed at the roots, climbed half way up the brick wall. The cold breath of autumn had stricken its leaves from the vine until its skeleton branches clung, almost bare, to the crumbling bricks.

'What is it, dear?' asked Sue.

'Six,' said Johnsy, in almost a whisper. 'They're falling faster now. Three days ago there were almost a hundred. It made my head ache to count them. But now it's easy. There goes another one. There are only five left now.'

'Five what, dear. Tell your Sudie.'

'Leaves. On the ivy vine. When the last one falls I must go, too. I've known that for three days. Didn't the doctor tell you?'

'Oh, I never heard of such nonsense,' complained Sue, with magnificent scorn. 'What have old ivy leaves to do with your getting well? And you used to love that vine so, you naughty girl. Don't be a goosey. Why, the doctor told me this morning that your chances for getting well real soon were—let's see exactly what he said—he said the chances were ten to one! Why that's almost as good a chance as we have in New York when we ride on the street cars or walk past a new building. Try to take some broth now, and let Sudie go back to her drawing, so she can sell the editor man with it, and buy port wine for her sick child, and pork chops for her greedy self.'

'You needn't get any more wine,' said Johnsy, keeping her eyes fixed on the window. 'There goes another. No, I don't want any broth. That leaves just four. I want to see the last one fall before it gets dark. Then I'll go, too.'

'Johnsy, dear,' said Sue, bending over her, 'will you promise me to keep your eyes closed, and not look out the window until I am done working? I must hand those drawings in by tomorrow. I need the light, or I could draw the shade down.'

'Couldn't you draw in the other room?' asked Johnsy, coldly.

'I'd rather be here by you,' said Sue. 'Besides, I don't want you to keep looking at those silly ivy leaves.'

'Tell me as soon as you have finished,' said Johnsy, closing her eyes, and lying white and still as a fallen statue, 'because I want to see the last one fall. I'm tired of waiting. I'm tired of thinking. I want to turn loose my hold on everything, and go sailing down, down, just like one of those poor, tired leaves.'

'Try to sleep,' said Sue. 'I must call Behrman up to be my model for the old hermit miner. I'll not be gone a minute. Don't try to move 'til I come back.'

Old Behrman was a painter who lived on the ground floor beneath them. He was past sixty and had a Michael Angelo's Moses beard curling down from the head of a satyr along the body of an imp. Behrman was a failure in art. Forty years he had wielded the brush without getting near enough to touch the hem of his Mistress's robe. He had been always about to paint a masterpiece, but had never yet begun it. For several years he had painted nothing except now and then a daub in the line of commerce or advertising. He earned a little by serving as a model to those young artists in the colony who could not pay the price of a professional. He drank gin to excess, and still talked of his coming masterpiece. For the rest he was a fierce little old man, who scoffed terribly at the softness in any one, and who regarded himself as especial mastiff-in-waiting to protect the two young artists in the studio above.

Sue found Behrman smelling strongly of juniper berries in his dimly lighted den below. In one corner was a blank canvas on an easel that had been waiting there for twenty-five years to receive the first line of the masterpiece. She told him of Johnsy's fancy, and how she feared she would, indeed light and fragile as a leaf herself, float away, when her slight hold upon the world grew weaker.

Old Behrman, with his red eyes plainly streaming, shouted his contempt and derision for such idiotic imaginings.

'Vass!' he cried. 'Is dere people in de world mit der foolishness to die because leafs dey drop off from a confounded vine? I haf not heard of such a thing. No, I will not bose as a model for your fool hermit-dunder head. Vy do you allow dot silly pusiness to come in der brain of her? Ach, dot poor leetle Miss Yohnsy.'

'She is very ill and weak,' said Sue, 'and the fever has left her mind morbid and full of strange fancies. Very well, Mr Behrman, if you do not care to pose for me, you needn't. But I think you are a horrid old—old flibbertigibbet.'

'You are just like a woman!' yelled Behrman. 'Who said I will not bose? Go on. I come mit you. For half and hour I haf peen trying to say dot I am ready to bose. Gott! dis is not any blace in which one so gooot as Miss Yohnsy shall lie sick. Some day I vill baint a masterpiece, and ve shall all go away. Gott! yes.'

Johnsy was sleeping when they went upstairs. Sue pulled the shade down to the window-sill, and motioned Behrman into the other room. In there they peered out the window fearfully at the ivy vine. Then they looked at each other for a moment without speaking. A persistent, cold rain was falling, mingled with snow. Behrman, in his old blue shirt, took his seat as the hermit miner on an upturned kettle for a rock.

When Sue awoke from an hour's sleep the next morning she found Johnsy with dull, wide-open eyes staring at the drawn green shade. 'Pull it up; I want to see,' she ordered, in a whisper. Wearily Sue obeyed.

But lo! after the beating rain and fierce gusts of wind that had endured through the livelong night, there yet stood out against the brick wall one ivy leaf. It was the last on the vine. Still dark green near its stem, but with its serrated edges tinted with the yellow of dissolution and decay, it hung bravely from a branch some twenty feet above the ground.

'It is the last one,' said Johnsy. 'I thought it would surely fall during the night. I heard the wind. It will fall today, and I shall die at the same time.'

'Dear, dear!' said Sue, leaning her worn face down to the pillow, 'think of me, if you won't think of yourself. What would I do?'

But Johnsy did not answer. The lonesomest thing in all the world is a soul when it is making ready to go on its mysterious, far journey. The fancy seemed to posses her more strongly as one by one the ties that bound her to friendship and to earth were loosed.

The day wore away, and even through the twilight they could see the lone ivy leaf clinging to its stem against the wall. And then, with the coming of the night the north wind was again down from the low Dutch eaves.

When it was light enough Johnsy, the merciless, commanded that the shade be raised.

The ivy leaf was still there.

Johnsy lay for a long time looking at it. And then she called to Sue, who was stirring her chicken broth over the gas stove.

'I've been a bad girl, Sudie,' said Johnsy. 'Something has made that last leaf stay there to show me how wicked I was. It is a sin to want to die. You may bring me a little broth now, and some milk with a little port in it, and—no; bring me a hand-mirror first, and then pack some pillows about me, and I will sit up and watch you cook.'

An hour later she said: 'Sudie, some day I hope to paint the Bay of Naples.'

The doctor came in the afternoon, and Sue had an excuse to go into the hallway as he left.

'Even chances,' said the doctor, taking Sue's thin shaking hand in his. 'With good nursing you'll win. And now I must see another case I have downstairs. Behrman, his name is—some kind of an artist, I believe. Pneumonia, too. He is an old, weak man, and the attack is acute. There is no hope for him; but he goes to the hospital today to be made more comfortable.'

The next day the doctor said to Sue: 'She's out of danger. You've won. Nutrition and care now—that's all.'

And that afternoon Sue came to the bed where Johnsy lay, contentedly knitting a very blue and very useless woollen shoulder scarf, and put one arm around her, pillows and all.

'I have something to tell you, white mouse,' she said. 'Mr Behrman died of pneumonia today in the hospital. He was ill only two days. The janitor found him on the morning of the first day in his room downstairs helpless with pain. His shoes and clothing were wet through and icy cold. They couldn't imagine where he had been on such a dreadful night. And then they found a lantern, still lighted, and a ladder that had been dragged from its place, and some scattered brushes, and a palette with green and yellow colors mixed on it, and—look out the window, dear, at the last ivy leaf on the wall. Didn't you wonder why it never fluttered or moved when the wind blew? Ah, darling, it's Behrman's masterpiece—he painted it there the night the last leaf fell.'

It's a masterpiece—painted the night the last leaf fell. The poet W.B. Yeats describes the art and artifact or the artifice of eternity as a golden bird sitting on a golden bough, singing to a drowsy emperor of the past, passing or to come. In this story, the 'last leaf' becomes an artifact of life overcoming two opposites—pessimism and optimism.

25

THE CONFESSION

GUY DE MAUPASSANT

Marguerite de Thérelles was dying. Although but fifty-six, she seemed like seventy-five at least. She panted, paler than the sheets, shaken by dreadful shiverings, her face convulsed, her eyes haggard, as if she had seen some horrible thing.

Her field est sister, Suzanne, six years older, sobbed on her knees beside the bed. A little table drawn close to the couch of the dying woman, and covered with a napkin, bore two lighted candles, the priest being momentarily expected to give extreme unction and the communion, which should be the last.

The apartment had that sinister aspect, that air of hopeless farewells, which belongs to the chambers of the dying. Medicine bottles stood about on the furniture, linen lay in the corners, pushed aside by foot or broom. The disordered chairs themselves seemed affrighted, as if they had run, in all the senses of the word. Death, the formidable, was there, hidden, waiting.

The story of the two sisters was very touching. It was quoted far and wide; it had made many eyes to weep.

Suzanne, the field er, had once been madly in love with a young man, who had also been in love with her. They were engaged, and were only waiting the day fixed for the contract, when Henry de Lampierre suddenly died.

The despair of the young girl was dreadful, and she vowed that she would never marry. She kept her word. She put on widow's weeds, which she never took off.

Then her sister, her little sister Marguérite, who was only twelve years old, came one morning to throw herself into the arms of the field er, and said: 'Big Sister, I do not want thee to be unhappy. I do not want thee to cry all thy life. I will never leave thee, never, never! I—I, too, shall never marry. I shall stay with thee always, always, always!'

Suzanne, touched by the devotion of the child, kissed her, but did not believe.

Yet the little one, also, kept her word, and despite the entreaties of her parents, despite the supplications of the field er, she never married. She was pretty, very pretty; she refused many a young man who seemed to love her truly; and she never left her sister any more.

They lived together all the days of their life, without ever being separated a single time. They went side by side, inseparably united. But Marguérite seemed always sad, oppressed, more melancholy than the field er, as though perhaps her sublime sacrifice had broken her spirit. She aged more quickly, had white hair from the age of thirty, and often suffering, seemed afflicted by some secret, gnawing trouble.

Now she was to be the first to die.

Since yesterday she was no longer able to speak. She had only said, at the first glimmers of day-dawn:

'Go fetch Monsieur le Curé, the moment has come.'

And she had remained since then upon her back, shaken with spasms, her lips agitated as though dreadful words were mounting from her heart without power of issue, her look mad with fear, terrible to see.

Her sister, torn by sorrow, wept wildly, her forehead resting on the edge of the bed, and kept repeating:

'Margot, my poor Margot, my little one!'

She had always called her, 'Little One,' just as the younger had always called her 'Big Sister.'

Steps were heard on the stairs. The door opened. A choir boy appeared, followed by an old priest in a surplice. As soon as she perceived him, the dying woman, with one shudder, sat up, opened her lips, stammered two or three words, and began to scratch the sheets with her nails as if she had wished to make a hole.

The Abbé Simon approached, took her hand, kissed her brow, and said with a soft voice:

'God pardon thee, my child; have courage, the moment is now come, speak.'

Then Marguérite, shivering from head to foot, shaking her whole couch with nervous movements, stammered:

'Sit down, Big Sister ... listen.'

The priest bent down toward Suzanne, who was still flung upon the bed's foot. He raised her, placed her in an armchair, and taking a hand of each of the sisters in one of his own, he pronounced:

'Lord, my God! Endue them with strength, cast Thy mercy upon them.'

And Marguérite began to speak. The words issued from her throat one by one, raucous, with sharp pauses, as though very feeble.

'Pardon, pardon, Big Sister; oh, forgive! If thou knewest how I have had fear of this moment all my life....'

Suzanne stammered through her tears:

'Forgive thee what, Little One? Thou hast given all to me, sacrificed everything; thou art an angel....'

But Marguérite interrupted her:

'Hush, hush! Let me speak ... do not stop me. It is dreadful ... let me tell all ... to the very end, without flinching. Listen. Thou rememberest ... thou rememberest ... Henry....'

Suzanne trembled and looked at her sister. The younger continued:

'Thou must hear all, to understand. I was twelve years old, only twelve years old; thou rememberest well, is it not so? And I was spoiled, I did everything that I liked! Thou rememberest, surely, how they spoiled me? Listen. The first time that he came he had varnished boots. He got down from his horse at the great steps, and he begged pardon for his costume, but he came to bring some news to papa. Thou rememberest, is it not so? Don't speak—listen. When I saw him I was completely carried away, I found him so very beautiful; and I remained standing in a corner of the *salon* all the time that he was talking. Children are strange ... and terrible. Oh yes ... I have dreamed of all that.

'He came back again ... several times ... I looked at him with all my eyes, with all my soul ... I was large of my age ... and very much more knowing than anyone thought. He came back often ... I thought only of him. I said, very low:

"Henry ... Henry de Lampierre!"

'Then they said that he was going to marry thee. It was a sorrow; oh, Big Sister, a sorrow ... a sorrow! I cried for three nights without sleeping. He came back every day, in the afternoon, after his lunch ... thou rememberest, is it not so? Say nothing ... listen. Thou madest him cakes which he liked ... with meal, with butter and milk. Oh, I know well how. I could make them yet if it were needed. He ate them at one mouthful, and ... and then he drank a glass of wine, and then he said, "It is delicious." Thou rememberest how he would say that?

'I was jealous, jealous! The moment of thy marriage approached. There were only two weeks more. I became crazy. I said to myself: "He shall not marry Suzanne, no, I will not have it! It is I whom he will marry when I am grown up. I shall never find anyone whom I love so much." But one night, ten days before the contract, thou tookest a walk with him in front of the chateau by moonlight ... and there ... under the fir, under the great fir ... he kissed thee ... kissed ... holding thee in his two arms ... so long. Thou rememberest, is it not so? It was probably the first time ... yes ... Thou wast so pale when thou earnest back to the *salon*.

'I had seen you two; I was there, in the shrubbery. I was angry! If I could I should have killed you both!

'I said to myself: "He shall not marry Suzanne, never! He shall marry no one. I should be too unhappy." And all of a sudden I began to hate him dreadfully.

'Then, dost thou know what I did? Listen. I had seen the gardener making little balls to kill strange dogs. He pounded up a bottle with a stone and put the powdered glass in a little ball of meat.

'I took a little medicine bottle that mamma had; I broke it small with a hammer, and I hid the glass in my pocket. It was a shining powder ... The next day, as soon as you had made the little cakes ... I split them with a knife and I put in the glass ... He ate three of them ... I too, I ate one ... I threw the other six into the pond. The two swans died three days after ... Dost thou remember? Oh, say nothing ... listen, listen. I, I alone did not die ... but I have always been sick. Listen ... He died—thou knowest well ... listen ... that, that is nothing. It is afterwards, later ... always ... the worst ... listen.

'My life, all my life ... what torture! I said to myself: "I will never leave my sister. And at the hour of death I will tell her all ..." There! And ever since, I have always thought of that moment when I should tell thee all. Now it is come. It is terrible. Oh ... Big Sister!

"I have always thought, morning and evening, by night and by day, "Some time I must tell her that ..." I waited ... What agony! ... It is done. Say nothing. Now I am afraid ... am afraid ... oh, I am afraid. If I am going to see him again, soon, when I am dead. See him again ... think of it! The first! Before thou! I shall not dare. I must ... I am going to die ... I want you to forgive me. I want it ... I cannot go off to meet him without that. Oh, tell her to forgive me, Monsieur le Curé, tell her ... I implore you to do it. I cannot die without that....'

She was silent, and remained panting, always scratching the sheet with her withered nails.

Suzanne had hidden her face in her hands, and did not move. She was thinking of him whom she might have loved so long! What a good life they should have lived together! She saw him once again in that vanished bygone time, in that old past which was put out forever. The beloved dead—how they tear your hearts! Oh, that kiss, his only kiss! She had hidden it in her soul. And after it nothing, nothing more her whole life long!

All of a sudden the priest stood straight, and, with a strong vibrant voice, he cried:

'Mademoiselle Suzanne, your sister is dying!'

Then Suzanne, opening her hands, showed her face soaked with tears, and throwing herself upon her sister, she kissed her with all her might, stammering:

'I forgive thee, I forgive thee, Little One.'

Several layers of multiple themes—guilt, jealousy, loss, grief, forgiveness and acceptance form the crux of the story ending with 'forgiveness' as the apex of all.

THE CACTUS

O. HENRY

The most notable thing about Time is that it is so purely relative. A large amount of reminiscence is, by common consent, conceded to the drowning man; and it is not past belief that one may review an entire courtship while removing one's gloves.

That is what Trysdale was doing, standing by a table in his bachelor apartments. On the table stood a singular-looking green plant in a red earthen jar. The plant was one of the species of cacti, and was provided with long, tentacular leaves that perpetually swayed with the slightest breeze with a peculiar beckoning motion.

Trysdale's friend, the brother of the bride, stood at a sideboard complaining at being allowed to drink alone. Both men were in evening dress. White favors like stars upon their coats shone through the gloom of the apartment.

As he slowly unbuttoned his gloves, there passed through Trysdale's mind a swift, scarifying retrospect of the last few hours. It seemed that in his nostrils was still the scent of the flowers that had been banked in odorous masses about the church, and in his ears the lowpitched hum of a thousand well-bred voices, the rustle of crisp garments, and, most insistently recurring, the drawling words of the minister irrevocably binding her to another.

From this last hopeless point of view he still strove, as if it had become a habit of his mind, to reach some conjecture as to why and how he had lost her. Shaken rudely by the uncompromising fact, he had suddenly found himself confronted by a thing he had never before faced—his own innermost, unmitigated, and unbedecked self. He saw all the garbs of pretence and egoism that he had worn now turn to rags of folly. He shuddered at the thought that to others, before now, the garments of his soul must have appeared sorry and threadbare. Vanity and conceit? These were the joints in his armor. And how free from either she had always been—But why—

As she had slowly moved up the aisle toward the altar he had felt an unworthy, sullen exultation that had served to support him. He had told himself that her paleness was from thoughts of another than the man to whom she was about to give herself. But even that poor consolation had been wrenched from him. For, when he saw that swift, limpid, upward look that she gave the man when he took her hand, he knew himself to be forgotten. Once that same look had been raised to him, and he had gauged its meaning. Indeed, his conceit had crumbled; its last prop was gone. Why had it ended thus? There had been no quarrel between them, nothing—

For the thousandth time he remarshalled in his mind the events of those last few days before the tide had so suddenly turned.

She had always insisted upon placing him upon a pedestal, and he had accepted her homage with royal grandeur. It had been a very sweet incense that she had burned before him; so modest (he told himself); so childlike and worshipful, and (he would once have sworn) so sincere. She had invested him with an almost supernatural number of high attributes and excellencies and talents, and he had absorbed the oblation as a desert drinks the rain that can coax from it no promise of blossom or fruit.

As Trysdale grimly wrenched apart the seam of his last glove, the crowning instance of his fatuous and tardily mourned egoism came vividly back to him. The scene was the night when he had asked her to come up on his pedestal with him and share his greatness. He could not, now, for the pain of it, allow his mind to dwell upon the memory of her convincing beauty that night—the careless wave of her hair, the tenderness and virginal charm of her looks and words. But they had been enough, and they had brought him to speak. During their conversation she had said:

'And Captain Carruthers tells me that you speak the Spanish language like a native. Why have you hidden this accomplishment from me? Is there anything you do not know?'

Now, Carruthers was an idiot. No doubt he (Trysdale) had been guilty (he sometimes did such things) of airing at the club some old, canting Castilian proverb dug from the hotchpotch at the back of dictionaries. Carruthers, who was one of his incontinent admirers, was the very man to have magnified this exhibition of doubtful erudition.

But, alas! the incense of her admiration had been so sweet and flattering. He allowed the imputation to pass without denial. Without protest, he allowed her to twine about his brow this spurious bay of Spanish scholarship. He let it grace his conquering head, and, among its soft convolutions, he did not feel the prick of the thorn that was to pierce him later.

How glad, how shy, how tremulous she was! How she fluttered like a snared bird when he laid his mightiness at her feet! He could have sworn, and he could swear now, that unmistakable consent was in her eyes, but, coyly, she would give him no direct answer. 'I will send you my answer tomorrow,' she said; and he, the indulgent, confident victor, smilingly granted the delay. The next day he waited, impatient, in his rooms for the word. At noon her groom came to the door and left the strange cactus in the red earthen jar. There was no note, no message, merely a tag upon the plant bearing a barbarous foreign or botanical name. He waited until night, but her answer did not come. His large pride and hurt vanity kept him from seeking her. Two evenings later they met at a dinner. Their greetings were conventional, but she looked at him, breathless, wondering, eager. He was courteous, adamant, waiting her explanation. With womanly swiftness she took her cue from his manner, and turned to snow and ice. Thus, and wider from this on, they had drifted apart. Where was his fault? Who had been to blame? Humbled now, he sought the answer amid the ruins of his self-conceit. If—

The voice of the other man in the room, querulously intruding upon his thoughts, aroused him.

'I say, Trysdale, what the deuce is the matter with you? You look unhappy as if you yourself had been married instead of having acted merely as an accomplice. Look at me, another accessory, come two thousand miles on a garlicky, cockroachy banana steamer all the way from South America to connive at the sacrifice—please to observe how lightly my guilt rests upon my shoulders. Only little sister I had, too, and now she's gone. Come now! take something to ease your conscience.'

'I don't drink just now, thanks,' said Trysdale.

'Your brandy,' resumed the other, coming over and joining him, 'is abominable. Run down to see me some time at Punta Redonda, and try some of our stuff that old Garcia smuggles in. It's worth the trip. Hallo! here's an old acquaintance. Wherever did you rake up this cactus, Trysdale?'

'A present,' said Trysdale, 'from a friend. Know the species?'

'Very well. It's a tropical concern. See hundreds of 'em around Punta every day. Here's the name on this tag tied to it. Know any Spanish, Trysdale?'

'No,' said Trysdale, with the bitter wraith of a smile—'Is it Spanish?'

'Yes. The natives imagine the leaves are reaching out and beckoning to you. They call it by this name—Ventomarme. Name means in English, "Come and take me."'

A white lie is a harmless lie but in this story it can hurt: a lie may cause a love connection to break. Thus it is like the cactus, as the song, goes 'I beg your pardon, I never promised a rose garden.'

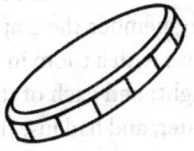

27
A SCHOOL STORY

M.R. JAMES

At night the narrator's friend sees a man sitting on Sampson's window-sill, but when he returns with the narrator he's gone. Sampson is missing the next day. Years later a body is found—with Sampson's coin—in a well that sits between four trees.

Two men in a smoking-room were talking of their private-school days. 'At our school,' said A., 'we had a ghost's footmark on the staircase. What was it like? Oh, very unconvincing. Just the shape of a shoe, with a square toe, if I remember right. The staircase was a stone one. I never heard any story about the thing. That seems odd, when you come to think of it. Why didn't somebody invent one, I wonder?'

'You never can tell with little boys. They have a mythology of their own. There's a subject for you, by the way—"The Folklore of Private Schools."'

'Yes; the crop is rather scanty, though. I imagine, if you were to investigate the cycle of ghost stories, for instance, which the boys at private schools tell each other, they would all turn out to be highly-compressed versions of stories out of books.'

'Nowadays the Strand and Pearson's, and so on, would be extensively drawn upon.'

'No doubt: they weren't born or thought of in my time. Let's see. I wonder if I can remember the staple ones that I was told. First, there was the house with a room in which a series of people insisted on passing a night; and each of them in the morning was found kneeling in a corner, and had just time to say, "I've seen it," and died.'

'Wasn't that the house in Berkeley Square?'

'I dare say it was. Then there was the man who heard a noise in the passage at night, opened his door, and saw someone crawling towards him on all fours with his eye hanging out on his cheek. There was besides, let me think——Yes! The room where a man was found dead in bed with a horseshoe mark on his forehead, and the floor under the bed was covered with marks of horseshoes also; I don't know why. Also there was the lady who, on locking her bedroom door in a strange house, heard a thin voice among the bed-curtains say, 'Now we're shut in for the night.' None of those had any explanation or sequel. I wonder if they go on still, those stories.'

'Oh, likely enough—with additions from the magazines, as I said. You never heard, did you, of a real ghost at a private school? I thought not; nobody has that ever I came across.'

'From the way in which you said that, I gather that you have.'

'I really don't know; but this is what was in my mind. It happened at my private school thirty odd years ago, and I haven't any explanation of it.

'The school I mean was near London. It was established in a large and fairly old house—a great white building with very fine grounds about it; there were large cedars in the garden, as there are in so many of the older gardens in the Thames valley, and ancient elms in the three or four fields which we used for our games. I think probably it was quite an attractive place, but boys seldom allow that their schools possess any tolerable features.

'I came to the school in a September, soon after the year 1870; and among the boys who arrived on the same day was one whom I took to: a Highland boy, whom I will call McLeod. I needn't spend time in describing him: the main thing is that I got to know him very well. He was not an exceptional boy in any way—not particularly good at books or games—but he suited me.

'The school was a large one: there must have been from 120 to 130 boys there as a rule, and so a considerable staff of masters was required, and there were rather frequent changes among them.

'One term—perhaps it was my third or fourth—a new master made his appearance. His name was Sampson. He was a tallish, stoutish, pale, black-bearded man. I think we liked him: he had travelled a good deal, and had stories which amused us on our school walks, so that there was some competition among us to get within earshot of him. I remember too—dear me, I have hardly thought of it since then!—that he had a charm on his watch-chain that attracted my attention one day, and he let me examine it. It was, I now suppose, a gold Byzantine coin; there was an effigy of some absurd emperor on one side; the other side had been worn practically smooth, and he had had cut on it—rather barbarously—his own initials, G.W.S., and a date, 24 July, 1865. Yes, I can see it now: he told me he had picked it up in Constantinople: it was about the size of a florin, perhaps rather smaller.

'Well, the first odd thing that happened was this. Sampson was doing Latin grammar with us. One of his favourite methods—perhaps it is rather a good one—was to make us construct sentences out of our own heads to illustrate the rules he was trying to make us learn. Of course that is a thing which gives a silly boy a chance of being impertinent: there are lots of school stories in which that happens—or anyhow there might be. But Sampson was too good a disciplinarian for us to think of trying that on with him. Now, on this occasion he was telling us how to express remembering in Latin: and he ordered us each to make a sentence bringing in the verb *memini*, "I remember." Well, most of us made up some ordinary sentence such as "I remember my father," or "He remembers his book," or something equally uninteresting: and I dare say a good many put down *memino librum meum*, and so forth: but the boy I mentioned—McLeod—

was evidently thinking of something more elaborate than that. The rest of us wanted to have our sentences passed, and get on to something else, so some kicked him under the desk, and I, who was next to him, poked him and whispered to him to look sharp. But he didn't seem to attend. I looked at his paper and saw he had put down nothing at all. So I jogged him again harder than before and upbraided him sharply for keeping us all waiting. That did have some effect. He started and seemed to wake up, and then very quickly he scribbled about a couple of lines on his paper, and showed it up with the rest. As it was the last, or nearly the last, to come in, and as Sampson had a good deal to say to the boys who had written *meminiscimus patri meo* and the rest of it, it turned out that the clock struck twelve before he had got to McLeod, and McLeod had to wait afterwards to have his sentence corrected. There was nothing much going on outside when I got out, so I waited for him to come. He came very slowly when he did arrive, and I guessed there had been some sort of trouble. "Well," I said, "what did you get?" "Oh, I don't know," said McLeod, "nothing much: but I think Sampson's rather sick with me." "Why, did you show him up some rot?" "No fear," he said. "It was all right as far as I could see: it was like this: *Memento*—that's right enough for remember, and it takes a genitive—*memento putei inter quatuor taxos*." "What silly rot!" I said. "What made you shove that down? What does it mean?" "That's the funny part," said McLeod. "I'm not quite sure what it does mean. All I know is, it just came into my head and I corked it down. I know what I think it means, because just before I wrote it down I had a sort of picture of it in my head: I believe it means 'Remember the well among the four'—what are those dark sort of trees that have red berries on them?" "Mountain ashes, I s'pose you mean." "I never heard of them," said McLeod; "No, I'll tell you—yews." Well, and what did Sampson say? Why, he was jolly odd about it. When he read it he got up and went to the mantelpiece and stopped quite a long time without saying anything, with his back to me. And then he said, without turning round, and rather quiet, "What do you suppose that means?" I told him what I thought; only I couldn't remember the name of the silly tree: and then he wanted to know why I put it down, and I had to say something or other. And after that he left off talking about it, and asked me how long I'd been here, and where my people lived, and things like that: and then I came away: but he wasn't looking a bit well.

'I don't remember any more that was said by either of us about this. Next day McLeod took to his bed with a chill or something of the kind, and it was a week or more before he was in school again. And as much as a month went by without anything happening that was noticeable. Whether or not Mr Sampson was really startled, as McLeod had thought, he didn't show it. I am pretty sure, of course, now, that there was something very curious in his past history, but I'm not going to pretend that we boys were sharp enough to guess any such thing.

'There was one other incident of the same kind as the last which I told you. Several times since that day we had had to make up examples in school to illustrate different rules, but there had never any row except when we did them wrong. At last there came a day when we were going through those dismal things which people call Conditional Sentences, and we were told to make a conditional sentence, expressing a future consequence. We did it, right or wrong, and showed up our bits of paper, and Sampson began looking through them. All at once he got up, made some odd sort of noise in his throat, and rushed out by a door that was just by his desk. We sat there for a minute or two, and then—I suppose it was incorrect—but we went up, I and one or two others, to look at the papers on his desk. Of course I thought someone must have put down some nonsense or other, and Sampson had gone off to report him. All the same, I noticed that he hadn't taken any of the papers with him when he ran out. Well, the top paper on the desk was written in red ink—which no one used—and it wasn't in anyone's hand who was in the class. They all looked at it—McLeod and all—and took their dying oaths that it wasn't theirs. Then I thought of counting the bits of paper.

And of this I made quite certain: that there were seventeen bits of paper on the desk, and sixteen boys in the form. Well, I bagged the extra paper, and kept it, and I believe I have it now. And now you will want to know what was written on it. It was simple enough, and harmless enough, I should have said, '"*Si tu non veneris ad me, ego veniam ad te,*" which means, I suppose, "If you don't come to me, I'll come to you."'

'Could you show me the paper?' interrupted the listener.

'Yes, I could: but there's another odd thing about it. That same afternoon I took it out of my locker—I know for certain it was the same bit, for I made a finger-mark on it—and no single trace of writing of any kind was there on it. I kept it, as I said, and since that time I have tried various experiments to see whether sympathetic ink had been used, but absolutely without result.

'So much for that. After about half an hour Sampson looked in again: said he had felt very unwell, and told us we might go. He came rather gingerly to his desk, and gave just one look at the uppermost paper: and I suppose he thought he must have been dreaming: anyhow, he asked no questions.

'That day was a half-holiday, and next day Sampson was in school again, much as usual. That night the third and last incident in my story happened.

'We—McLeod and I—slept in a dormitory at right angles to the main building. Sampson slept in the main building on the first floor. There was a very bright full moon. At an hour which I can't tell exactly, but some time between one and two, I was woken up by somebody shaking me. It was McLeod; and a nice state of mind he seemed to be in. "Come," he said,—"come! there's a burglar getting in through Sampson's window." As soon as I could speak, I said, "Well, why not call out and wake everybody up?" "No, no," he said, "I'm not sure who it is: don't make a row: come and look." Naturally I came and looked, and naturally there was no one there. I was cross enough, and should have called McLeod plenty of names: only—I couldn't tell why—it seemed to me that there was something wrong—something that made me very glad

I wasn't alone to face it. We were still at the window looking out, and as soon as I could, I asked him what he had heard or seen. "I didn't hear anything at all," he said, "but about five minutes before I woke you, I found myself looking out of this window here, and there was a man sitting or kneeling on Sampson's window-sill, and looking in, and I thought he was beckoning." "What sort of man?" McLeod wriggled. "I don't know," he said, "but I can tell you one thing—he was beastly thin: and he looked as if he was wet all over: and," he said, looking round and whispering as if he hardly liked to hear himself, "I'm not at all sure that he was alive."

'We went on talking in whispers some time longer, and eventually crept back to bed. No one else in the room woke or stirred the whole time. I believe we did sleep a bit afterwards, but we were very cheap next day.

'And next day Mr Sampson was gone: not to be found: and I believe no trace of him has ever come to light since. In thinking it over, one of the oddest things about it all has seemed to me to be the fact that neither McLeod nor I ever mentioned what we had seen to any third person whatever. Of course no questions were asked on the subject, and if they had been, I am inclined to believe that we could not have made any answer: we seemed unable to speak about it.

'That is my story,' said the narrator. 'The only approach to a ghost story connected with a school that I know, but still, I think, an approach to such a thing.'

The sequel to this may perhaps be reckoned highly conventional; but a sequel there is, and so it must be produced. There had been more than one listener to the story, and, in the latter part of that same year, or of the next, one such listener was staying at a country house in Ireland.

One evening his host was turning over a drawer full of odds and ends in the smoking-room. Suddenly he put his hand upon a little box. 'Now,' he said, 'you know about old things; tell me what that is.' My friend opened the little box, and found in it a thin gold chain with an object attached to it. He glanced at the object and then took off his spectacles to examine it more narrowly. 'What's the history of this?' he asked. 'Odd enough,' was the answer. 'You know the yew thicket in the shrubbery: well, a year or two back we were cleaning out the old well that used to be in the clearing here, and what do you suppose we found?'

'Is it possible that you found a body?' said the visitor, with an odd feeling of nervousness.

'We did that: but what's more, in every sense of the word, we found two.'

'Good Heavens! Two? Was there anything to show how they got there? Was this thing found with them?'

'It was. Amongst the rags of the clothes that were on one of the bodies. A bad business, whatever the story of it may have been. One body had the arms tight round the other. They must have been there thirty years or more—long enough before we came to this place. You may judge we filled the well up fast enough. Do you make anything of what's cut on that gold coin you have there?'

'I think I can,' said my friend, holding it to the light (but he read it without much difficulty); 'it seems to be G.W.S., 24 July, 1865.'

∞

The setting is divided into two parts: social and physical. A ghost story set in a school, the plot and character enable the reader to be there!

28

MY OWN TRUE GHOST STORY

RUDYARD KIPLING

As I came through the Desert thus it was—
As I came through the Desert. The City of Dreadful Night.

Somewhere in the Other World, where there are books and pictures and plays and shop windows to look at, and thousands of men who spend their lives in building up all four, lives a gentleman who writes real stories about the real insides of people; and his name is Mr Walter Besant. But he will insist upon treating his ghosts—he has published half a workshopful of them—with levity. He makes his ghost–seers talk familiarly, and, in some cases, flirt outrageously, with the phantoms. You may treat anything, from a Viceroy to a Vernacular Paper, with levity; but you must behave reverently towards a ghost, and particularly an Indian one. There are, in this land, ghosts who take the form of fat, cold, pobby corpses, and hide in trees near the roadside till a traveller passes. Then they drop upon his neck and remain. There are also terrible ghosts of women who have died in child-bed. These wander along the pathways at dusk, or hide in the crops near a village, and call seductively. But to answer their call is death in this world and the next. Their feet are turned backwards that all sober men may recognise them. There are ghosts of little children who have been thrown into wells. These haunt well-curbs and the fringes of jungles, and wail under the stars, or catch women by the wrist and beg to be taken up and carried. These and the corpse ghosts, however, are only vernacular articles and do not attack Sahibs. No native ghost has yet been authentically reported to have frightened an Englishman; but many English ghosts have scared the life out of both white and black. Nearly every other Station owns a ghost. There are said to be two at Simla, not counting the woman who blows the bellows at Syree dak-bungalow on the Old Road; Mussoorie has a house haunted of a very lively Thing; a White Lady is supposed to do night-watchman round a house in Lahore; Dalhousie says that one of her houses 'repeats' on autumn evenings all the incidents of a horrible horse-and-precipice accident; Murree has a merry ghost, and, now that she has been swept by cholera, will have room for a sorrowful one; there are Officers' Quarters in Mian Mir whose doors open without reason, and whose furniture is guaranteed to creak, not with the heat of June but with the weight of Invisibles who come to lounge in the chairs; Peshawar possesses houses that none will willingly rent; and there is something—not fever—wrong with a big bungalow in Allahabad. The older Provinces simply bristle with haunted houses, and march phantom armies along their main thoroughfares. Some of the dak-bungalows on the Grand Trunk Road have handy little cemeteries in their compound—witnesses to the 'changes and chances of this mortal life' in the days when men drove from Calcutta to the Northwest. These bungalows are objectionable places to put up in. They are generally very old, always dirty, while the *khansamah* is as ancient as the bungalow. He either chatters senilely, or falls into the long trances of age. In both moods he is useless. If you get angry with him, he refers to some Sahib dead and buried these thirty years, and says that when he was in that Sahib's service not a *khansamah* in the Province could touch him. Then he jabbers and mows and trembles and fidgets among the dishes, and you repent of your irritation. In these dak-bungalows, ghosts are most likely to be found, and when found, they should be made a note of. Not long ago it was my business to live in dak-bungalows. I never inhabited the same house for three nights running, and grew to be learned in the breed. I lived in Government-built ones with red brick walls and rail ceilings, an inventory of the furniture posted in every room, and an excited snake at the threshold to give welcome. I lived in 'converted' ones—old houses officiating as dak-bungalows—where nothing was in its proper place and there wasn't even a fowl for dinner. I lived in second-hand palaces where the wind blew through open-work marble tracery just as uncomfortably as through a broken pane. I lived in dak-bungalows where the last entry in the visitors' book was fifteen months old, and where they slashed off the curry-kid's head with a sword. It was my good luck to meet all sorts of men, from sober travelling missionaries and deserters flying from British Regiments, to drunken loafers who threw whisky bottles at all who passed; and my still greater good fortune just to escape a maternity case. Seeing that a fair proportion of the tragedy of our lives out here acted itself in dak-bungalows, I wondered that I had met no ghosts. A ghost that would voluntarily hang about a dak–bungalow would be mad of course; but so many men have died mad in dak-bungalows that there must be a fair percentage of lunatic ghosts. In due time I found my ghost, or ghosts rather, for there were two of them. Up till that hour I had sympathised with Mr Besant's method of handling them, as shown in *The Strange Case of Mr Lucraft and Other Stories.* I am now in the Opposition. We will call the bungalow Katmal dak–bungalow. But that was the smallest part of the horror. A man with a sensitive hide has no right to sleep in dak-bungalows. He should marry. Katmal dak-bungalow was old and rotten and unrepaired. The floor was of worn brick, the walls were filthy, and the windows were nearly black with grime. It stood on a bypath largely used by native Sub-Deputy Assistants of all kinds, from Finance to Forests; but real Sahibs were rare.

The *khansamah*, who was nearly bent double with old age, said so. When I arrived, there was a fitful, undecided rain on the face of the land, accompanied by a restless wind, and every gust made a noise like the rattling of dry bones in the stiff toddy palms outside. The *khansamah* completely lost his head on my arrival. He had served a Sahib once. Did I know that Sahib? He gave me the name of a well-known man who has been buried for more than a quarter of a century, and showed me an ancient daguerreotype of that man in his prehistoric youth. I had seen a steel engraving of him at the head of a double volume of Memoirs a month before, and I felt ancient beyond telling. The day shut in and the *khansamah* went to get me food. He did not go through the pretense of calling it '*khana*'—man's victuals. He said '*ratub*,' and that means, among other things, 'grub'—dog's rations. There was no insult in his choice of the term. He had forgotten the other word, I suppose. While he was cutting up the dead bodies of animals, I settled myself down, after exploring the dak–bungalow. There were three rooms, beside my own, which was a corner kennel, each giving into the other through dingy white doors fastened with long iron bars. The bungalow was a very solid one, but the partition walls of the rooms were almost jerry-built in their flimsiness. Every step or bang of a trunk echoed from my room down the other three, and every footfall came back tremulously from the far walls. For this reason I shut the door. There were no lamps—only candles in long glass shades. An oil wick was set in the bathroom. For bleak, unadulterated misery that dak–bungalow was the worst of the many that I had ever set foot in. There was no fireplace, and the windows would not open; so a brazier of charcoal would have been useless. The rain and the wind splashed and gurgled and moaned round the house, and the toddy palms rattled and roared. Half a dozen jackals went through the compound singing, and a hyena stood afar off and mocked them. A hyena would convince a Sadducee of the Resurrection of the Dead—the worst sort of Dead. Then came the *ratub*—a curious meal, half native and half English in composition—with the old *khansamah* babbling behind my chair about dead and gone English people, and the wind-blown candles playing shadow-bo-peep with the bed and the mosquito-curtains. It was just the sort of dinner and evening to make a man think of every single one of his past sins, and of all the others that he intended to commit if he lived. Sleep, for several hundred reasons, was not easy. The lamp in the bathroom threw the most absurd shadows into the room, and the wind was beginning to talk nonsense. Just when the reasons were drowsy with blood-sucking I heard the regular— 'Let-us-take-and-heave-him-over' grunt of doolie-bearers in the compound. First one doolie came in, then a second, and then a third. I heard the doolies dumped on the ground, and the shutter in front of my door shook. 'That's some one trying to come in,' I said. But no one spoke, and I persuaded myself that it was the gusty wind. The shutter of the room next to mine was attacked, flung back, and the inner door opened. 'That's some Sub-Deputy Assistant,' I said, 'and he has brought his friends with him. Now they'll talk and spit and smoke for an hour.' But there were no voices and no footsteps. No one was putting his luggage into the next room. The door shut, and I thanked Providence that I was to be left in peace. But I was curious to know where the doolies had gone. I got out of bed and looked into the darkness. There was never a sign of a doolie. Just as I was getting into bed again, I heard, in the next room, the sound that no man in his senses can possibly mistake—the whir of a billiard ball down the length of the slates when the striker is stringing for break. No other sound is like it. A minute afterwards there was another whir, and I got into bed. I was not frightened—indeed I was not. I was very curious to know what had become of the doolies. I jumped into bed for that reason. Next minute I heard the double click of a cannon and my hair sat up. It is a mistake to say that hair stands up. The skin of the head tightens and you can feel a faint, prickly, bristling all over the scalp. That is the hair sitting up. There was a whir and a click, and both sounds could only have been made by one thing—a billiard ball. I argued the matter out at great length with myself; and the more I argued the less probable it seemed that one bed, one table, and two chairs—all the furniture of the room next to mine—could so exactly duplicate the sounds of a game of billiards. After another cannon, a three-cushion one to judge by the whir, I argued no more. I had found my ghost and would have given worlds to have escaped from that dak-bungalow. I listened, and with each listen the game grew clearer. There was whir on whir and click on click. Sometimes there was a double click and a whir and another click. Beyond any sort of doubt, people were playing billiards in the next room. And the next room was not big enough to hold a billiard table! Between the pauses of the wind I heard the game go forward—stroke after stroke. I tried to believe that I could not hear voices; but that attempt was a failure. Do you know what fear is? Not ordinary fear of insult, injury or death, but abject, quivering dread of something that you cannot see—fear that dries the inside of the mouth and half of the throat—fear that makes you sweat on the palms of the hands, and gulp in order to keep the uvula at work? This is a fine Fear—a great cowardice, and must be felt to be appreciated. The very improbability of billiards in a dak–bungalow proved the reality of the thing. No man—drunk or sober—could imagine a game at billiards, or invent the spitting crack of a 'screw-cannon.' A severe course of dak-bungalows has this disadvantage—it breeds infinite credulity. If a man said to a confirmed dak-bungalow-haunter:—'There is a corpse in the next room, and there's a mad girl in the next but one, and the woman and man on that camel have just eloped from a place sixty miles away,' the hearer would not disbelieve because he would know that nothing is too wild, grotesque, or horrible to happen in a dak–bungalow. This credulity, unfortunately, extends to ghosts. A rational person fresh from his own house would have turned on his side and slept. I did not. So surely as I was given up as a bad carcass by the scores of things in the bed because the bulk of my blood was in my heart, so surely did I hear every stroke of a long game at billiards played in the echoing room behind the iron-barred door. My dominant fear was that the players might want a marker. It was an absurd fear;

because creatures who could play in the dark would be above such superfluities. I only know that that was my terror; and it was real. After a long, long while the game stopped, and the door banged. I slept because I was dead tired. Otherwise I should have preferred to have kept awake. Not for everything in Asia would I have dropped the door-bar and peered into the dark of the next room. When the morning came, I considered that I had done well and wisely, and inquired for the means of departure. 'By the way, *khansamah*,' I said, 'what were those three doolies doing in my compound in the night?' 'There were no doolies,' said the *khansamah*. I went into the next room and the daylight streamed through the open door. I was immensely brave. I would, at that hour, have played Black Pool with the owner of the big Black Pool down below. 'Has this place always been a dak–bungalow?' I asked. 'No,' said the *khansamah*. 'Ten or twenty years ago, I have forgotten how long, it was a billiard room.' 'A how much?' 'A billiard room for the Sahibs who built the Railway. I was *khansamah* then in the big house where all the Railway-Sahibs lived, and I used to come across with brandy-*sharab*. These three rooms were all one, and they held a big table on which the Sahibs played every evening. But the Sahibs are all dead now, and the Railway runs, you say, nearly to Kabul.' 'Do you remember anything about the Sahibs?' 'It is long ago, but I remember that one Sahib, a fat man and always angry, was playing here one night, and he said to me:—'Mangal Khan, brandy-*pani do*,' and I filled the glass, and he bent over the table to strike, and his head fell lower and lower till it hit the table, and his spectacles came off, and when we—the Sahibs and I myself—ran to lift him he was dead. I helped to carry him out. Aha, he was a strong Sahib! But he is dead and I, old Mangal Khan, am still living, by your favor.' That was more than enough! I had my ghost—a firsthand, authenticated article. I would write to the Society for Psychical Research—I would paralyse the Empire with the news! But I would, first of all, put eighty miles of assessed crop land between myself and that dak–bungalow before nightfall. The Society might send their regular agent to investigate later on. I went into my own room and prepared to pack after noting down the facts of the case. As I smoked I heard the game begin again,—with a miss in balk this time, for the whir was a short one. The door was open and I could see into the room. *Click—click!* That was a cannon. I entered the room without fear, for there was sunlight within and a fresh breeze without. The unseen game was going on at a tremendous rate. And well it might, when a restless little rat was running to and fro inside the dingy ceiling-cloth, and a piece of loose window-sash was making fifty breaks off the window-bolt as it shook in the breeze! Impossible to mistake the sound of billiard balls! Impossible to mistake the whir of a ball over the slate! But I was to be excused. Even when I shut my enlightened eyes the sound was marvellously like that of a fast game. Entered angrily the faithful partner of my sorrows, Kadir Baksh. 'This bungalow is very bad and low-caste! No wonder the Presence was disturbed and is speckled. Three sets of doolie-bearers came to the bungalow late last night when I was sleeping outside, and said that it was their custom to rest in the rooms set apart for the English people! What honour has the *khansamah*? They tried to enter, but I told them to go. No wonder, if these *Oorias* have been here, that the Presence is sorely spotted. It is shame, and the work of a dirty man!' Kadir Baksh did not say that he had taken from each gang two annas for rent in advance, and then, beyond my earshot, had beaten them with the big green umbrella whose use I could never before divine. But Kadir Baksh has no notions of morality. There was an interview with the *khansamah*, but as he promptly lost his head, wrath gave place to pity, and pity led to a long conversation, in the course of which he put the fat Engineer-sahib's tragic death in three separate stations—two of them fifty miles away. The third shift was to Calcutta, and there the Sahib died while driving a dogcart. If I had encouraged him the *khansamah* would have wandered all through Bengal with his corpse. I did not go away as soon as I intended. I stayed for the night, while the wind and the rat and the sash and the window-bolt played a ding-dong 'hundred and fifty up.' Then the wind ran out and the billiards stopped, and I felt that I had ruined my one genuine, hall-marked ghost story. Had I only stopped at the proper time, I could have made *anything* out of it. That was the bitterest thought of all!

―∞―

The language and theme of the story indeed stands out as set in the times of the British Raj in India. It is set in a decrepit old bungalow. 'Bungalow' etymologically is from the Bengali word 'bangla,' a mansion with khansamahs, et al.

29

THE LOTTERY TICKET

ANTON CHEKHOV

Ivan Dmitritch, a middle-class man who lived with his family on an income of twelve hundred a year and was very well satisfied with his lot, sat down on the sofa after supper and began reading the newspaper.

'I forgot to look at the newspaper today,' his wife said to him as she cleared the table. 'Look and see whether the list of drawings is there.'

'Yes, it is,' said Ivan Dmitritch; 'but hasn't your ticket lapsed?'

'No; I took the interest on Tuesday.'

'What is the number?'

'Series 9,499, number 26.'

'All right ... we will look ... 9,499 and 26.'

Ivan Dmitritch had no faith in lottery luck, and would not, as a rule, have consented to look at the lists of winning numbers, but now, as he had nothing else to do and as the newspaper was before his eyes, he passed his finger downwards along the column of numbers. And immediately, as though in mockery of his scepticism, no further than the second line from the top, his eye was caught by the figure 9,499! Unable to believe his eyes, he hurriedly dropped the paper on his knees without looking to see the number of the ticket, and, just as though some one had given him a douche of cold water, he felt an agreeable chill in the pit of the stomach; tingling and terrible and sweet!

'Masha, 9,499 is there!' he said in a hollow voice.

His wife looked at his astonished and panic-stricken face, and realized that he was not joking.

'9,499?' she asked, turning pale and dropping the folded tablecloth on the table.

'Yes, yes ... it really is there!'

'And the number of the ticket?'

'Oh, yes! There's the number of the ticket too. But stay ... wait! No, I say! Anyway, the number of our series is there! Anyway, you understand....'

Looking at his wife, Ivan Dmitritch gave a broad, senseless smile, like a baby when a bright object is shown it. His wife smiled too; it was as pleasant to her as to him that he only mentioned the series, and did not try to find out the number of the winning ticket. To torment and tantalize oneself with hopes of possible fortune is so sweet, so thrilling!

'It is our series,' said Ivan Dmitritch, after a long silence. 'So there is a probability that we have won. It's only a probability, but there it is!'

'Well, now look!'

'Wait a little. We have plenty of time to be disappointed. It's on the second line from the top, so the prize is seventy-five thousand. That's not money, but power, capital! And in a minute I shall look at the list, and there—26! Eh? I say, what if we really have won?'

The husband and wife began laughing and staring at one another in silence. The possibility of winning bewildered them; they could not have said, could not have dreamed, what they both needed that seventy-five thousand for, what they would buy, where they would go. They thought only of the figures 9,499 and 75,000 and pictured them in their imagination, while somehow they could not think of the happiness itself which was so possible.

Ivan Dmitritch, holding the paper in his hand, walked several times from corner to corner, and only when he had recovered from the first impression began dreaming a little.

'And if we have won,' he said—'why, it will be a new life, it will be a transformation! The ticket is yours, but if it were mine I should, first of all, of course, spend twenty-five thousand on real property in the shape of an estate; ten thousand on immediate expenses, new furnishing ... travelling ... paying debts, and so on.... The other forty thousand I would put in the bank and get interest on it.'

'Yes, an estate, that would be nice,' said his wife, sitting down and dropping her hands in her lap.

'Somewhere in the Tula or Oryol provinces.... In the first place we shouldn't need a summer villa, and besides, it would always bring in an income.'

And pictures came crowding on his imagination, each more gracious and poetical than the last. And in all these pictures he saw himself well-fed, serene, healthy, felt warm, even hot! Here, after eating a summer soup, cold as ice, he lay on his back on the burning sand close to a stream or in the garden under a lime-tree.... It is hot.... His little boy and girl are crawling about near him, digging in the sand or catching ladybirds in the grass. He dozes sweetly, thinking of nothing, and feeling all over that he need not go to the office today, tomorrow, or the day after. Or, tired of lying still, he goes to the hayfield, or to the forest for mushrooms, or watches the peasants catching fish with a net. When the sun sets he takes a towel and soap and saunters to the bathing-shed, where he undresses at his leisure, slowly rubs his bare chest with his hands, and goes into the water. And in the water, near the opaque soapy circles, little fish flit to and fro and green water-weeds nod their heads. After bathing there is tea with cream and milk rolls.... In the evening a walk or vint with the neighbours.

'Yes, it would be nice to buy an estate,' said his wife, also dreaming, and from her face it was evident that she was enchanted by her thoughts.

Ivan Dmitritch pictured to himself autumn with its rains, its cold evenings, and its St. Martin's summer. At that season he would have to take longer walks about the garden and beside the river, so as to get thoroughly chilled, and then drink a big glass of vodka and eat a salted mushroom or a soused cucumber, and then—drink another.... The children would come running from the kitchen-garden, bringing a carrot and a radish smelling of fresh earth.... And then, he would lie stretched full length on the sofa, and in leisurely fashion turn over the pages of some illustrated magazine, or, covering his face with it and unbuttoning his waistcoat, give himself up to slumber.

The St. Martin's summer is followed by cloudy, gloomy weather. It rains day and night, the bare trees weep, the wind is damp and cold. The dogs, the horses, the fowls—all are wet, depressed, downcast. There is nowhere to walk; one can't go out for days together; one has to pace up and down the room, looking despondently at the grey window. It is dreary!

Ivan Dmitritch stopped and looked at his wife.

'I should go abroad, you know, Masha,' he said.

And he began thinking how nice it would be in late autumn to go abroad somewhere to the South of France ... to Italy.... to India!

'I should certainly go abroad too,' his wife said. 'But look at the number of the ticket!'

'Wait, wait! ...'

He walked about the room and went on thinking. It occurred to him: what if his wife really did go abroad? It is pleasant to travel alone, or in the society of light, careless women who live in the present, and not such as think and talk all the journey about nothing but their children, sigh, and tremble with dismay over every farthing. Ivan Dmitritch imagined his wife in the train with a multitude of parcels, baskets, and bags; she would be sighing over something, complaining that the train made her head ache, that she had spent so much money.... At the stations he would continually be having to run for boiling water, bread and butter.... She wouldn't have dinner because of it being too dear....

'She would begrudge me every farthing,' he thought, with a glance at his wife. 'The lottery ticket is hers, not mine! Besides, what is the use of her going abroad? What does she want there? She would shut herself up in the hotel, and not let me out of her sight.... I know!'

And for the first time in his life his mind dwelt on the fact that his wife had grown field erly and plain, and that she was saturated through and through with the smell of cooking, while he was still young, fresh, and healthy, and might well have got married again.

'Of course, all that is silly nonsense,' he thought; 'but ... why should she go abroad? What would she make of it? And yet she would go, of course.... I can fancy ... In reality it is all one to her, whether it is Naples or Klin. She would only be in my way. I should be dependent upon her. I can fancy how, like a regular woman, she will lock the money up as soon as she gets it.... She will hide it from me.... She will look after her relations and grudge me every farthing.'

Ivan Dmitritch thought of her relations. All those wretched brothers and sisters and aunts and uncles would come crawling about as soon as they heard of the winning ticket, would begin whining like beggars, and fawning upon them with oily, hypocritical smiles. Wretched, detestable people! If they were given anything, they would ask for more; while if they were refused, they would swear at them, slander them, and wish them every kind of misfortune.

Ivan Dmitritch remembered his own relations, and their faces, at which he had looked impartially in the past, struck him now as repulsive and hateful.

'They are such reptiles!' he thought.

And his wife's face, too, struck him as repulsive and hateful. Anger surged up in his heart against her, and he thought malignantly:

'She knows nothing about money, and so she is stingy. If she won it she would give me a hundred roubles, and put the rest away under lock and key.'

And he looked at his wife, not with a smile now, but with hatred. She glanced at him too, and also with hatred and anger. She had her own daydreams, her own plans, her own reflections; she understood perfectly well what her husband's dreams were. She knew who would be the first to try and grab her winnings.

'It's very nice making daydreams at other people's expense!' is what her eyes expressed. 'No, don't you dare!'

Her husband understood her look; hatred began stirring again in his breast, and in order to annoy his wife he glanced quickly, to spite her, at the fourth page on the newspaper and read out triumphantly:

'Series 9,499, number 46! Not 26!'

Hatred and hope both disappeared at once, and it began immediately to seem to Ivan Dmitritch and his wife that their rooms were dark and small and low-pitched, that the supper they had been eating was not doing them good, but lying heavy on their stomachs, that the evenings were long and wearisome....

'What the devil's the meaning of it?' said Ivan Dmitritch, beginning to be ill-humoured. 'Wherever one steps there are bits of paper under one's feet, crumbs, husks. The rooms are never swept! One is simply forced to go out. Damnation take my soul entirely! I shall go and hang myself on the first aspen-tree!'

Anton Chekhov expounds the theme of hope, aspiration, selfishness, power, greed, control, freedom and satisfaction. It is ironical how the once loving family became resentful towards each other towards the end of the story.

30

SALVATORE

SOMERSET MAUGHAM

I wonder if I can do it.

I knew Salvatore first when he was a boy of fifteen with a pleasant face, a laughing mouth and care-free eyes. He used to spend the morning lying about the beach with next to nothing on and his brown body was as thin as a rail. He was full of grace. He was in and out of the sea all the time swimming with the clumsy, effortless stroke common to the fisher boat.

Scrambling up the jagged rocks on his hard feet, for except on Sundays he never wore shoes, he would throw himself into the deep water with a scream of delight. His father was a fisherman who owned his own little vineyard and Salvatore acted as nursemaid to his two younger brothers. He shouted to them to come inshore when they ventured out too far and made them dress when it was time to climb the hot, vineclad hill for the frugal midday meal.

But boys in those Southern parts grow apace and in a little while he was madly in love with a pretty girl who lived on the Grande Marina. She had eyes like forest pools and held herself like a daughter of the Caesars. They were affianced, but they could not marry till Salvatore had done his military service, and when he left the island which he had never left in his life before, to become a sailor in the navy of King Victor Emmanuel, he wept like a child. It was hard for one who had never been less free than the birds to be at the beck and call of others, it was harder still to live in a battleship with strangers instead of in a little white cottage among the vines; and when he was ashore, to walk in noisy, friendless cities with streets so crowded that he was frightened to cross them, when he had been used to silent paths and the mountains and the sea. I suppose it had never struck him that Ischia, which he looked at every evening (it was like a fairy island in the sunset) to see what the weather would be like next day, or Vesuvius, pearly in the dawn, had anything to do with him at all; but when he ceased to have them before his eyes he realized in some dim fashion that they were as much part of him as his hands and his feet. He was dreadfully homesick. But it was hardest of all to be parted from the girl he loved with all his passionate young heart. He wrote to her (in his childlike handwriting) long, ill-spelt letters in which he told her how constantly he thought of her and how much he longed to be back. He was sent here and there, to Spezzia, to Venice, to Bari and finally to China. Here he fell ill of some mysterious ailment that kept him in hospital for months. He bore it with the mute and uncomprehending patience of a dog. When he learnt that it was a form of rheumatism that made him unfit for further service his heart exulted, for he could go home; and he did not bother, in fact he scarcely listened, when the doctors told him that he would never again be quite well. What did he care when he was going back to the little island he loved so well and the girl who was waiting for him?

When he got into the rowing-boat that met the steamer from Naples and was rowed ashore he saw his father and mother standing on the jetty and his two brothers, big boys now, and he waved to them. His eyes searched among the crowd that waited there, for the girl. He could not see her. There was a great deal of kissing when he jumped up the steps and they all, emotional creatures, cried a little when they exchanged their greetings. He asked where the girl was. His mother told him that she did not know; they had not seen her for two or three weeks; so in the evening when the moon was shining over the placid sea and the lights of Naples twinkled in the distance he walked down to the Grande Marina to her house. She was sitting on the doorstep with her mother. He was a little shy because he had not seen her for so long. He asked her if she had not received the letter that he had written to her to say that he was coming home. Yes, they had received a letter, and they had been told by another of the island boys that he was ill. Yes, that was why he was back; was it not a piece of luck? Oh, but they had heard that he would never be quite well again. The doctor talked a lot of nonsense, but he knew very well that now he was home again he would recover. They were silent for a little, and then the mother nudged the girl. She did not try to soften the blow. She told him straight out, with the blunt directness of her race that she could not marry a man who would never be strong enough to work like a man. They had made up their minds, her mother and father and she, and her father would never give consent.

When Salvatore went home he found that they all knew. The girl's father had been to tell them what they had decided, but they had lacked the courage to tell him themselves. He wept on his mother's bosom. He was terribly unhappy, but he did not blame the girl. A fisherman's life is hard and it needs strength and endurance. He knew very well that a girl could not afford to marry a man who might not be able to support her. His smile was very sad and his eyes had the look of a dog that has been beaten, but he did not complain, and he never said a hard word of the girl he had loved so well.

Then, a few months later, when he had settled down to the common round, working in his father's vineyard and fishing, his mother told him that there was a young woman in the village who was willing to marry him. Her name was Assunta.

'She's as ugly as the devil,' he said.

She was older than he, twenty-four or twenty-five, and she had been engaged to a man who, while doing his military service, had been killed in Africa. She had a little money of her own and if Salvatore married her she could buy him a boat of his own and they could take a vineyard that by happy chance happened at that moment to be without a tenant. His mother told him that Assunta had seen him at the *festa* and had fallen in love with him. Salvatore smiled his sweet smile and said he would think about it. On the following Sunday, dressed in the stiff black clothes in which he looked so much less well than in the ragged shirt and trousers of every day, he went up to High Mass at the parish church and placed himself so that he could have a good look at the young woman. When he came down again he told his mother that he was willing.

Well, they were married and they settled down in a tiny whitewashed house in the middle of a handsome vineyard. Salvatore was now a great, big husky fellow, tall and broad, but still with that ingenuous smile and those trusting, kindly eyes that he had as a boy. He had the most beautiful manners I have ever seen in my life. Assunta was a grim-visaged female, with decided features, and she looked old for her years. But she had a good heart and she was no fool. I used to be amused by the little smile of devotion that she gave her husband when he was being very masculine and masterful; she never ceased to be touched by his gentle sweetness. But she could not bear the girl who had thrown him over, and notwithstanding Salvatore's smiling expostulations she had nothing but harsh words for her. Presently children were born to them.

It was a hard enough life. All through the fishing season towards evening he set out in his boat with one of his brothers for the fishing grounds. It was a long pull of six or seven miles, and he spent the night catching the profitable cuttlefish. Then there was the long row back again in order to sell the catch in time for it to go on the early boat to Naples. At other times he was working in his vineyard from dawn till the heat drove him to rest and then again, when it was a trifle cooler, till dusk. Often his rheumatism prevented him from doing anything at all and then he would lie about the beach, smoking cigarettes, with a pleasant word for everyone notwithstanding the pain that racked his limbs. The foreigners who came down to bathe and saw him there said that these Italian fishermen were lazy devils.

Sometimes he used to bring his children down to give them a bath. They were both boys and at this time the field er was three and the younger less than two. They sprawled about at the water's edge stark naked and Salvatore standing on a rock would dip them in the water. The field er one bore it with stoicism, but the baby screamed lustily. Salvatore had enormous hands, like legs of mutton, coarse and hard from constant toil, but when he bathed his children, holding them so tenderly, drying them with delicate care; upon my word they were like flowers. He would seat the naked baby on the palm of his hand and hold him up, laughing a little at his smallness, and his laugh was like the laughter of an angel. His eyes then were as candid as his child's.

I started by saying that I wondered if I could do it and now I must tell you what it is that I have tried to do. I wanted to see whether I could hold your attention for a few pages while I drew for you the portrait of a man, just an ordinary fisherman who possessed nothing in the world except a quality which is the rarest, the most precious and the loveliest that anyone can have. Heaven only knows why he should so strangely and unexpectedly have possessed it. All I know is that it shone in him with a radiance that, if it had not been unconscious and so humble, would have been to the common run of men hardly bearable. And in case you have not guessed what the quality was, I will tell you. Goodness, just goodness.

The message of this story is loud and clear: That which is beautiful may be good but that which is good is always beautiful!

31

THE DREAM

O. HENRY

MURRAY dreamed a dream.

Both psychology and science grope when they would explain to us the strange adventures of our immaterial selves when wandering in the realm of 'Death's twin brother, Sleep.' This story will not attempt to be illuminative; it is no more than a record of Murray's dream. One of the most puzzling phases of that strange waking sleep is that dreams which seem to cover months or even years may take place within a few seconds or minutes.

Murray was waiting in his cell in the ward of the condemned. An electric arc light in the ceiling of the corridor shone brightly upon his table. On a sheet of white paper an ant crawled wildly here and there as Murray blocked its way with an envelope. The electrocution was set for eight o'clock in the evening. Murray smiled at the antics of the wisest of insects.

There were seven other condemned men in the chamber. Since he had been there Murray had seen three taken out to their fate; one gone mad and fighting like a wolf caught in a trap; one, no less mad, offering up a sanctimonious lip-service to Heaven; the third, a weakling, collapsed and strapped to a board. He wondered with what credit to himself his own heart, foot, and face would meet his punishment; for this was his evening. He thought it must be nearly eight o'clock.

Opposite his own in the two rows of cells was the cage of Bonifacio, the Sicilian slayer of his betrothed and of two officers who came to arrest him. With him Murray had played checkers many a long hour, each calling his move to his unseen opponent across the corridor.

Bonifacio's great booming voice with its indestructible singing quality called out:

'Eh, Meestro Murray; how you feel—all-a right—yes?'

'All right, Bonifacio,' said Murray steadily, as he allowed the ant to crawl upon the envelope and then dumped it gently on the stone floor.

'Dat's good-a, Meestro Murray. Men like us, we must-a die like-a men. My time come nex'-a week. All-a right. Remember, Meestro Murray, I beat-a you dat las' game of de check. Maybe we play again some-a time. I don'-a know. Maybe we have to call-a de move damn-a loud to play de check where dey goin' send us.'

Bonifacio's hardened philosophy, followed closely by his deafening, musical peal of laughter, warmed rather than chilled Murray's numbed heart. Yet, Bonifacio had until next week to live.

The cell-dwellers heard the familiar, loud click of the steel bolts as the door at the end of the corridor was opened. Three men came to Murray's cell and unlocked it. Two were prison guards; the other was 'Len'—no; that was in the old days; now the Reverend Leonard Winston, a friend and neighbor from their barefoot days.

'I got them to let me take the prison chaplain's place,' he said, as he gave Murray's hand one short, strong grip. In his left hand he held a small Bible, with his forefinger marking a page.

Murray smiled slightly and arranged two or three books and some penholders orderly on his small table. He would have spoken, but no appropriate words seemed to present themselves to his mind.

The prisoners had christened this cellhouse, eighty feet long, twenty-eight feet wide, Limbo Lane. The regular guard of Limbo Lane, an immense, rough, kindly man, drew a pint bottle of whiskey from his pocket and offered it to Murray, saying:

'It's the regular thing, you know. All has it who feel like they need a bracer. No danger of it becoming a habit with 'em, you see.'

Murray drank deep into the bottle.

'That's the boy!' said the guard. 'Just a little nerve tonic, and everything goes smooth as silk.'

They stepped into the corridor, and each one of the doomed seven knew. Limbo Lane is a world on the outside of the world; but it had learned, when deprived of one or more of the five senses, to make another sense supply the deficiency. Each one knew that it was nearly eight, and that Murray was to go to the chair at eight. There is also in the many Limbo Lanes an aristocracy of crime. The man who kills in the open, who beats his enemy or pursuer down, flushed by the primitive emotions and the ardor of combat, holds in contempt the human rat, the spider, and the snake.

So, of the seven condemned only three called their farewells to Murray as he marched down the corridor between the two guards—Bonifacio, Marvin, who had killed a guard while trying to escape from the prison, and Bassett, the train-robber, who was driven to it because the express-messenger wouldn't raise his hands when ordered to do so. The remaining four smoldered, silent, in their cells, no doubt feeling their social ostracism in Limbo Lane society more keenly than they did the memory of their less picturesque offences against the law.

Murray wondered at his own calmness and nearly indifference. In the execution room were about twenty men, a congregation made up of prison officers, newspaper reporters, and lookers-on who had succeeded

Here, in the very middle of a sentence, the hand of Death interrupted the telling of O. Henry's last story. He had planned to make this story different from his others, the beginning of a new series in a style he had not previously attempted. 'I want to show the public,' he said, 'that I can write something new—new for me, I mean—a story without slang, a straightforward dramatic plot treated in a way that will come nearer my idea of real story-writing.' Before starting to write the present story, he outlined briefly how he intended to develop it: Murray, the criminal accused and convicted of the brutal murder of his sweetheart—a murder prompted by jealous rage—at first faces the death penalty, calm, and, to all outward appearances, indifferent to his fate. As he nears the electric chair he is overcome by a revulsion of feeling. He is left dazed, stupefied, stunned. The entire scene in the death-chamber—the witnesses, the spectators, the preparations for execution—become unreal to him. The thought flashes through his brain that a terrible mistake is being made. Why is he being strapped to the chair? What has he done? What crime has he committed? In the few moments while the straps are being adjusted a vision comes to him. He dreams a dream. He sees a little country cottage, bright, sun-lit, nestling in a bower of flowers. A woman is there, and a little child. He speaks with them and finds that they are his wife, his child—and the cottage their home. So, after all, it is a mistake. Someone has frightfully, irretrievably blundered. The accusation, the trial, the conviction, the sentence to death in the electric chair—all a dream. He takes his wife in his arms and kisses the child. Yes, here is happiness. It was a dream. Then—at a sign from the prison warden the fatal current is turned on.

Murray had dreamed the wrong dream.

∞

The story explores the theme of indifference. The irony is breathtaking. Murray sees a little country cottage, bright, sun-lit, nestling in a bower of flowers. A woman is there, and a little child. He had dreamed the wrong dream. Death is his final toll.

32

A VERY OLD MAN WITH ENORMOUS WINGS

GABRIEL GARCÍA MÁRQUEZ

On the third day of rain they had killed so many crabs inside the house that Pelayo had to cross his drenched courtyard and throw them into the sea, because the newborn child had a temperature all night and they thought it was due to the stench. The world had been sad since Tuesday. Sea and sky were a single ash-gray thing and the sands of the beach, which on March nights glimmered like powdered light, had become a stew of mud and rotten shellfish. The light was so weak at noon that when Pelayo was coming back to the house after throwing away the crabs, it was hard for him to see what it was that was moving and groaning in the rear of the courtyard. He had to go very close to see that it was an old man, a very old man, lying face down in the mud, who, in spite of his tremendous efforts, couldn't get up, impeded by his enormous wings.

Frightened by that nightmare, Pelayo ran to get Elisenda, his wife, who was putting compresses on the sick child, and he took her to the rear of the courtyard. They both looked at the fallen body with a mute stupor. He was dressed like a ragpicker. There were only a few faded hairs left on his bald skull and very few teeth in his mouth, and his pitiful condition of a drenched great-grandfather took away any sense of grandeur he might have had. His huge buzzard wings, dirty and half-plucked, were forever entangled in the mud. They looked at him so long and so closely that Pelayo and Elisenda very soon overcame their surprise and in the end found him familiar. Then they dared speak to him, and he answered in an incomprehensible dialect with a strong sailor's voice. That was how they skipped over the inconvenience of the wings and quite intelligently concluded that he was a lonely castaway from some foreign ship wrecked by the storm. And yet, they called in a neighbor woman who knew everything about life and death to see him, and all she needed was one look to show them their mistake.

'He's an angel,' she told them. 'He must have been coming for the child, but the poor fellow is so old that the rain knocked him down.'

On the following day everyone knew that a flesh-and-blood angel was held captive in Pelayo's house. Against the judgment of the wise neighbor woman, for whom angels in those times were the fugitive survivors of a celestial conspiracy, they did not have the heart to club him to death. Pelayo watched over him all afternoon from the kitchen, armed with his bailiff's club, and before going to bed he dragged him out of the mud and locked him up with the hens in the wire chicken coop. In the middle of the night, when the rain stopped, Pelayo and Elisenda were still killing crabs. A short time afterward the child woke up without a fever and with a desire to eat. Then they felt magnanimous and decided to put the angel on a raft with fresh water and provisions for three days and leave him to his fate on the high seas. But when they went out into the courtyard with the first light of dawn, they found the whole neighborhood in front of the chicken coop having fun with the angel, without the slightest reverence, tossing him things to eat through the openings in the wire as if he weren't a supernatural creature but a circus animal.

Father Gonzaga arrived before seven o'clock, alarmed at the strange news. By that time onlookers less frivolous than those at dawn had already arrived and they were making all kinds of conjectures concerning the captive's future. The simplest among them thought that he should be named mayor of the world. Others of sterner mind felt that he should be promoted to the rank of five-star general in order to win all wars. Some visionaries hoped that he could be put to stud in order to implant on the earth a race of winged wise men who could take charge of the universe. But Father Gonzaga, before becoming a priest, had been a robust woodcutter. Standing by the wire, he reviewed his catechism in an instant and asked them to open the door so that he could take a close look at that pitiful man who looked more like a huge decrepit hen among the fascinated chickens. He was lying in the corner drying his open wings in the sunlight among the fruit peels and breakfast leftovers that the early risers had thrown him. Alien to the impertinences of the world, he only lifted his antiquarian eyes and murmured something in his dialect when Father Gonzaga went into the chicken coop and said good morning to him in Latin. The parish priest had his first suspicion of an imposter when he saw that he did not understand the language of God or know how to greet His ministers. Then he noticed that seen close up he was much too human: he had an unbearable smell of the outdoors, the back side of his wings was strewn with parasites and his main feathers had been mistreated by terrestrial winds, and nothing about him measured up to the proud dignity of angels. Then he came out of the chicken coop and in a brief sermon warned the curious against the risks of being ingenuous. He reminded them that the devil had the bad habit of making use of carnival tricks in order to confuse the unwary. He argued that if wings were not the essential element in determining the difference between a hawk and an airplane, they were even less so in the recognition of angels. Nevertheless, he promised to write a letter to his bishop so that the latter would write his primate so that the latter would write to the Supreme Pontiff in order to get the final verdict from the highest courts.

His prudence fell on sterile hearts. The news of the captive angel spread with such rapidity that after a few hours the courtyard had the bustle of a marketplace and they had to call in troops with fixed bayonets to disperse the mob that was about to knock the house down. Elisenda, her spine all twisted from sweeping up so much marketplace trash, then got the idea of fencing in the yard and charging five cents admission to see the angel.

The curious came from far away. A traveling carnival arrived with a flying acrobat who buzzed over the crowd several times, but no one paid any attention to him because his wings were not those of an angel but, rather, those of a sidereal bat. The most unfortunate invalids on earth came in search of health: a poor woman who since childhood has been counting her heartbeats and had run out of numbers; a Portuguese man who couldn't sleep because the noise of the stars disturbed him; a sleepwalker who got up at night to undo the things he had done while awake; and many others with less serious ailments. In the midst of that shipwreck disorder that made the earth tremble, Pelayo and Elisenda were happy with fatigue, for in less than a week they had crammed their rooms with money and the line of pilgrims waiting their turn to enter still reached beyond the horizon.

The angel was the only one who took no part in his own act. He spent his time trying to get comfortable in his borrowed nest, befuddled by the hellish heat of the oil lamps and sacramental candles that had been placed along the wire. At first they tried to make him eat some mothballs, which, according to the wisdom of the wise neighbor woman, were the food prescribed for angels. But he turned them down, just as he turned down the papal lunches that the pentinents brought him, and they never found out whether it was because he was an angel or because he was an old man that in the end ate nothing but eggplant mush. His only supernatural virtue seemed to be patience. Especially during the first days, when the hens pecked at him, searching for the stellar parasites that proliferated in his wings, and the cripples pulled out feathers to touch their defective parts with, and even the most merciful threw stones at him, trying to get him to rise so they could see him standing. The only time they succeeded in arousing him was when they burned his side with an iron for branding steers, for he had been motionless for so many hours that they thought he was dead. He awoke with a start, ranting in his hermetic language and with tears in his eyes, and he flapped his wings a couple of times, which brought on a whirlwind of chicken dung and lunar dust and a gale of panic that did not seem to be of this world. Although many thought that his reaction had not been one of rage but of pain, from then on they were careful not to annoy him, because the majority understood that his passivity was not that of a hero taking his ease but that of a cataclysm in repose.

Father Gonzaga held back the crowd's frivolity with formulas of maidservant inspiration while awaiting the arrival of a final judgment on the nature of the captive. But the mail from Rome showed no sense of urgency. They spent their time finding out if the prisoner had a navel, if his dialect had any connection with Aramaic, how many times he could fit on the head of a pin, or whether he wasn't just a Norwegian with wings. Those meager letters might have come and gone until the end of time if a providential event had not put and end to the priest's tribulations.

It so happened that during those days, among so many other carnival attractions, there arrived in the town the traveling show of the woman who had been changed into a spider for having disobeyed her parents. The admission to see her was not only less than the admission to see the angel, but people were permitted to ask her all manner of questions about her absurd state and to examine her up and down so that no one would ever doubt the truth of her horror. She was a frightful tarantula the size of a ram and with the head of a sad maiden. What was most heartrending, however, was not her outlandish shape but the sincere affliction with which she recounted the details of her misfortune. While still practically a child she had sneaked out of her parents' house to go to a dance, and while she was coming back through the woods after having danced all night without permission, a fearful thunderclap rent the sky in two and through the crack came the lightning bolt of brimstone that changed her into a spider. Her only nourishment came from the meatballs that charitable souls chose to toss into her mouth. A spectacle like that, full of so much human truth and with such a fearful lesson, was bound to defeat without even trying, that of a haughty angel who scarcely deigned to look at mortals. Besides, the few miracles attributed to the angel showed a certain mental disorder, like the blind man who didn't recover his sight but grew three new teeth, or the paralytic who didn't get to walk but almost won the lottery, and the leper whose sores sprouted sunflowers. Those consolation miracles, which were more like mocking fun, had already ruined the angel's reputation when the woman who had been changed into a spider finally crushed him completely. That was how Father Gonzaga was cured forever of his insomnia and Pelayo's courtyard went back to being as empty as during the time it had rained for three days and crabs walked through the bedrooms.

The owners of the house had no reason to lament. With the money they saved they built a two-story mansion with balconies and gardens and high netting so that crabs wouldn't get in during the winter, and with iron bars on the windows so that angels wouldn't get in. Pelayo also set up a rabbit warren close to town and gave up his job as a bailiff for good, and Elisenda bought some satin pumps with high heels and many dresses of iridescent silk, the kind worn on Sunday by the most desirable women in those times. The chicken coop was the only thing that didn't receive any attention. If they washed it down with creolin and burned tears of myrrh inside it every so often, it was not in homage to the angel but to drive away the dungheap stench that still hung everywhere like a ghost and was turning the new house into an old one. At first, when the child learned to walk, they were careful that he not get too close to the chicken coop. But then they began to lose their fears and got used to the smell, and before the child got his second teeth he'd gone inside the chicken coop to play, where the wires were falling apart. The angel was no less standoffish with him than with the other mortals, but he tolerated the most ingenious infamies with the patience of a dog who had no illusions. They both came down with the chicken pox at the same time. The doctor who took care of the child couldn't resist the temptation to listen to the angel's heart, and he found so much whistling in the heart and so many sounds in his kidneys that it seemed impossible for him to be alive. What surprised him most, however, was the logic of his wings. They seemed so natural on that completely human organism that he couldn't understand why other men didn't have them too.

When the child began school it had been some time since the sun and rain had caused the collapse of the chicken coop. The angel went dragging himself about here and there like a stray dying man. They would drive him out of the bedroom with a broom and a moment later find him in the kitchen. He seemed to be in so many places at the same time that they grew to think that he'd be duplicated, that he was reproducing himself all through the house, and the exasperated and unhinged Elisenda shouted that it was awful living in that hell full of angels. He could scarcely eat and his antiquarian eyes had also become so foggy that he went about bumping into posts. All he had left were the bare cannulae of his last feathers. Pelayo threw a blanket over him and extended him the charity of letting him sleep in the shed, and only then did they notice that he had a temperature at night, and was delirious with the tongue twisters of an old Norwegian. That was one of the few times they became alarmed, for they thought he was going to die and not even the wise neighbor woman had been able to tell them what to do with dead angels.

And yet he not only survived his worst winter, but seemed improved with the first sunny days. He remained motionless for several days in the farthest corner of the courtyard, where no one would see him, and at the beginning of December some large, stiff feathers began to grow on his wings, the feathers of a scarecrow, which looked more like another misfortune of decreptitude. But he must have known the reason for those changes, for he was quite careful that no one should notice them, that no one should hear the sea chanteys that he sometimes sang under the stars. One morning Elisenda was cutting some bunches of onions for lunch when a wind that seemed to come from the high seas blew into the kitchen. Then she went to the window and caught the angel in his first attempts at flight. They were so clumsy that his fingernails opened a furrow in the vegetable patch and he was on the point of knocking the shed down with the ungainly flapping that slipped on the light and couldn't get a grip on the air. But he did manage to gain altitude. Elisenda let out a sigh of relief, for herself and for him, when she watched him pass over the last houses, holding himself up in some way with the risky flapping of a senile vulture. She kept watching him even when she was through cutting the onions and she kept on watching until it was no longer possible for her to see him, because then he was no longer an annoyance in her life but an imaginary dot on the horizon of the sea.

The wings usually represent speed and limitless motion. But ironically, they symbolically represent a sense of age and disease in this story.

33

THE BET

ANTON CHEKHOV

It was a dark autumn night. The old banker was walking up and down his study and remembering how, fifteen years before, he had given a party one autumn evening. There had been many clever men there, and there had been interesting conversations. Among other things they had talked of capital punishment. The majority of the guests, among whom were many journalists and intellectual men, disapproved of the death penalty. They considered that form of punishment out of date, immoral, and unsuitable for Christian States. In the opinion of some of them the death penalty ought to be replaced everywhere by imprisonment for life. 'I don't agree with you,' said their host the banker. 'I have not tried either the death penalty or imprisonment for life, but if one may judge *a priori*, the death penalty is more moral and more humane than imprisonment for life. Capital punishment kills a man at once, but lifelong imprisonment kills him slowly. Which executioner is the more humane, he who kills you in a few minutes or he who drags the life out of you in the course of many years?'

'Both are equally immoral,' observed one of the guests, 'for they both have the same object—to take away life. The State is not

God. It has not the right to take away what it cannot restore when it wants to.'

Among the guests was a young lawyer, a young man of five-and-twenty. When he was asked his opinion, he said, 'The death sentence and the life sentence are equally immoral, but if I had to choose between the death penalty and imprisonment for life, I would certainly choose the second. To live anyhow is better than not at all.'

A lively discussion arose. The banker, who was younger and more nervous in those days, was suddenly carried away by excitement; he struck the table with his fist and shouted at the young man:

'It's not true! I'll bet you two million you wouldn't stay in solitary confinement for five years.'

'If you mean that in earnest,' said the young man, 'I'll take the bet, but I would stay not five but fifteen years.'

'Fifteen? Done!' cried the banker. 'Gentlemen, I stake two million!'

'Agreed! You stake your millions and I stake my freedom!' said the young man.

And this wild, senseless bet was carried out! The banker, spoilt and frivolous, with millions beyond his reckoning, was delighted at the bet. At supper he made fun of the young man, and said:

'Think better of it, young man, while there is still time. To me two million is a trifle, but you are losing three or four of the best years of your life. I say three or four, because you won't stay longer. Don't forget either, you unhappy man, that voluntary confinement is a great deal harder to bear than compulsory. The thought that you have the right to step out in liberty at any moment will poison your whole existence in prison. I am sorry for you.'

And now the banker, walking to and fro, remembered all this, and asked himself: 'What was the object of that bet? What is the good of that man's losing fifteen years of his life and my throwing away two million? Can it prove that the death penalty is better or worse than imprisonment for life? No, no. It was all nonsensical and meaningless. On my part it was the caprice of a pampered man, and on his part simple greed for money ...'

Then he remembered what followed that evening. It was decided that the young man should spend the years of his captivity under the strictest supervision in one of the lodges in the banker's garden. It was agreed that for fifteen years he should not be free to cross the threshold of the lodge, to see human beings, to hear the human voice, or to receive letters and newspapers. He was allowed to have a musical instrument and books, and was allowed to write letters, to drink wine, and to smoke. By the terms of the agreement, the only relations he could have with the outer world were by a little window made purposely for that object. He might have anything he wanted—books, music, wine, and so on—in any quantity he desired by writing an order, but could only receive them through the window. The agreement provided for every detail and every trifle that would make his imprisonment strictly solitary, and bound the young man to stay there exactly fifteen years, beginning from twelve o'clock of November 14, 1870, and ending at twelve o'clock of November 14, 1885. The slightest attempt on his part to break the conditions, if only two minutes before the end, released the banker from the obligation to pay him the two million.

For the first year of his confinement, as far as one could judge from his brief notes, the prisoner suffered severely from loneliness and depression. The sounds of the piano could be heard continually day and night from his lodge. He refused wine and tobacco. Wine, he wrote, excites the desires, and desires are the worst foes of the prisoner; and besides, nothing could be more dreary than drinking good wine and seeing no one. And tobacco spoilt the air of his room. In the first year the books he sent for were principally of a light character; novels with a complicated love plot, sensational and fantastic stories, and so on.

In the second year the piano was silent in the lodge, and the prisoner asked only for the classics. In the fifth year music was audible again, and the prisoner asked for wine. Those who watched him through the window said that all that year he spent doing nothing but eating and drinking and lying on his bed, frequently yawning and angrily talking to himself. He did not read books. Sometimes at night he would sit down to write; he would spend hours writing, and in the morning tear up all that he had written. More than once he could be heard crying.

In the second half of the sixth year the prisoner began zealously studying languages, philosophy, and history. He threw himself eagerly into these studies—so much so that the banker had enough to do to get him the books he ordered. In the course of four years some six hundred volumes were procured at his request. It was during this period that the banker received the following letter from his prisoner:

'My dear Jailer, I write you these lines in six languages. Show them to people who know the languages. Let them read them. If they find not one mistake I implore you to fire a shot in the garden. That shot will show me that my efforts have not been thrown away. The geniuses of all ages and of all lands speak different languages, but the same flame burns in them all. Oh, if you only knew what unearthly happiness my soul feels now from being able to understand them!' The prisoner's desire was fulfilled. The banker ordered two shots to be fired in the garden.

Then after the tenth year, the prisoner sat immovably at the table and read nothing but the Gospel. It seemed strange to the banker that a man who in four years had mastered six hundred learned volumes should waste nearly a year over one thin book easy of comprehension. Theology and histories of religion followed the Gospels.

In the last two years of his confinement the prisoner read an immense quantity of books quite indiscriminately. At one time he was busy with the natural sciences, then he would ask for Byron or Shakespeare. There were notes in which he demanded at the same time books on chemistry, and a manual of medicine, and a novel, and some treatise on philosophy or theology. His reading suggested a man swimming in the sea among the wreckage of his ship, and trying to save his life by greedily clutching first at one spar and then at another.

The old banker remembered all this, and thought:

'Tomorrow at twelve o'clock he will regain his freedom. By our agreement I ought to pay him two million. If I do pay him, it is all over with me: I shall be utterly ruined.'

Fifteen years before, his millions had been beyond his reckoning; now he was afraid to ask himself which were greater, his debts or his assets. Desperate gambling on the Stock Exchange, wild speculation and the excitability which he could not get over even in advancing years, had by degrees led to the decline of his fortune and the proud, fearless, self-confident millionaire had become a banker of middling rank, trembling at every rise and fall in his investments. 'Cursed bet!' muttered the old man, clutching his head in despair 'Why didn't the man die? He is only forty now. He will take my last penny from me, he will marry, will enjoy life, will gamble on the Exchange; while I shall look at him with envy like a beggar, and hear from him every day the same sentence: 'I am indebted to you for the happiness of my life, let me help you!' No, it is too much! The one means of being saved from bankruptcy and disgrace is the death of that man!'

It struck three o'clock, the banker listened; everyone was asleep in the house and nothing could be heard outside but the rustling of the chilled trees. Trying to make no noise, he took from a fireproof safe the key of the door which had not been opened for fifteen years, put on his overcoat, and went out of the house.

It was dark and cold in the garden. Rain was falling. A damp cutting wind was racing about the garden, howling and giving the trees no rest. The banker strained his eyes, but could see neither the earth nor the white statues, nor the lodge, nor the trees. Going to the spot where the lodge stood, he twice called the watchman. No answer followed. Evidently the watchman had sought shelter from the weather, and was now asleep somewhere either in the kitchen or in the greenhouse.

'If I had the pluck to carry out my intention,' thought the old man, 'Suspicion would fall first upon the watchman.'

He felt in the darkness for the steps and the door, and went into the entry of the lodge. Then he groped his way into a little passage and lighted a match. There was not a soul there. There was a bedstead with no bedding on it, and in the corner there was a dark cast-iron stove. The seals on the door leading to the prisoner's rooms were intact.

When the match went out the old man, trembling with emotion, peeped through the little window. A candle was burning dimly in the prisoner's room. He was sitting at the table. Nothing could be seen but his back, the hair on his head, and his hands. Open books were lying on the table, on the two easy-chairs, and on the carpet near the table.

Five minutes passed and the prisoner did not once stir. Fifteen years' imprisonment had taught him to sit still. The banker tapped at the window with his finger, and the prisoner made no movement whatever in response. Then the banker cautiously broke the seals off the door and put the key in the keyhole. The rusty lock gave a grating sound and the door creaked. The banker expected to hear at once footsteps and a cry of astonishment, but three minutes passed and it was as quiet as ever in the room. He made up his mind to go in.

At the table a man unlike ordinary people was sitting motionless. He was a skeleton with the skin drawn tight over his bones, with long curls like a woman's and a shaggy beard. His face was yellow with an earthy tint in it, his cheeks were hollow, his back long and narrow, and the hand on which his shaggy head was propped was so thin and delicate that it was dreadful to look at it. His hair was already streaked with silver, and seeing his emaciated, aged-looking face, no one would have believed that he was only forty. He was asleep ... In front of his bowed head there lay on the table a sheet of paper on which there was something written in fine handwriting.

'Poor creature!' thought the banker, 'he is asleep and most likely dreaming of the millions. And I have only to take this half-dead man, throw him on the bed, stifle him a little with the pillow, and the most conscientious expert would find no sign of a violent death. But let us first read what he has written here ...'

The banker took the page from the table and it read as follows:

'Tomorrow at twelve o'clock I regain my freedom and the right to associate with other men, but before I leave this room and see the sunshine, I think it necessary to say a few words to you. With a clear conscience I tell you, as before God, who beholds me, that I despise freedom and life and health, and all that in your books is called the good things of the world.

'For fifteen years I have been intently studying earthly life. It is true I have not seen the earth nor men, but in your books I have drunk fragrant wine, I have sung songs, I have hunted stags and wild boars in the forests, have loved women ... Beauties as ethereal as clouds, created by the magic of your poets and geniuses, have visited me at night, and have whispered in my ears wonderful tales that have set my brain in a whirl. In your books I have climbed to the peaks of Elburz and Mont Blanc, and from there I have seen the sun rise and have watched it at evening flood the sky, the ocean, and the mountain-tops with gold and crimson. I have watched from there the lightning flashing over my head and cleaving the storm-clouds. I have seen green forests, fields, rivers, lakes, towns. I have heard the singing of the sirens, and the strains of the shepherds' pipes; I have touched the wings of comely devils who flew down to converse with me of God ... In your books I have flung myself into the bottomless pit, performed miracles, slain, burned towns, preached new religions, conquered whole kingdoms ...

'Your books have given me wisdom. All that the unresting thought of man has created in the ages is compressed into a small compass in my brain. I know that I am wiser than all of you.

'And I despise your books, I despise wisdom and the blessings of this world. It is all worthless, fleeting, illusory, and deceptive, like a mirage. You may be proud, wise, and fine, but death will wipe you off the face of the earth as though you were no more than mice burrowing under the floor, and your posterity, your history, your immortal geniuses will burn or freeze together with the earthly globe.

'You have lost your reason and taken the wrong path. You have taken lies for truth, and hideousness for beauty. You would marvel if, owing to strange events of some sorts, frogs and lizards suddenly grew on apple and orange trees instead of fruit, or if roses began to smell like a sweating horse; so I marvel at you who exchange heaven for earth. I don't want to understand you.

'To prove to you in action how I despise all that you live by, I renounce the two million of which I once dreamed as of paradise and which now I despise. To deprive myself of the right to the money I shall go out from here five hours before the time fixed, and so break the contract ...'

When the banker had read this he laid the page on the table, kissed the strange man on the head, and went out of the lodge, weeping. At no other time, even when he had lost heavily on the Stock Exchange, had he felt so great a contempt for himself. When he got home he lay on his bed, but his tears and emotion kept him for hours from sleeping.

Next morning the watchmen ran in with pale faces, and told him they had seen the man who lived in the lodge climb out of the window into the garden, go to the gate, and disappear. The banker went at once with the servants to the lodge and made sure of the flight of his prisoner. To avoid arousing unnecessary talk, he took from the table the writing in which the millions were renounced, and when he got home locked it up in the fireproof safe.

∞

The debate is whether death penalty or life imprisonment is better. A man has to spend fifteen years in isolation in order to win a bet. The uniqueness of this story is that it leaves the reader with a kind of unfinished narrative.

34

A RETRIEVED REFORMATION

O. HENRY

A guard came to the prison shoe-shop, where Jimmy Valentine was assiduously stitching uppers, and escorted him to the front office. There the warden handed Jimmy his pardon, which had been signed that morning by the governor. Jimmy took it in a tired kind of way. He had served nearly ten months of a four year sentence. He had expected to stay only about three months, at the longest. When a man with as many friends on the outside as Jimmy Valentine had is received in the 'stir' it is hardly worth while to cut his hair.

'Now, Valentine,' said the warden, 'you'll go out in the morning. Brace up, and make a man of yourself. You're not a bad fellow at heart. Stop cracking safes, and live straight.'

'Me?' said Jimmy, in surprise. 'Why, I never cracked a safe in my life.'

'Oh, no,' laughed the warden. 'Of course not. Let's see, now. How was it you happened to get sent up on that Springfield job? Was it because you wouldn't prove an alibi for fear of compromising somebody in extremely high-toned society? Or was it simply a case of a mean old jury that had it in for you? It's always one or the other with you innocent victims.'

'Me?' said Jimmy, still blankly virtuous. 'Why, warden, I never was in Springfield in my life!'

'Take him back, Cronin!' said the warden, 'and fix him up with outgoing clothes. Unlock him at seven in the morning, and let him come to the bull-pen. Better think over my advice, Valentine.'

At a quarter past seven on the next morning Jimmy stood in the warden's outer office. He had on a suit of the villainously fitting, ready-made clothes and a pair of the stiff, squeaky shoes that the state furnishes to its discharged compulsory guests.

The clerk handed him a railroad ticket and the five-dollar bill with which the law expected him to rehabilitate himself into good citizenship and prosperity. The warden gave him a cigar, and shook hands. Valentine, 9762, was chronicled on the books 'Pardoned by Governor,' and Mr James Valentine walked out into the sunshine.

Disregarding the song of the birds, the waving green trees, and the smell of the flowers, Jimmy headed straight for a restaurant. There he tasted the first sweet joys of liberty in the shape of a broiled chicken and a bottle of white wine—followed by a cigar a grade better than the one the warden had given him. From there he proceeded leisurely to the depot. He tossed a quarter into the hat of a blind man sitting by the door, and boarded his train. Three hours set him down in a little town near the state line. He went to the cafe of one Mike Dolan and shook hands with Mike, who was alone behind the bar.

'Sorry we couldn't make it sooner, Jimmy, me boy,' said Mike. 'But we had that protest from Springfield to buck against, and the governor nearly balked. Feeling all right?'

'Fine,' said Jimmy. 'Got my key?'

He got his key and went upstairs, unlocking the door of a room at the rear. Everything was just as he had left it. There on the floor was still Ben Price's collar-button that had been torn from that eminent detective's shirt-band when they had overpowered Jimmy to arrest him.

Pulling out from the wall a folding-bed, Jimmy slid back a panel in the wall and dragged out a dust-covered suit-case. He opened this and gazed fondly at the finest set of burglar's tools in the East. It was a complete set, made of specially tempered steel, the latest designs in drills, punches, braces and bits, jimmies, clamps, and augers, with two or three novelties, invented by Jimmy himself, in which he took pride. Over nine hundred dollars they had cost him to have made at—, a place where they make such things for the profession.

In half an hour Jimmy went downstairs and through the cafe. He was now dressed in tasteful and well-fitting clothes, and carried his dusted and cleaned suit-case in his hand.

'Got anything on?' asked Mike Dolan, genially.

'Me?' said Jimmy, in a puzzled tone. 'I don't understand. I'm representing the New York Amalgamated Short Snap Biscuit Cracker and Frazzled Wheat Company.'

This statement delighted Mike to such an extent that Jimmy had to take a seltzer-and-milk on the spot. He never touched 'hard' drinks.

A week after the release of Valentine, 9762, there was a neat job of safe-burglary done in Richmond, Indiana, with no clue to the author. A scant eight hundred dollars was all that was secured. Two weeks after that a patented, improved, burglar-proof safe in Logansport was opened like a cheese to the tune of fifteen hundred dollars, currency; securities and silver untouched. That began to interest the rogue-catchers. Then an old-fashioned bank-safe in Jefferson City became active and threw out of its crater an eruption of bank-notes amounting to five thousand dollars. The losses were now high enough to bring the matter up into Ben Price's class of work. By comparing notes, a remarkable similarity in the methods of the burglaries was noticed. Ben Price investigated the scenes of the robberies, and was heard to remark:

'That's Dandy Jim Valentine's autograph. He's resumed business. Look at that combination knob—jerked out as easy as pulling up a radish in wet weather. He's got the only clamps that can do it. And look how clean those tumblers were punched out! Jimmy never has to drill but one hole. Yes, I guess I want Mr Valentine. He'll do his bit next time without any short-time or clemency foolishness.'

Ben Price knew Jimmy's habits. He had learned them while working on the Springfield case. Long jumps, quick get-aways, no confederates, and a taste for good society—these ways had helped Mr Valentine to become noted as a successful dodger of retribution. It was given out that Ben Price had taken up the trail of the elusive cracksman, and other people with burglar-proof safes felt more at ease.

One afternoon Jimmy Valentine and his suit-case climbed out of the mail-hack in Elmore, a little town five miles off the railroad down in the black-jack country of Arkansas. Jimmy, looking like an athletic young senior just home from college, went down the board side-walk toward the hotel.

A young lady crossed the street, passed him at the corner and entered a door over which was the sign 'The Elmore Bank.' Jimmy Valentine looked into her eyes, forgot what he was, and became another man. She lowered her eyes and colored slightly. Young men of Jimmy's style and looks were scarce in Elmore.

Jimmy collared a boy that was loafing on the steps of the bank as if he were one of the stockholders, and began to ask him questions about the town, feeding him dimes at intervals. By and by the young lady came out, looking royally unconscious of the young man with the suit-case, and went her way.

'Isn't that young lady Miss Polly Simpson?' asked Jimmy, with specious guile.

'Naw,' said the boy. 'She's Annabel Adams. Her pa owns this bank. What'd you come to Elmore for? Is that a gold watch-chain? I'm going to get a bulldog. Got any more dimes?'

Jimmy went to the Planters' Hotel, registered as Ralph D.

Spencer, and engaged a room. He leaned on the desk and declared his platform to the clerk. He said he had come to Elmore to look for a location to go into business. How was the shoe business, now, in the town? He had thought of the shoe business. Was there an opening?

The clerk was impressed by the clothes and manner of Jimmy. He, himself, was something of a pattern of fashion to the thinly gilded youth of Elmore, but he now perceived his shortcomings. While trying to figure out Jimmy's manner of tying his four-in-hand he cordially gave information.

Yes, there ought to be a good opening in the shoe line. There wasn't an exclusive shoe-store in the place. The dry-goods and general stores handled them. Business in all lines was fairly good. Hoped Mr Spencer would decide to locate in Elmore. He would find it a pleasant town to live in, and the people very sociable.

Mr Spencer thought he would stop over in the town a few days and look over the situation. No, the clerk needn't call the boy. He would carry up his suit-case, himself; it was rather heavy.

Mr Ralph Spencer, the phoenix that arose from Jimmy Valentine's ashes—ashes left by the flame of a sudden and alterative attack of love—remained in Elmore, and prospered. He opened a shoe-store and secured a good run of trade.

Socially he was also a success, and made many friends. And he accomplished the wish of his heart. He met Miss Annabel Adams, and became more and more captivated by her charms.

At the end of a year the situation of Mr Ralph Spencer was this: he had won the respect of the community, his shoe-store was flourishing, and he and Annabel were engaged to be married in two weeks. Mr Adams, the typical, plodding, country banker, approved of Spencer. Annabel's pride in him almost equaled her affection. He was as much at home in the family of Mr Adams and that of Annabel's married sister as if he were already a member.

One day Jimmy sat down in his room and wrote this letter, which he mailed to the safe address of one of his old friends in St. Louis:

Dear Old Pal,

I want you to be at Sullivan's place, in Little Rock, next Wednesday night, at nine o'clock. I want you to wind up some little matters for me. And, also, I want to make you a present of my kit of tools. I know you'll be glad to get them—you couldn't duplicate the lot for a thousand dollars. Say, Billy, I've quit the old business—a year ago. I've got a nice store. I'm making an honest living, and I'm going to marry the finest girl on earth two weeks from now. It's the only life, Billy—the straight one. I wouldn't touch a dollar of another man's money now for a million. After I get married I'm going to sell out and go West, where there won't be so much danger of having old scores brought up against me. I tell you, Billy, she's an angel. She believes in me; and I wouldn't do another crooked thing for the whole world. Be sure to be at Sully's, for I must see you. I'll bring along the tools with me.

Your old friend,
Jimmy.

On the Monday night after Jimmy wrote this letter, Ben Price jogged unobtrusively into Elmore in a livery buggy. He lounged about town in his quiet way until he found out what he wanted to know. From the drug-store across the street from Spencer's shoe-store he got a good look at Ralph D. Spencer.

'Going to marry the banker's daughter are you, Jimmy?' said Ben to himself, softly. 'Well, I don't know!'

The next morning Jimmy took breakfast at the Adamses. He was going to Little Rock that day to order his wedding-suit and buy something nice for Annabel. That would be the first time he had left town since he came to Elmore. It had been more than a year now since those last professional 'jobs,' and he thought he could safely venture out.

After breakfast quite a family party went downtown together—Mr Adams, Annabel, Jimmy, and Annabel's married sister with her two little girls, aged five and nine. They came by the hotel where Jimmy still boarded, and he ran up to his room and brought along his suit-case. Then they went on to the bank. There stood Jimmy's horse and buggy and Dolph Gibson, who was going to drive him over to the railroad station.

All went inside the high, carved oak railings into the banking-room—Jimmy included, for Mr Adams's future son-in-law was welcome anywhere. The clerks were pleased to be greeted by the good-looking, agreeable young man who was going to marry Miss Annabel. Jimmy set his suit-case down. Annabel, whose heart was bubbling with happiness and lively youth, put on Jimmy's hat, and picked up the suit-case. 'Wouldn't I make a nice drummer?' said Annabel. 'My! Ralph, how heavy it is. Feels like it was full of gold bricks.'

'Lot of nickel-plated shoe-horns in there,' said Jimmy, coolly, 'that I'm going to return. Thought I'd save express charges by taking them up. I'm getting awfully economical.'

The Elmore Bank had just put in a new safe and vault. Mr Adams was very proud of it, and insisted on an inspection by every one. The vault was a small one, but it had a new, patented door. It fastened with three solid steel bolts thrown simultaneously with a single handle, and had a time-lock. Mr Adams beamingly explained its workings to Mr Spencer, who showed a courteous but not too intelligent interest. The two children, May and Agatha, were delighted by the shining metal and funny clock and knobs.

While they were thus engaged Ben Price sauntered in and leaned on his elbow, looking casually inside between the railings. He told the teller that he didn't want anything; he was just waiting for a man he knew.

Suddenly there was a scream or two from the women, and a commotion. Unperceived by the field ers, May, the nine-year-old girl, in a spirit of play, had shut Agatha in the vault. She had then shot the bolts and turned the knob of the combination as she had seen Mr Adams do.

The old banker sprang to the handle and tugged at it for a moment. 'The door can't be opened,' he groaned. 'The clock hasn't been wound nor the combination set.'

Agatha's mother screamed again, hysterically.

'Hush!' said Mr Adams, raising his trembling hand. 'All be quite for a moment. Agatha!' he called as loudly as he could. 'Listen to me.' During the following silence they could just hear the faint sound of the child wildly shrieking in the dark vault in a panic of terror.

'My precious darling!' wailed the mother. 'She will die of fright! Open the door! Oh, break it open! Can't you men do something?'

'There isn't a man nearer than Little Rock who can open that door,' said Mr Adams, in a shaky voice. 'My God! Spencer, what shall we do? That child—she can't stand it long in there. There isn't enough air, and, besides, she'll go into convulsions from fright.'

Agatha's mother, frantic now, beat the door of the vault with her hands. Somebody wildly suggested dynamite. Annabel turned to Jimmy, her large eyes full of anguish, but not yet despairing. To a woman nothing seems quite impossible to the powers of the man she worships.

'Can't you do something, Ralph—try, won't you?'

He looked at her with a queer, soft smile on his lips and in his keen eyes.

'Annabel,' he said, 'give me that rose you are wearing, will you?'

Hardly believing that she heard him aright, she unpinned the bud from the bosom of her dress, and placed it in his hand. Jimmy stuffed it into his vest-pocket, threw off his coat and pulled up his shirt-sleeves. With that act Ralph D. Spencer passed away and Jimmy Valentine took his place.

'Get away from the door, all of you,' he commanded, shortly.

He set his suit-case on the table, and opened it out flat. From that time on he seemed to be unconscious of the presence of any one else. He laid out the shining, queer implements swiftly and orderly, whistling softly to himself as he always did when at work. In a deep silence and immovable, the others watched him as if under a spell.

In a minute Jimmy's pet drill was biting smoothly into the steel door. In ten minutes—breaking his own burglarious record—he threw back the bolts and opened the door.

Agatha, almost collapsed, but safe, was gathered into her mother's arms.

Jimmy Valentine put on his coat, and walked outside the railings toward the front door. As he went he thought he heard a far-away voice that he once knew call 'Ralph!' But he never hesitated.

At the door a big man stood somewhat in his way.

'Hello, Ben!' said Jimmy, still with his strange smile. 'Got around at last, have you? Well, let's go. I don't know that it makes much difference, now.'

And then Ben Price acted rather strangely.

'Guess you're mistaken, Mr Spencer,' he said. 'Don't believe I recognize you. Your buggy's waiting for you, ain't it?'

And Ben Price turned and strolled down the street.

The magic of love can even change a cold-hearted criminal! The conflict in this story—Valentine's decision whether or not to save Annabel's niece—is intriguing. If he saves her, he gives himself up as a criminal. If he doesn't, he will end up with a lifetime of guilt for not saving the girl's life.

35

QUALITY

JOHN GALSWORTHY

I knew him from the days of my extreme youth, because he made my father's boots; inhabiting with his field er brother two little shops let into one, in a small by-street—now no more, but then most fashionably placed in the West End.

That tenement had a certain quiet distinction; there was no sign upon its face that he made for any of the Royal Family— merely his own German name of Gessler Brothers: and in the window a few pairs of boots. I remember that it always troubled me to account for those unvarying boots in the window, for he made only what was ordered, reaching nothing down, and it seemed so inconceivable that what he made could ever have failed to fit. Had he bought them to put there? That, too, seemed inconceivable. He would never have tolerated in his house leather on which he had not worked himself. Besides, they were too beautiful—the pair of pumps, so inexpressibly slim, the patent leathers with cloth tops, making water come into one's mouth, the tall brown riding boots with marvellous sooty glow, as if, though new, they had been worn a hundred years. Those pairs could only have been made by one who saw before him the Soul of Boot—so truly were they prototypes incarnating the very spirit of all footgear. These thoughts, of course, came to me later, though even when I was promoted to him, at the age of perhaps fourteen, some inkling haunted me of the dignity of himself and brother. For to make boots—such boots as he made—seemed to me then, and still seems to me, mysterious and wonderful.

I remember well my shy remark, one day, while stretching out to him my youthful foot: 'Isn't it awfully hard to do, Mr Gessler?' And his answer, given with a sudden smile from out of the sardonic redness of his beard: 'Id is an Ardt!'

Himself, he was a little as if made from leather, with his yellow crinkly face, and crinkly reddish hair and beard, and neat folds slanting down his cheeks to the corners of his mouth, and his guttural and one-toned voice; for leather is a sardonic substance, and stiff and slow of purpose. And that was the character of his face, save that his eyes, which were gray-blue, had in them the simple gravity of one secretly possessed by the Ideal. His field er brother was so very like him—though watery, paler in every way, with a great industry—that sometimes in early days I was not quite sure of him until the interview was over. Then I knew that it was he, if the words, 'I will ask my brudder,' had not been spoken; and that, if they had, it was his field er brother.

When one grew old and wild and ran up bills, one somehow never ran them up with Gessler Brothers. It would not have seemed becoming to go in there and stretch out one's foot to that blue iron-spectacled glance, owing him for more than—say—two pairs, just the comfortable reassurance that one was still his client.

For it was not possible to go to him very often—his boots lasted terribly, having something beyond the temporary—some, as it were, essence of boot stitched into them.

One went in, not as into most shops, in the mood of: 'Please serve me, and let me go!' but restfully, as one enters a church; and, sitting on the single wooden chair, waited—for there was never anybody there. Soon, over the top edge of that sort of well—rather dark, and smelling soothingly of leather—which formed the shop, there would be seen his face, or that of his field er brother, peering down.

A guttural sound, and the tip-tap of bast slippers beating the narrow wooden stairs, and he would stand before one without coat, a little bent, in leather apron, with sleeves turned back, blinking—as if awakened from some dream of boots, or like an owl surprised in daylight and annoyed at this interruption.

And I would say: 'How do you do, Mr Gessler? Could you make me a pair of Russia leather boots?' Without a word he would leave me, retiring whence he came, or into the other portion of the shop, and I would continue to rest in the wooden chair, inhaling the incense of his trade. Soon he would come back, holding in his thin, veined hand a piece of gold-brown leather. With eyes fixed on it, he would remark: 'What a beaudiful biece!' When I, too, had admired it, he would speak again. 'When do you wand dem?' And I would answer: 'Oh! As soon as you conveniently can.' And he would say: 'Tomorrow fordnighd?' Or if he were his field er brother: 'I will ask my brudder!'

Then I would murmur: 'Thank you! Good-morning, Mr Gessler.' 'Goot-morning!' he would reply, still looking at the leather in his hand. And as I moved to the door, I would hear the tip-tap of his bast slippers restoring him, up the stairs, to his dream of boots. But if it were some new kind of foot-gear that he had not yet made me, then indeed he would observe ceremony—divesting me of my boot and holding it long in his hand, looking at it with eyes at once critical and loving, as if recalling the glow with which he had created it, and rebuking the way in which one had disorganised this masterpiece. Then, placing my foot on a piece of paper, he would two or three times tickle the outer edges with a pencil and pass his nervous fingers over my toes, feeling himself into the heart of my requirements.

I cannot forget that day on which I had occasion to say to him: 'Mr Gessler, that last pair of town walking-boots creaked, you know.'

He looked at me for a time without replying, as if expecting me to withdraw or qualify the statement, then said: 'Id shouldn'd 'ave greaked.'

'It did, I'm afraid.'

'You goddem wed before dey found demselves?'

'I don't think so.'

At that he lowered his eyes, as if hunting for memory of those boots, and I felt sorry I had mentioned this grave thing. 'Zend dem back!' he said; 'I will look at dem.'

A feeling of compassion for my creaking boots surged up in me, so well could I imagine the sorrowful long curiosity of regard which he would bend on them. 'Zome boods,' he said slowly, 'are bad from birdt. If I can do noding wid dem, I dake dem off your bill.'

Once (once only) I went absent-mindedly into his shop in a pair of boots bought in an emergency at some large firm's. He took my order without showing me any leather, and I could feel his eyes penetrating the inferior integument of my foot. At last he said: 'Dose are nod my boods.' The tone was not one of anger, nor of sorrow, not even of contempt, but there was in it something quiet that froze the blood. He put his hand down and pressed a finger on the place where the left boot, endeavoring to be fashionable, was not quite comfortable.

'Id 'urds you dere,' he said. 'Dose big virms 'ave no selfrespect. Drash!' And then, as if something had given way within him, he spoke long and bitterly. It was the only time I ever heard him discuss the conditions and hardships of his trade.

'Dey get id all,' he said, 'dey get id by adverdisement, nod by work. Dey dake it away from us, who lofe our boods. Id gomes to this—bresently I haf no work. Every year id gets less—you will see.'

And looking at his lined face I saw things I had never noticed before, bitter things and bitter struggle—and what a lot of gray hairs there seemed suddenly in his red beard! As best I could, I explained the circumstances of the purchase of those ill-omened boots. But his face and voice made so deep impression that during the next few minutes I ordered many pairs. Nemesis fell! They lasted more terribly than ever. And I was not able conscientiously to go to him for nearly two years.

When at last I went I was surprised to find that outside one of the two little windows of his shop another name was painted, also that of a bootmaker—making, of course, for the Royal Family. The old familiar boots, no longer in dignified isolation, were huddled in the single window. Inside, the now contracted well of the one little shop was more scented and darker than ever. And it was longer than usual, too, before a face peered down, and the tip-tap of the bast slippers began.

At last he stood before me, and, gazing through those rusty iron spectacles, said: 'Mr—, isn'd it?'

'Ah! Mr Gessler,' I stammered, 'but your boots are really *too* good, you know! See, these are quite decent still!' And I stretched out to him my foot. He looked at it.

'Yes,' he said, 'beople do nod wand good boods, id seems.'

To get away from his reproachful eyes and voice I hastily remarked: 'What have you done to your shop?'

He answered quietly: 'Id was too exbensif. Do you wand some boods?'

I ordered three pairs, though I had only wanted two, and quickly left. I had, I do not know quite what feeling of being part, in his mind, of a conspiracy against him; or not perhaps so much against him as against his idea of boots.

One does not, I suppose, care to feel like that; for it was again many months before my next visit to his shop, paid, I remember, with the feeling: 'Oh! well, I can't leave the old boy—so here goes! Perhaps it'll be his field er brother!' For his field er brother, I knew, had not character enough to reproach me, even dumbly. And, to my relief, in the shop there did appear to be his field er brother, handling a piece of leather.

'Well, Mr Gessler,' I said, 'how are you?'

He came close, and peered at me.

'I am breddy well,' he said slowly; 'but my field er brudder is dead.'

And I saw that it was indeed himself—but how aged and wan! And never before had I heard him mention his brother. Much shocked, I murmured: 'Oh! I am sorry!'

'Yes,' he answered, 'he was a good man, he made a good bood; but he is dead.' And he touched the top of his head, where the hair had suddenly gone as thin as it had been on that of his poor brother, to indicate, I suppose, the cause of death. 'He could nod ged over losing de oder shop. Do you wand any boods?' And he held up the leather in his hand: 'Id's a beaudiful biece.'

I ordered several pairs. It was very long before they came—but they were better than ever. One simply could not wear them out. And soon after that I went abroad. It was over a year before I was again in London. And the first shop I went to was my old friend's. I had left a man of sixty, I came back to one of seventy-five, pinched and worn and tremulous, who genuinely, this time, did not at first know me.

'Oh! Mr Gessler,' I said, sick at heart; 'how splendid your boots are! See, I've been wearing this pair nearly all the time I've been abroad; and they're not half worn out, are they?'

He looked long at my boots—a pair of Russia leather, and his face seemed to regain steadiness. Putting his hand on my instep, he said: 'Do dey vid you here? I 'ad drouble wid dat bair, I remember.' I assured him that they had fitted beautifully.

'Do you wand any boods?' he said. 'I can make dem quickly; id is a slack dime.'

I answered: 'Please, please! I want boots all round— every kind!'

'I will make a vresh model. Your food must be bigger.'

And with utter slowness, he traced round my foot, and felt my toes, only once looking up to say: 'Did I dell you my brudder was dead?'

To watch him was painful, so feeble had he grown; I was glad to get away.

I had given those boots up, when one evening they came. Opening the parcel, I set the four pairs out in a row. Then one by one I tried them on. There was no doubt about it. In shape and fit, in finish and quality of leather, they were the best he had ever made me. And in the mouth of one of the town walking-boots I found his bill. The amount was the same as usual, but it gave me quite a shock. He had never before sent it in till quarter day. I flew downstairs, and wrote a check, and posted it at once with my own hand. A week later, passing the little street, I thought I would go in and tell him how splendidly the new boots fitted. But when I came to where his shop had been, his name was gone. Still there, in the window, were the slim pumps, the patent leathers with cloth tops, the sooty riding boots.

I went in, very much disturbed. In the two little shops—again made into one—was a young man with an English face. 'Mr Gessler in?' I said.

He gave me a strange, ingratiating look. 'No, sir,' he said, 'no. But we can attend to anything with pleasure. We've taken the shop over. You've seen our name, no doubt, next door. We make for some very good people.'

'Yes, yes,' I said; 'but Mr Gessler?'

'Oh!' he answered; 'dead.'

'Dead! But I only received these boots from him last Wednesday week.'

'Ah!' he said; 'a shockin' go. Poor old man starved 'imself.'

'Good God!'

'Slow starvation, the doctor called it! You see he went to work in such a way! Would keep the shop on; wouldn't have a soul touch his boots except himself. When he got an order, it took him such a time. People won't wait. He lost everybody. And there he'd sit, goin' on and on—I will say that for him—not a man in London made a better boot! But look at the competition! He never advertised! Would 'ave the best leather, too, and do it all 'imself. Well, there it is. What could you expect with his ideas?'

'But starvation—!'

'That may be a bit flowery, as the sayin' is—but I know myself he was sittin' over his boots day and night, to the very last. You see I used to watch him. Never gave 'imself time to eat; never had a penny in the house. All went in rent and leather. How he lived so long I don't know. He regular let his fire go out. He was a character. But he made good boots.'

'Yes,' I said, 'he made good boots.'

And I turned and went out quickly, for I did not want that youth to know that I could hardly see.

⸻

This story is 'mysterious and wonderful'. Doing business without advertising, in a light vein, is like winking at someone in the dark. Indeed, advertising is the modern substitute for argument; its function is to make the worse appear better. And often quality takes a beating in the corporate world.

A CUP OF TEA

KATHERINE MANSFIELD

Rosemary Fell was not exactly beautiful. No, you couldn't have called her beautiful. Pretty? Well, if you took her to pieces... But why be so cruel as to take anyone to pieces? She was young, brilliant, extremely modern, exquisitely well dressed, amazingly well read in the newest of the new books, and her parties were the most delicious mixture of the really important people and ... artists—quaint creatures, discoveries of hers, some of them too terrifying for words, but others quite presentable and amusing.

Rosemary had been married two years. She had a duck of a boy. No, not Peter—Michael. And her husband absolutely adored her. They were rich, really rich, not just comfortably well off, which is odious and stuffy and sounds like one's grandparents. But if Rosemary wanted to shop she would go to Paris as you and I would go to Bond Street. If she wanted to buy flowers, the car pulled up at that perfect shop in Regent Street, and Rosemary inside the shop just gazed in her dazzled, rather exotic way, and said: 'I want those and those and those. Give me four bunches of those. And that jar of roses. Yes, I'll have all the roses in the jar. No, no lilac. I hate lilac. It's got no shape.' The attendant bowed and put the lilac out of sight, as though this was only too true; lilac was dreadfully shapeless. 'Give me those stumpy little tulips. Those red and white ones.' And she was followed to the car by a thin shop-girl staggering under an immense white paper armful that looked like a baby in long clothes....

One winter afternoon she had been buying something in a little antique shop in Curzon Street. It was a shop she liked. For one thing, one usually had it to oneself. And then the man who kept it was ridiculously fond of serving her. He beamed whenever she came in. He clasped his hands; he was so gratified he could scarcely speak. Flattery, of course. All the same, there was something....

'You see, madam,' he would explain in his low respectful tones, 'I love my things. I would rather not part with them than sell them to someone who does not appreciate them, who has not that fine feeling which is so rare...' And, breathing deeply, he unrolled a tiny square of blue velvet and pressed it on the glass counter with his pale finger-tips.

Today it was a little box. He had been keeping it for her. He had shown it to nobody as yet. An exquisite little enamel box with a glaze so fine it looked as though it had been baked in cream. On the lid a minute creature stood under a flowery tree, and a more minute creature still had her arms round his neck. Her hat, really no bigger than a geranium petal, hung from a branch; it had green ribbons.

And there was a pink cloud like a watchful cherub floating above their heads. Rosemary took her hands out of her long gloves. She always took off her gloves to examine such things. Yes, she liked it very much. She loved it; it was a great duck.

She must have it. And, turning the creamy box, opening and shutting it, she couldn't help noticing how charming her hands were against the blue velvet. The shopman, in some dim cavern of his mind, may have dared to think so too. For he took a pencil, leant over the counter, and his pale, bloodless fingers crept timidly towards those rosy, flashing ones, as he murmured gently:

'If I may venture to point out to madam, the flowers on the little lady's bodice.'

'Charming!' Rosemary admired the flowers. But what was the price? For a moment the shopman did not seem to hear. Then a murmur reached her. 'Twenty-eight guineas, madam.' 'Twenty-eight guineas.' Rosemary gave no sign. She laid the little box down; she buttoned her gloves again. Twenty-eight guineas. Even if one is rich...

She looked vague. She stared at a plump tea-kettle like a plump hen above the shopman's head, and her voice was dreamy as she answered: 'Well, keep it for me—will you? I'll...'

But the shopman had already bowed as though keeping it for her was all any human being could ask. He would be willing, of course, to keep it for her for ever.

The discreet door shut with a click. She was outside on the step, gazing at the winter afternoon. Rain was falling, and with the rain it seemed the dark came too, spinning down like ashes. There was a cold bitter taste in the air, and the newlighted lamps looked sad. Sad were the lights in the houses opposite. Dimly they burned as if regretting something. And people hurried by, hidden under their hateful umbrellas. Rosemary felt a strange pang. She pressed her muff against her breast; she wished she had the little box, too, to cling to. Of course the car was there. She'd only to cross the pavement. But still she waited. There are moments, horrible moments in life, when one emerges from shelter and looks out, and it's awful. One oughtn't to give way to them. One ought to go home and have an extra special tea. But at the very instant of thinking that, a young girl, thin, dark, shadowy—where had she come from—was standing at Rosemary's elbow and a voice like a sigh, almost like a sob, breathed: 'Madam, may I speak to you a moment?'

'Speak to me?' Rosemary turned. She saw a little battered creature with enormous eyes, someone quite young, no older than herself, who clutched at her coat-collar with reddened hands, and shivered as though she had just come out of the water.

'M-madam,' stammered the voice. 'Would you let me have the price of a cup of tea?'

'A cup of tea?' There was something simple, sincere in that voice; it wasn't in the least the voice of a beggar. 'Then have you no money at all?' asked Rosemary.

'None, madam,' came the answer.

'How extraordinary!' Rosemary peered through the dusk and the girl gazed back at her. How more than extraordinary! And suddenly it seemed to Rosemary such an adventure. It was like something out of a novel by Dostoevsky, this meeting in the dusk. Supposing she took the girl home? Supposing she did do one of those things she was always reading about or seeing on the stage, what would happen? It would be thrilling. And she heard herself saying afterwards to the amazement of her friends: 'I simply took her home with me,' as she stepped forward and said to that dim person beside her: 'Come home to tea with me.'

The girl drew back startled. She even stopped shivering for a moment.

Rosemary put out a hand and touched her arm. 'I mean it,' she said, smiling. And she felt how simple and kind her smile was. 'Why won't you? Do. Come home with me now in my car and have tea.'

'You—you don't mean it, madam,' said the girl, and there was pain in her voice.

'But I do,' cried Rosemary. 'I want you to. To please me. Come along.'

The girl put her fingers to her lips and her eyes devoured Rosemary. 'You're—you're not taking me to the police station?' she stammered.

'The police station!' Rosemary laughed out. 'Why should I be so cruel? No, I only want to make you warm and to hear—anything you care to tell me.'

Hungry people are easily led. The footman held the door of the car open, and a moment later they were skimming through the dusk.

'There!' said Rosemary. She had a feeling of triumph as she slipped her hand through the velvet strap. She could have said, 'Now I've got you,' as she gazed at the little captive she had netted. But of course she meant it kindly. Oh, more than kindly. She was going to prove to this girl that—wonderful things did happen in life, that—fairy godmothers were real, that—rich people had hearts, and that women *were* sisters.

She turned impulsively, saying, 'Don't be frightened. After all, why shouldn't you come back with me? We're both women. If I'm the more fortunate, you ought to expect...'

But happily at that moment, for she didn't know how the sentence was going to end, the car stopped. The bell was rung, the door opened, and with a charming, protecting, almost embracing movement, Rosemary drew the other into the hall.

Warmth, softness, light, a sweet scent, all those things so familiar to her she never even thought about them, she watched that other receive. It was fascinating. She was like the rich little girl in her nursery with all the cupboards to open, all the boxes to unpack.

'Come, come upstairs,' said Rosemary, longing to begin to be generous.

'Come up to my room.' And, besides, she wanted to spare this poor little thing from being stared at by the servants; she decided as they mounted the stairs she would not even ring to Jeanne, but take off her things by herself. The great thing was to be natural!

And 'There!' cried Rosemary again, as they reached her beautiful big bedroom with the curtains drawn, the fire leaping on her wonderful lacquer furniture, her gold cushions and the primrose and blue rugs.

The girl stood just inside the door; she seemed dazed. But Rosemary didn't mind that.

'Come and sit down,' she cried, dragging her big chair up to the fire, 'in this comfy chair. Come and get warm. You look so dreadfully cold.'

'I daren't, madam,' said the girl, and she edged backwards.

'Oh, please,'—Rosemary ran forward—'you mustn't be frightened, you mustn't, really. Sit down, when I've taken off my things we shall go into the next room and have tea and be cozy. Why are you afraid?' And gently she half pushed the thin figure into its deep cradle.

But there was no answer. The girl stayed just as she had been put, with her hands by her sides and her mouth slightly open. To be quite sincere, she looked rather stupid. But Rosemary wouldn't acknowledge it. She leant over her, saying:

'Won't you take off your hat? Your pretty hair is all wet. And one is so much more comfortable without a hat, isn't one?'

There was a whisper that sounded like 'Very good, madam,' and the crushed hat was taken off.

'And let me help you off with your coat, too,' said Rosemary.

The girl stood up. But she held on to the chair with one hand and let Rosemary pull. It was quite an effort. The other scarcely helped her at all. She seemed to stagger like a child, and the thought came and went through Rosemary's mind, that if people wanted helping they must respond a little, just a little, otherwise it became very difficult indeed. And what was she to do with the coat now? She left it on the floor, and the hat too. She was just going to take a cigarette off the mantelpiece when the girl said quickly, but so lightly and strangely: 'I'm very sorry, madam, but I'm going to faint. I shall go off, madam, if I don't have something.'

'Good heavens, how thoughtless I am!' Rosemary rushed to the bell.

'Tea! Tea at once! And some brandy immediately!'

The maid was gone again, but the girl almost cried out: 'No, I don't want no brandy. I never drink brandy. It's a cup of tea I want, madam.' And she burst into tears.

It was a terrible and fascinating moment. Rosemary knelt beside her chair.

'Don't cry, poor little thing,' she said. 'Don't cry.' And she gave the other her lace handkerchief. She really was touched beyond words. She put her arm round those thin, bird-like shoulders.

Now at last the other forgot to be shy, forgot everything except that they were both women, and gasped out: 'I can't go on no longer like this. I can't bear it. I can't bear it. I shall do away with myself. I can't bear no more.'

'You shan't have to. I'll look after you. Don't cry any more. Don't you see what a good thing it was that you met me? We'll have tea and you'll tell me everything. And I shall arrange something. I promise. Do stop crying. It's so exhausting. Please!'

The other did stop just in time for Rosemary to get up before the tea came. She had the table placed between them. She plied the poor little creature with everything, all the sandwiches, all the bread and butter, and every time her cup was empty she filled it with tea, cream and sugar. People always said sugar was so nourishing. As for herself she didn't eat; she smoked and looked away tactfully so that the other should not be shy.

And really the effect of that slight meal was marvellous. When the tea-table was carried away a new being, a light, frail creature with tangled hair, dark lips, deep, lighted eyes, lay back in the big chair in a kind of sweet languor, looking at the blaze. Rosemary lit a fresh cigarette; it was time to begin.

'And when did you have your last meal?' she asked softly.

But at that moment the door-handle turned.

'Rosemary, may I come in?' It was Philip.

'Of course.'

He came in. 'Oh, I'm so sorry,' he said, and stopped and stared.

'It's quite all right,' said Rosemary, smiling. 'This is my friend, Miss—'

'Smith, madam,' said the languid figure, who was strangely still and unafraid.

'Smith,' said Rosemary. 'We are going to have a little talk.'

'Oh yes,' said Philip. 'Quite,' and his eye caught sight of the coat and hat on the floor. He came over to the fire and turned his back to it. 'It's a beastly afternoon,' he said curiously, still looking at that listless figure, looking at its hands and boots, and then at Rosemary again.

'Yes, isn't it?' said Rosemary enthusiastically. 'Vile.'

Philip smiled his charming smile. 'As a matter of fact,' said he, 'I wanted you to come into the library for a moment. Would you? Will Miss Smith excuse us?'

The big eyes were raised to him, but Rosemary answered for her: 'Of course she will.' And they went out of the room together.

'I say,' said Philip, when they were alone. 'Explain. Who is she? What does it all mean?'

Rosemary, laughing, leaned against the door and said: 'I picked her up in Curzon Street. Really. She's a real pick-up. She asked me for the price of a cup of tea, and I brought her home with me.'

'But what on earth are you going to do with her?' cried Philip.

'Be nice to her,' said Rosemary quickly. 'Be frightfully nice to her. Look after her. I don't know how. We haven't talked yet. But show her—treat her—make her feel—'

'My darling girl,' said Philip, 'you're quite mad, you know. It simply can't be done.'

'I knew you'd say that,' retorted Rosemary. 'Why not? I want to. Isn't that a reason? And besides, one's always reading about these things. I decided—'

'But,' said Philip slowly, and he cut the end of a cigar, 'she's so astonishingly pretty.'

'Pretty?' Rosemary was so surprised that she blushed. 'Do you think so? I—I hadn't thought about it.'

'Good Lord!' Philip struck a match. 'She's absolutely lovely. Look again, my child. I was bowled over when I came into your room just now. However... I think you're making a ghastly mistake. Sorry, darling, if I'm crude and all that. But let me know if Miss Smith is going to dine with us in time for me to look up *The Milliner's Gazette*.'

'You absurd creature!' said Rosemary, and she went out of the library, but not back to her bedroom. She went to her writing-room and sat down at her desk.

Pretty! Absolutely lovely! Bowled over! Her heart beat like a heavy bell. Pretty! Lovely! She drew her cheque book towards her. But no, cheques would be no use, of course. She opened a drawer and took out five pound notes, looked at them, put two back, and holding the three squeezed in her hand, she went back to her bedroom.

Half an hour later Philip was still in the library, when Rosemary came in.

'I only wanted to tell you,' said she, and she leaned against the door again and looked at him with her dazzled exotic gaze, 'Miss Smith won't dine with us tonight.' Philip put down the paper. 'Oh, what's happened? Previous engagement?'

Rosemary came over and sat down on his knee. 'She insisted on going,' said she, 'so I gave the poor little thing a present of money. I couldn't keep her against her will, could I?' she added softly. Rosemary had just done her hair, darkened her eyes a little and put on her pearls. She put up her hands and touched Philip's cheeks.

'Do you like me?' said she, and her tone, sweet, husky, troubled him.

'I like you awfully,' he said, and he held her tighter. 'Kiss me.' There was a pause. Then Rosemary said dreamily: 'I saw a fascinating little box today. It cost twenty-eight guineas. May I have it?' Philip jumped her on his knee. 'You may, little wasteful one,' said he.

But that was not really what Rosemary wanted to say.

'Philip,' she whispered, and she pressed his head against her bosom, 'am I *pretty*?'

―∞―

The theme of jealousy, insecurity, materialism and class form the epicenter of this story. A narrative over a cup of tea turns out with many questions of insecurity. To be vulgarly good can be fragile also.

37
A CHAMELEON
ANTON CHEKHOV

The police superintendent Otchumyelov is walking across the market square wearing a new overcoat and carrying a parcel under his arm. A red-haired policeman strides after him with a sieve full of confiscated gooseberries in his hands. There is silence all around. Not a soul in the square.... The open doors of the shops and taverns look out upon God's world disconsolately, like hungry mouths; there is not even a beggar near them.

'So you bite, you damned brute?' Otchumyelov hears suddenly. 'Lads, don't let him go! Biting is prohibited nowadays! Hold him! ah ... ah!'

There is the sound of a dog yelping. Otchumyelov looks in the direction of the sound and sees a dog, hopping on three legs and looking about her, run out of Pitchugin's timber-yard. A man in a starched cotton shirt, with his waistcoat unbuttoned, is chasing her. He runs after her, and throwing his body forward falls down and seizes the dog by her hind legs. Once more there is a yelping and a shout of 'Don't let go!' Sleepy countenances are protruded from the shops, and soon a crowd, which seems to have sprung out of the earth, is gathered round the timber-yard.

'It looks like a row, your honour ... ' says the policeman.

Otchumyelov makes a half turn to the left and strides towards the crowd.

He sees the aforementioned man in the unbuttoned waistcoat standing close by the gate of the timber-yard, holding his right hand in the air and displaying a bleeding finger to the crowd. On his half-drunken face there is plainly written: 'I'll pay you out, you rogue!' and indeed the very finger has the look of a flag of victory. In this man Otchumyelov recognises Hryukin, the goldsmith. The culprit who has caused the sensation, a white borzoy puppy with a sharp muzzle and a yellow patch on her back, is sitting on the ground with her fore-paws outstretched in the middle of the crowd, trembling all over. There is an expression of misery and terror in her tearful eyes.

'What's it all about?' Otchumyelov inquires, pushing his way through the crowd. 'What are you here for? Why are you waving your finger ... ? Who was it shouted?'

'I was walking along here, not interfering with anyone, your honour,' Hryukin begins, coughing into his fist. 'I was talking about firewood to Mitry Mitritch, when this low brute for no rhyme or reason bit my finger .... You must excuse me, I am a working man.... Mine is fine work. I must have damages, for I shan't be able to use this finger for a week, may be.... It's not even the law, your honour, that one should put up with it from a beast.... If everyone is going to be bitten, life won't be worth living ....'

'H'm. Very good,' says Otchumyelov sternly, coughing and raising his eyebrows. 'Very good. Whose dog is it? I won't let this pass! I'll teach them to let their dogs run all over the place! It's time these gentry were looked after, if they won't obey the regulations! When he's fined, the blackguard, I'll teach him what it means to keep dogs and such stray cattle! I'll give him a lesson! ... Yeldyrin,' cries the superintendent, addressing the policeman, 'find out whose dog this is and draw up a report! And the dog must be strangled. Without delay! It's sure to be mad.... Whose dog is it, I ask?'

'I fancy it's General Zhigalov's,' says someone in the crowd.

'General Zhigalov's, h'm .... Help me off with my coat, Yeldyrin ... it's frightfully hot! It must be a sign of rain .... There's one thing I can't make out, how it came to bite you?' Otchumyelov turns to Hryukin. 'Surely it couldn't reach your finger. It's a little dog, and you are a great hulking fellow! You must have scratched your finger with a nail, and then the idea struck you to get damages for it. We all know ... your sort! I know you devils!'

'He put a cigarette in her face, your honour, for a joke, and she had the sense to snap at him .... He is a nonsensical fellow, your honour!'

'That's a lie, Squinteye! You didn't see, so why tell lies about it? His honour is a wise gentleman, and will see who is telling lies and who is telling the truth, as in God's sight.... And if I am lying let the court decide. It's written in the law .... We are all equal nowadays. My own brother is in the *gendarmes* ... let me tell you....'

'Don't argue!'

'No, that's not the General's dog,' says the policeman, with profound conviction, 'the General hasn't got one like that. His are mostly setters.'

'Do you know that for a fact?'

'Yes, your honour.'

'I know it, too. The General has valuable dogs, thoroughbred, and this is goodness knows what! No coat, no shape... A low creature. And to keep a dog like that! ... where's the sense of it. If a dog like that were to turn up in Petersburg or Moscow, do you know what would happen? They would not worry about the law, they would strangle it in a twinkling! You've been injured, Hryukin, and we can't let the matter drop ... We must give them a lesson! It is high time ...!'

'Yet maybe it is the General's,' says the policeman, thinking aloud. 'It's not written on its face .... I saw one like it the other day in his yard.'

'It is the General's, that's certain!' says a voice in the crowd.

'H'm, help me on with my overcoat, Yeldyrin, my lad ... the wind's getting up... I am cold .... You take it to the General's, and inquire there. Say I found it and sent it. And tell them not to let it out into the street.... It may be a valuable dog, and if every swine goes sticking a cigar in its mouth, it will soon be ruined. A dog is a delicate animal.... And you put your hand down, you blockhead. It's no use your displaying your fool of a finger. It's your own fault....'

'Here comes the General's cook, ask him ... Hi, Prohor! Come here, my dear man! Look at this dog.... Is it one of yours?'

'What an idea! We have never had one like that!'

'There's no need to waste time asking,' says Otchumyelov. 'It's a stray dog! There's no need to waste time talking about it.... Since he says it's a stray dog, a stray dog it is.... It must be destroyed, that's all about it.'

'It is not our dog,' Prohor goes on. 'It belongs to the General's brother, who arrived the other day. Our master does not care for hounds. But his honour is fond of them....'

You don't say his Excellency's brother is here? Vladimir Ivanitch?' inquires Otchumyelov, and his whole face beams with an ecstatic smile. 'Well, I never! And I didn't know! Has he come on a visit?'

'Yes.'

'Well, I never ... He couldn't stay away from his brother.... And there I didn't know! So this is his honour's dog? Delighted to hear it ... Take it. It's not a bad pup ... A lively creature ... Snapped at this fellow's finger! Ha-ha-ha... Come, why are you shivering? Rrr ... Rrrr... The rogue's angry ... a nice little pup.'

Prohor calls the dog, and walks away from the timber-yard with her. The crowd laughs at Hryukin.

'I'll make you smart yet!' Otchumyelov threatens him, and wrapping himself in his greatcoat, goes on his way across the square.

'The Chameleon' expresses a deep truth about human behaviour in a detailed setting. The title refers to a police officer who changes his mind several times about how to act in a situation where he doesn't know all the facts.

38

THE OUTSIDER

H.P. LOVECRAFT

That night the Baron dreamt of many a woe;
And all his warrior-guests, with shade and form
Of witch, and demon, and large coffin-worm,
Were long be-nightmared.
—*Keats.*

Unhappy is he to whom the memories of childhood bring only fear and sadness. Wretched is he who looks back upon lone hours in vast and dismal chambers with brown hangings and maddening rows of antique books, or upon awed watches in twilight groves of grotesque, gigantic, and vine-encumbered trees that silently wave twisted branches far aloft. Such a lot the gods gave to me—to me, the dazed, the disappointed; the barren, the broken. And yet I am strangely content, and cling desperately to those sere memories, when my mind momentarily threatens to reach beyond to the other.

I know not where I was born, save that the castle was infinitely old and infinitely horrible; full of dark passages and having high ceilings where the eye could find only cobwebs and shadows. The stones in the crumbling corridors seemed always hideously damp, and there was an accursed smell everywhere, as of the piled-up corpses of dead generations. It was never light, so that I used sometimes to light candles and gaze steadily at them for relief; nor was there any sun outdoors, since the terrible trees grew high above the topmost accessible tower. There was one black tower which reached above the trees into the unknown outer sky, but that was partly ruined and could not be ascended save by a well-nigh impossible climb up the sheer wall, stone by stone.

I must have lived years in this place, but I cannot measure the time. Beings must have cared for my needs, yet I cannot recall any person except myself; or anything alive but the noiseless rats and bats and spiders. I think that whoever nursed me must have been shockingly aged, since my first conception of a living person was that of something mockingly like myself, yet distorted, shriveled, and decaying like the castle. To me there was nothing grotesque in the bones and skeletons that strowed some of the stone crypts deep down among the foundations. I fantastically associated these things with every-day events, and thought them more natural than the colored pictures of living beings which I found in many of the moldy books. From such books I learned all that I know. No teacher urged or guided me, and I do not recall hearing any human voice in all those years—not even my own; for although I had read of speech, I had never thought to try to speak aloud. My aspect was a matter equally unthought of, for there were no mirrors in the castle, and I merely regarded myself by instinct as akin to the youthful figures I saw drawn and painted in the books. I felt conscious of youth because I remembered so little.

Outside, across the putrid moat and under the dark mute trees, I would often lie and dream for hours about what I read in the books; and would longingly picture myself amidst gay crowds in the sunny world beyond the endless forest. Once I tried to escape from the forest, but as I went farther from the castle the shade grew denser and the air more filled with brooding fear; so that I ran frantically back lest I lose my way in a labyrinth of nighted silence.

So through endless twilights I dreamed and waited, though I knew not what I waited for. Then in the shadowy solitude my longing for light grew so frantic that I could rest no more, and I lifted entreating hands to the single black ruined tower that reached above the forest into the unknown outer sky. And at last I resolved to scale that tower, fall though I might; since it were better to glimpse the sky and perish, than to live without ever beholding day.

In the dank twilight I climbed the worn and aged stone stairs till I reached the level where they ceased, and thereafter clung perilously to small footholds leading upward. Ghastly and terrible was that dead, stairless cylinder of rock; black, ruined, and deserted, and sinister with startled bats whose wings made no noise. But more ghastly and terrible still was the slowness of my progress; for climb as I might, the darkness overhead grew no thinner, and a new chill as of haunted and venerable mold assailed me. I shivered as I wondered why I did not reach the light, and would have looked down had I dared. I fancied that night had come suddenly upon me, and vainly groped with one free hand for a window embrasure, that I might peer out and above, and try to judge the height I had attained.

All at once, after an infinity of awesome, sightless crawling up that concave and desperate precipice, I felt my head touch a solid thing, and I knew I must have gained the roof, or at least some kind of floor. In the darkness I raised my free hand and tested the barrier, finding it stone and immovable. Then came a deadly circuit of the tower, clinging to whatever holds the slimy wall could give; till finally my testing hand found the barrier yielding, and I turned upward again, pushing the slab or door with my head as I used both hands in my fearful ascent. There was no light revealed above, and as my hands went higher I knew that my climb was for the nonce ended; since the slab was the trap-door of an aperture leading to a level stone surface of greater circumference than the lower tower, no doubt the floor of some lofty and capacious observation chamber. I crawled through carefully, and tried to prevent the heavy slab from falling back into place; but failed in the latter attempt. As I lay exhausted on the stone floor I heard the eerie echoes of its fall, but hoped when necessary to pry it open again.

Believing I was now at a prodigious height, far above the accursed branches of the wood, I dragged myself up from the floor and fumbled about for windows, that I might look for the first time upon the sky, and the moon and stars of which I had read. But on every hand I was disappointed; since all that I found were vast shelves of marble, bearing odious oblong boxes of disturbing size. More and more I reflected, and wondered what hoary secrets might abide in this high apartment so many eons cut off from the castle below. Then unexpectedly my hands came upon a doorway, where hung a portal of stone, rough with strange chiseling. Trying it, I found it locked; but with a supreme burst of strength I overcame all obstacles and dragged it open inward. As I did so there came to me the purest ecstasy I have ever known; for shining tranquilly through an ornate grating of iron, and down a short stone passageway of steps that ascended from the newly found doorway, was the radiant full moon, which I had never before seen save in dreams and in vague visions I dared not call memories.

Fancying now that I had attained the very pinnacle of the castle, I commenced to rush up the few steps beyond the door; but the sudden veiling of the moon by a cloud caused me to stumble, and I felt my way more slowly in the dark. It was still very dark when I reached the grating—which I tried carefully and found unlocked, but which I did not open for fear of falling from the amazing height to which I had climbed. Then the moon came out.

Most demoniacal of all shocks is that of the abysmally unexpected and grotesquely unbelievable. Nothing I had before undergone could compare in terror with what I now saw; with the bizarre marvels that sight implied. The sight itself was as simple as it was stupefying, for it was merely this: instead of a dizzying prospect of treetops seen from a lofty eminence, there stretched around me on a level through the grating nothing less than the solid ground, decked and diversified by marble slabs and columns, and overshadowed by an ancient stone church, whose ruined spire gleamed spectrally in the moonlight.

Half unconscious, I opened the grating and staggered out upon the white gravel path that stretched away in two directions. My mind, stunned and chaotic as it was, still held the frantic craving for light; and not even the fantastic wonder which had happened could stay my course. I neither knew nor cared whether my experience was insanity, dreaming, or magic; but was determined to gaze on brilliance and gaiety at any cost. I knew not who I was or what I was, or what my surroundings might be; though as I continued to stumble along I became conscious of a kind of fearsome latent memory that made my progress not wholly fortuitous. I passed under an arch out of that region of slabs and columns, and wandered through the open country; sometimes following the visible road, but sometimes leaving it curiously to tread across meadows where only occasional ruins bespoke the ancient presence of a forgotten road. Once I swam across a swift river where crumbling, mossy masonry told of a bridge long vanished.

Over two hours must have passed before I reached what seemed to be my goal, a venerable ivied castle in a thickly wooded park; maddeningly familiar, yet full of perplexing strangeness to me. I saw that the moat was filled in, and that some of the well-known towers were demolished; whilst new wings existed to confuse the beholder. But what I observed with chief interest and delight were the open windows—gorgeously ablaze with light and sending forth sound of the gayest revelry. Advancing to one of these I looked in and saw an oddly dressed company, indeed; making merry, and speaking brightly to one another. I had never, seemingly, heard human speech before; and could guess only vaguely what was said. Some of the faces seemed to hold expressions that brought up incredibly remote recollections; others were utterly alien.

I now stepped through the low window into the brilliantly lighted room, stepping as I did so from my single bright moment of hope to my blackest convulsion of despair and realization. The nightmare was quick to come; for as I entered, there occurred immediately one of the most terrifying demonstrations I had ever conceived. Scarcely had I crossed the sill when there descended upon the whole company a sudden and unheralded fear of hideous intensity, distorting every face and evoking the most horrible screams from nearly every throat. Flight was universal, and in the clamor and panic several fell in a swoon and were dragged away by their madly fleeing companions. Many covered their eyes with their hands, and plunged blindly and awkwardly in their race to escape; overturning furniture and stumbling against the walls before they managed to reach one of the many doors.

The cries were shocking; and as I stood in the brilliant apartment alone and dazed, listening to their vanishing echoes, I trembled at the thought of what might be lurking near me unseen. At a casual inspection the room seemed deserted, but when I moved toward one of the alcoves I thought I detected a presence there—a hint of motion beyond the golden-arched doorway leading to another and somewhat similar room. As I approached the arch I began to perceive the presence more clearly; and then, with the first and last sound I ever uttered—a ghastly ululation that revolted me almost as poignantly as its noxious cause—I beheld in full, frightful vividness the inconceivable, indescribable, and unmentionable monstrosity which had by its simple appearance changed a merry company to a herd of delirious fugitives.

I cannot even hint what it was like, for it was a compound of all that is unclean, uncanny, unwelcome, abnormal, and detestable. It was the ghoulish shade of decay, antiquity, and desolation; the putrid, dripping eidolon of unwholesome revelation; the awful baring of that which the merciful earth should always hide. God knows it was not of this world—or no longer of this world—yet to my horror I saw in its eaten-away and bone-revealing outlines a leering, abhorrent travesty on the human shape; and in its moldy, disintegrating apparel an unspeakable quality that chilled me even more.

I was almost paralyzed, but not too much so to make a feeble effort toward flight; a backward stumble which failed to break the spell in which the nameless, voiceless monster held me. My eyes, bewitched by the glassy orbs which stared loathsomely into them, refused to close; though they were mercifully blurred, and shewed the terrible object but indistinctly after the first shock. I tried to raise my hand to shut out the sight, yet so stunned were my nerves that my arm could not fully obey my will. The attempt, however, was enough to disturb my balance; so that I had to stagger forward several steps to avoid falling. As I did so I became suddenly and agonizingly aware of the nearness of the carrion thing, whose hideous hollow breathing I half fancied I could hear. Nearly mad, I found myself yet able to throw out a hand to ward off the fetid apparition which pressed so close; when in one cataclysmic second of cosmic nightmarishness and hellish accident my fingers touched the rotting outstretched paw of the monster beneath the golden arch.

I did not shriek, but all the fiendish ghouls that ride the night-wind shrieked for me as in that same second there crashed down upon my mind a single and fleeting avalanche of soul-annihilating memory. I knew in that second all that had been; I remembered beyond the frightful castle and the trees, and recognized the altered edifice in which I now stood; I recognized, most terrible of all, the unholy abomination that stood leering before me as I withdrew my sullied fingers from its own.

But in the cosmos there is balm as well as bitterness, and that balm is nepenthe. In the supreme horror of that second I forgot what had horrified me, and the burst of black memory vanished in a chaos of echoing images. In a dream I fled from that haunted and accursed pile, and ran swiftly and silently in the moonlight. When I returned to the churchyard place of marble and went down the steps I found the stone trap-door immovable; but I was not sorry, for I had hated the antique castle and the trees. Now I ride with the mocking and friendly ghouls on the night-wind, and play by day amongst the catacombs of Nephren-Ka in the sealed and unknown valley of Hadoth by the Nile. I know that light is not for me, save that of the moon over the rock tombs of Neb, nor any gaiety save the unnamed feasts of Nitokris beneath the Great Pyramid; yet in my new wildness and freedom I almost welcome the bitterness of alienage.

For although nepenthe has calmed me, I know always that I am an outsider; a stranger in this century and among those who are still men. This I have known ever since I stretched out my fingers to the abomination within that great gilded frame; stretched out my fingers and touched a cold and unyielding surface of polished glass.

∞

Nightmare: 'I must have lived years in this place, but I cannot measure the time"... the horror world of noiseless rats and bats and spiders.

THE PICTURE IN THE HOUSE

H.P. LOVECRAFT

Searchers after horror haunt strange, far places. For them are the catacombs of Ptolemais, and the carven mausolea of the nightmare countries. They climb to the moonlit towers of ruined Rhine castles, and falter down black cobwebbed steps beneath the scattered stones of forgotten cities in Asia. The haunted wood and the desolate mountain are their shrines, and they linger around the sinister monoliths on uninhabited islands. But the true epicure in the terrible, to whom a new thrill of unutterable ghastliness is the chief end and justification of existence, esteems most of all the ancient, lonely farmhouses of backwoods New England; for there the dark elements of strength, solitude, grotesqueness, and ignorance combine to form the perfection of the hideous.

Most horrible of all sights are the little unpainted wooden houses remote from traveled ways, usually squatted upon some damp, grassy slope or leaning against some gigantic outcropping of rock. Two hundred years and more they have leaned or squatted there, while the vines have crawled and the trees have swelled and spread. They are almost hidden now in lawless luxuriances of green and guardian shrouds of shadow; but the small-paned windows still stare shockingly, as if blinking through a lethal stupor which wards off madness by dulling the memory of unutterable things.

In such houses have dwelt generations of strange people, whose like the world has never seen. Seized with a gloomy and fanatical belief which exiled them from their kind, their ancestors sought the wilderness for freedom. There the scions of a conquering race indeed flourished free from the restrictions of their fellows, but cowered in an appalling slavery to the dismal phantasms of their own minds. Divorced from the enlightenment of civilization, the strength of these Puritans turned into singular channels; and in their isolation, morbid self-repression, and struggle for life with relentless Nature, there came to them dark furtive traits from the prehistoric depths of their cold Northern heritage. By necessity practical and by philosophy stern, these folk were not beautiful in their sins. Erring as all mortals must, they were forced by their rigid code to seek concealment above all else; so that they came to use less and less taste in what they concealed. Only the silent, sleepy, staring houses in the backwoods can tell all that has lain hidden since the early days; and they are not communicative, being loath to shake off the drowsiness which helps them forget. Sometimes one feels that it would be merciful to tear down these houses, for they must often dream.

It was to a time-battered edifice of this description that I was driven one afternoon in November, 1896, by a rain of such chilling copiousness that any shelter was preferable to exposure. I had been traveling for some time amongst the people of the Miskatonic Valley in quest of certain genealogical data; and from the remote, devious, and problematical nature of my course, had deemed it convenient to employ a bicycle despite the lateness of the season. Now I found myself upon an apparently abandoned road which I had chosen as the shortest cut to Arkham; overtaken by the storm at a point far from any town, and confronted with no refuge save the antique and repellent wooden building which blinked with bleared windows from between two huge leafless elms near the foot of a rocky hill. Distant though it was from the remnant of a road, the house none the less impressed me unfavorably the very moment I espied it. Honest, wholesome structures do not stare at travelers so slyly and hauntingly, and in my genealogical researches I had encountered legends of a century before which biased me against places of this kind. Yet the force of the elements was such as to overcome my scruples, and I did not hesitate to wheel my machine up the weedy rise to the closed door which seemed at once so suggestive and secretive.

I had somehow taken it for granted that the house was abandoned, yet as I approached it I was not so sure; for though the walks were indeed overgrown with weeds, they seemed to retain their nature a little too well to argue complete desertion. Therefore instead of trying the door I knocked, feeling as I did so a trepidation I could scarcely explain. As I waited on the rough, mossy rock which served as a doorstep, I glanced at the neighboring windows and the panes of the transom above me, and noticed that although old, rattling, and almost opaque with dirt, they were not broken. The building, then, must still be inhabited, despite its isolation and general neglect. However, my rapping evoked no response, so after repeating the summons I tried the rusty latch and found the door unfastened. Inside was a little vestibule with walls from which the plaster was falling, and through the doorway came a faint but peculiarly hateful odor. I entered, carrying my bicycle, and closed the door behind me. Ahead rose a narrow staircase, flanked by a small door probably leading to the cellar, while to the left and right were closed doors leading to rooms on the ground floor.

Leaning my cycle against the wall I opened the door at the left, and crossed into a small low-ceiled chamber but dimly lighted by its two dusty windows and furnished in the barest and most primitive possible way. It appeared to be a kind of sitting-room, for it had a table and several chairs, and an immense fireplace above which ticked an antique clock on a mantel. Books and papers were very few, and in the prevailing gloom I could not readily discern the titles. What interested me was the uniform air of archaism as displayed in every visible detail. Most of the houses in this region I had found rich in relics of the past, but here the antiquity was curiously complete; for in all the room I could not discover a single article of definitely post-revolutionary date. Had the furnishings been less humble, the place would have been a collector's paradise.

As I surveyed this quaint apartment, I felt an increase in that aversion first excited by the bleak exterior of the house. Just what it was that I feared or loathed, I could by no means define; but something in the whole atmosphere seemed redolent of unhallowed age, of unpleasant crudeness, and of secrets which should be forgotten. I felt disinclined to sit down, and wandered about examining the various articles which I had noticed. The first object of my curiosity was a book of medium size lying upon the table and presenting such an antediluvian aspect that I marveled at beholding it outside a museum or library. It was bound in leather with metal fittings, and was in an excellent state of preservation; being altogether an unusual sort of volume to encounter in an abode so lowly. When I opened it to the title page my wonder grew even greater, for it proved to be nothing less rare than Pigafetta's account of the Congo region, written in Latin from the notes of the sailor Lopez and printed at Frankfort in 1598. I had often heard of this work, with its curious illustrations by the brothers De Bry, hence for a moment forgot my uneasiness in my desire to turn the pages before me. The engravings were indeed interesting, drawn wholly from imagination and careless descriptions, and represented negroes with white skins and Caucasian features; nor would I soon have closed the book had not an exceedingly trivial circumstance upset my tired nerves and revived my sensation of disquiet. What annoyed me was merely the persistent way in which the volume tended to fall open of itself at Plate XII, which represented in gruesome detail a butcher's shop of the cannibal Anziques. I experienced some shame at my susceptibility to so slight a thing, but the drawing nevertheless disturbed me, especially in connexion with some adjacent passages descriptive of Anzique gastronomy.

I had turned to a neighboring shelf and was examining its meagre literary contents—an eighteenth-century Bible, a *Pilgrim's Progress* of like period, illustrated with grotesque woodcuts and printed by the almanack-maker Isaiah Thomas, the rotting bulk of Cotton Mather's *Magnalia Christi Americana,* and a few other books of evidently equal age—when my attention was aroused by the unmistakable sound of walking in the room overhead. At first astonished and startled, considering the lack of response to my recent knocking at the door, I immediately afterward concluded that the walker had just awakened from a sound sleep; and listened with less surprise as the footsteps sounded on the creaking stairs. The tread was heavy, yet seemed to contain a curious quality of cautiousness; a quality which I disliked the more because the tread was heavy. When I had entered the room I had shut the door behind me. Now, after a moment of silence during which the walker may have been inspecting my bicycle in the hall, I heard a fumbling at the latch and saw the paneled portal swing open again.

In the doorway stood a person of such singular appearance that I should have exclaimed aloud but for the restraints of good breeding. Old, white-bearded, and ragged, my host possessed a countenance and physique which inspired equal wonder and respect. His height could not have been less than six feet, and despite a general air of age and poverty he was stout and powerful in proportion. His face, almost hidden by a long beard which grew high on the cheeks, seemed abnormally ruddy and less wrinkled than one might expect; while over a high forehead fell a shock of white hair little thinned by the years. His blue eyes, though a trifle bloodshot, seemed inexplicably keen and burning. But for his horrible unkemptness the man would have been as distinguished-looking as he was impressive. This unkemptness, however, made him offensive despite his face and figure. Of what his clothing consisted I could hardly tell, for it seemed to me no more than a mass of tatters surmounting a pair of high, heavy boots; and his lack of cleanliness surpassed description.

The appearance of this man, and the instinctive fear he inspired, prepared me for something like enmity; so that I almost shuddered through surprise and a sense of uncanny incongruity when he motioned me to a chair and addressed me in a thin, weak voice full of fawning respect and ingratiating hospitality.

His speech was very curious, an extreme form of Yankee dialect I had thought long extinct; and I studied it closely as he sat down opposite me for conversation.

'Ketched in the rain, be ye?' he greeted. 'Glad ye was nigh the haouse en' hed the sense ta come right in. I calc'late I was asleep, else I'd a heerd ye—I ain't as young as I uster be, an' I need a paowerful sight o' naps naowadays. Trav'lin' fur? I hain't seed many folks 'long this rud since they tuk off the Arkham stage.'

I replied that I was going to Arkham, and apologized for my rude entry into his domicile, whereupon he continued.

'Glad ta see ye, young Sir—new faces is scurce arount here, an' I hain't got much ta cheer me up these days. Guess yew hail from Bosting, don't ye? I never ben thar, but I kin tell a taown man when I see 'im—we hed one fer deestrick schoolmaster in 'eighty-four, but he quit suddent an' no one never heerd on 'im sence—' Here the old man lapsed into a kind of chuckle, and made no explanation when I questioned him. He seemed to be in an aboundingly good humour, yet to possess those eccentricities which one might guess from his grooming. For some time he rambled on with an almost feverish geniality, when it struck me to ask him how he came by so rare a book as Pigafetta's *Regnum Congo*. The effect of this volume had not left me, and I felt a certain hesitancy in speaking of it; but curiosity overmastered all the vague fears which had steadily accumulated since my first glimpse of the house. To my relief, the question did not seem an awkward one; for the old man answered freely and volubly.

'Oh, thet Afriky book? Cap'n Ebenezer Holt traded me thet in 'sixty-eight—him as was kilt in the war.' Something about the name of Ebenezer Holt caused me to look up sharply. I had encountered it in my genealogical work, but not in any record since the Revolution. I wondered if my host could help me in the task at which I was laboring, and resolved to ask him about it later on. He continued.

'Ebenezer was on a Salem merchantman for years, an' picked up a sight o' queer stuff in every port. He got this in London, I guess—he uster like ter buy things at the shops. I was up ta his haouse onct, on the hill, tradin' hosses, when I see this book. I relished the picters, so he give it in on a swap. 'Tis a queer book—here, leave me git on my spectacles—' The old man fumbled among his rags, producing a pair of dirty and amazingly antique glasses with small octagonal lenses and steel bows. Donning these, he reached for the volume on the table and turned the pages lovingly.

'Ebenezer cud read a leetle o' this—'tis Latin—but I can't. I hed two er three schoolmasters read me a bit, and Passon Clark, him they say got draownded in the pond—kin yew make anything outen it?' I told him that I could, and translated for his benefit a paragraph near the beginning. If I erred, he was not scholar enough to correct me; for he seemed childishly pleased at my English version. His proximity was becoming rather obnoxious, yet I saw no way to escape without offending him. I was amused at the childish fondness of this ignorant old man for the pictures in a book he could not read, and wondered how much better he could read the few books in English which adorned the room. This revelation of simplicity removed much of the ill-defined apprehension I had felt, and I smiled as my host rambled on:

'Queer haow picters kin set a body thinkin'. Take this un here near the front. Hev yew ever seed trees like thet, with big leaves a-floppin' over an' daown? And them men—them can't be niggers—they dew beat all. Kinder like Injuns, I guess, even ef they be in Afriky. Some o' these here critters looks like monkeys, or half monkeys an' half men, but I never heerd o' nothing like this un.' Here he pointed to a fabulous creature of the artist, which one might describe as a sort of dragon with the head of an alligator.

'But naow I'll shew ye the best un—over here nigh the middle—' The old man's speech grew a trifle thicker and his eyes assumed a brighter glow; but his fumbling hands, though seemingly clumsier than before, were entirely adequate to their mission. The book fell open, almost of its own accord and as if from frequent consultation at this place, to the repellent twelfth plate shewing a butcher's shop amongst the Anzique cannibals. My sense of restlessness returned, though I did not exhibit it. The especially bizarre thing was that the artist had made his Africans look like white men—the limbs and quarters hanging about the walls of the shop were ghastly, while the butcher with his axe was hideously incongruous. But my host seemed to relish the view as much as I disliked it.

'What d'ye think o' this—ain't never see the like hereabouts, eh? When I see this I telled Eb Holt, "That's suthin' ta stir ye up an' make yer blood tickle!" When I read in Scripter about slayin'—like them Midianites was slew—I kinder think things, but I ain't got no picter of it. Here a body kin see all they is to it—I s'pose 'tis sinful, but ain't we all born an' livin' in sin?—Thet feller bein' chopped up gives me a tickle every time I look at 'im—I hev ta keep lookin' at 'im—see whar the butcher cut off his feet? Thar's his head on thet bench, with one arm side of it, an' t'other arm's on the graound side o' the meat block.'

As the man mumbled on in his shocking ecstasy the expression on his hairy, spectacled face became indescribable, but his voice sank rather than mounted. My own sensations can scarcely be recorded. All the terror I had dimly felt before rushed upon me actively and vividly, and I knew that I loathed the ancient and abhorrent creature so near me with an infinite intensity. His madness, or at least his partial perversion, seemed beyond dispute. He was almost whispering now, with a huskiness more terrible than a scream, and I trembled as I listened.

'As I says, 'tis queer haow picters sets ye thinkin'. D'ye know, young Sir, I'm right sot on this un here. Arter I got the book off Eb I uster look at it a lot, especial when I'd heerd Passon Clark rant o' Sundays in his big wig. Onct I tried suthin' funny—here, young Sir, don't git skeert—all I done was ter look at the picter afore I kilt the sheep for market—killin' sheep was kinder more fun arter lookin' at it—' The tone of the old man now sank very low, sometimes becoming so faint that his words were hardly audible. I listened to the rain, and to the rattling of the bleared, small-paned windows, and marked a rumbling of approaching thunder quite unusual for the season. Once a terrific flash and peal shook the frail house to its foundations, but the whisperer seemed not to notice it.

'Killin' sheep was kinder more fun—but d'ye know, 'twan't quite *satisfyin'*. Queer haow a *cravin'* gits a holt on ye—As ye love the Almighty, young man, don't tell nobody, but I swar ter Gawd thet picter begun ta make me *hungry fer victuals I couldn't raise nor buy*—here, set still, what's ailin' ye?—I didn't do nothin', only I wondered haow 'twud be ef I *did*—They say meat makes blood an' flesh, an' gives ye new life, so I wondered ef 'twudn't make a man live longer an' longer ef 'twas *more the same*—' But the whisperer never continued. The interruption was not produced by my fright, nor by the rapidly increasing storm amidst whose fury I was presently to open my eyes on a smoky solitude of blackened ruins. It was produced by a very simple though somewhat unusual happening.

The open book lay flat between us, with the picture staring repulsively upward. As the old man whispered the words *'more the same'* a tiny spattering impact was heard, and something shewed on the yellowed paper of the upturned volume. I thought of the rain and of a leaky roof, but rain is not red. On the butcher's shop of the Anzique cannibals a small red spattering glistened picturesquely, lending vividness to the horror of the engraving. The old man saw it, and stopped whispering even before my expression of horror made it necessary; saw it and glanced quickly toward the floor of the room he had left an hour before. I followed his glance, and beheld just above us on the loose plaster of the ancient ceiling a large irregular spot of wet crimson which seemed to spread even as I viewed it. I did not shriek or move, but merely shut my eyes. A moment later came the titanic thunderbolt of thunderbolts; blasting that accursed house of unutterable secrets and bringing the oblivion which alone saved my mind.

༺∞༻

Suddenly, a drop of blood falls from the ceiling, clearly coming from the floor above, and splashes onto a page in the book. At that moment, a bolt of lightning destroys the house. Fortunately, the narrator survives to tell of his ordeal.

40

THE HAND

GUY DE MAUPASSANT

All were crowding around M. Bermutier, the judge, who was giving his opinion about the Saint-Cloud mystery. For a month this inexplicable crime had been the talk of Paris. Nobody could make head or tail of it.

M. Bermutier, standing with his back to the fireplace, was talking, citing the evidence, discussing the various theories, but arriving at no conclusion.

Some women had risen, in order to get nearer to him, and were standing with their eyes fastened on the clean-shaven face of the judge, who was saying such weighty things. They were shaking and trembling, moved by fear and curiosity, and by the eager and insatiable desire for the horrible, which haunts the soul of every woman. One of them, paler than the others, said during a pause:

'It's terrible. It verges on the supernatural. The truth will never be known.'

The judge turned to her: 'True, madame, it is likely that the actual facts will never be discovered. As for the word 'supernatural' which you have just used, it has nothing to do with the matter. We are in the presence of a very cleverly conceived and executed crime, so well enshrouded in mystery that we cannot disentangle it from the involved circumstances which surround it. But once I had to take charge of an affair in which the uncanny seemed to play a part. In fact, the case became so confused that it had to be given up.'

Several women exclaimed at once:

'Oh! Tell us about it!'

M. Bermutier smiled in a dignified manner, as a judge should, and went on:

'Do not think, however, that I, for one minute, ascribed anything in the case to supernatural influences. I believe only in normal causes. But if, instead of using the word 'supernatural' to express what we do not understand, we were simply to make use of the word 'inexplicable,' it would be much better. At any rate, in the affair of which I am about to tell you, it is especially the surrounding, preliminary circumstances which impressed me. Here are the facts:

'I was, at that time, a judge at Ajaccio, a little white city on the edge of a bay which is surrounded by high mountains. The majority of the cases which came up before me concerned vendettas. There were some that are superb, dramatic, ferocious, heroic. We find there the most beautiful causes for revenge of which one could dream, enmities hundreds of years old, quieted for a time but never extinguished; abominable stratagems, murders becoming massacres and almost deeds of glory. For two years I heard of nothing but the price of blood, of this terrible Corsican prejudice which compels revenge for insults meted out to the offending person and all his descendants and relatives. I had seen old men, children, cousins murdered; my head was full of these stories.

'One day I learned that an Englishman had just hired a little villa at the end of the bay for several years. He had brought with him a French servant, whom he had engaged on the way at Marseilles.

'Soon this peculiar person, living alone, only going out to hunt and fish, aroused a widespread interest. He never spoke to any one, never went to the town, and every morning he would practice for an hour or so with his revolver and rifle.

'Legends were built up around him. It was said that he was some high personage, fleeing from his fatherland for political reasons; then it was affirmed that he was in hiding after having committed some abominable crime. Some particularly horrible circumstances were even mentioned.

'In my judicial position I thought it necessary to get some information about this man, but it was impossible to learn anything. He called himself Sir John Rowell.

'I therefore had to be satisfied with watching him as closely as I could, but I could see nothing suspicious about his actions.

'However, as rumours about him were growing and becoming more widespread, I decided to try to see this stranger myself, and I began to hunt regularly in the neighbourhood of his grounds.

'For a long time I watched without finding an opportunity. At last it came to me in the shape of a partridge which I shot and killed right in front of the Englishman. My dog fetched it for me, but, taking the bird, I went at once to Sir John Rowell and, begging his pardon, asked him to accept it.

'He was a big man, with red hair and beard, very tall, very broad, a kind of calm and polite Hercules. He had nothing of the so-called British stiffness, and in a broad English accent he thanked me warmly for my attention. At the end of a month we had had five or six conversations.

'One night, at last, as I was passing before his door, I saw him in the garden, seated astride a chair, smoking his pipe. I bowed and he invited me to come in and have a glass of beer. I needed no urging.

'He received me with the most punctilious English courtesy, sang the praises of France and of Corsica, and declared that he was quite in love with this country.

'Then, with great caution and under the guise of a vivid interest, I asked him a few questions about his life and his plans. He answered without embarrassment, telling me that he had travelled a great deal in Africa, in the Indies, in America. He added, laughing: "I have had many adventures."

'Then I turned the conversation on hunting, and he gave me the most curious details on hunting the hippopotamus, the tiger, the elephant and even the gorilla.

'I said, "Are all these animals dangerous?"

'He smiled, "Oh, no! Man is the worst."

'And he laughed a good broad laugh, the wholesome laugh of a contented Englishman.

"I have also frequently been man-hunting."

'Then he began to talk about weapons, and he invited me to come in and see different makes of guns.

'His parlour was draped in black, black silk embroidered in gold. Big yellow flowers, as brilliant as fire, were worked on the dark material.

'He said, "It is a Japanese material."

'But in the middle of the widest panel a strange thing attracted my attention. A black object stood out against a square of red velvet. I went up to it; it was a hand, a human hand. Not the clean white hand of a skeleton, but a dried black hand, with yellow nails, the muscles exposed and traces of old blood on the bones, which were cut off as clean as though it had been chopped off with an axe, near the middle of the forearm.

'Around the wrist, an enormous iron chain, riveted and soldered to this unclean member, fastened it to the wall by a ring, strong enough to hold an elephant in leash.

'I asked, "What is that?"

'The Englishman answered quietly, "That is my best enemy. It comes from America, too. The bones were severed by a sword and the skin cut off with a sharp stone and dried in the sun for a week."

'I touched these human remains, which must have belonged to a giant. The uncommonly long fingers were attached by enormous tendons which still had pieces of skin hanging to them in places. This hand was terrible to see; it made one think of some savage vengeance.

'I said, "This man must have been very strong."

'The Englishman answered quietly, "Yes, but I was stronger than he. I put on this chain to hold him."

'I thought that he was joking. I said, "This chain is useless now, the hand won't run away."

'Sir John Rowell answered seriously, "It always wants to go away. This chain is needed."

'I glanced at him quickly, questioning his face, and I asked myself, "Is he an insane man or a practical joker?"

'But his face remained inscrutable, calm and friendly. I turned to other subjects, and admired his rifles.

'However, I noticed that he kept three loaded revolvers in the room, as though constantly in fear of some attack.

'I paid him several calls. Then I did not go any more. People had become used to his presence; everybody had lost interest in him.

'A whole year rolled by. One morning, towards the end of November, my servant awoke me and announced that Sir John Rowell had been murdered during the night.

'Half an hour later I entered the Englishman's house, together with the police commissioner and the captain of the *gendarmes*. The servant, bewildered and in despair, was crying before the door. At first I suspected this man, but he was innocent.'

'The guilty party could never be found.

'On entering Sir John's parlour, I noticed the body, stretched out on its back, in the middle of the room.

'His vest was torn, the sleeve of his jacket had been pulled off, everything pointed to a violent struggle.

'The Englishman had been strangled! His face was black, swollen and frightful, and seemed to express a terrible fear. He held something between his teeth, and his neck, pierced by five or six holes which looked as though they had been made by some iron instrument, was covered with blood.

'A physician joined us. He examined the finger marks on the neck for a long time and then made this strange announcement, "It looks as though he had been strangled by a skeleton."

'A cold chill seemed to run down my back, and I looked over to where I had formerly seen the terrible hand. It was no longer there. The chain was hanging down, broken.

'I bent over the dead man and, in his contracted mouth, I found one of the fingers of this vanished hand, cut—or rather sawed off by the teeth down to the second knuckle.

'Then the investigation began. Nothing could be discovered. No door, window or piece of furniture had been forced. The two watch dogs had not been aroused from their sleep.

'Here, in a few words, is the testimony of the servant:

'For a month his master had seemed excited. He had received many letters, which he would immediately burn.

'Often, in a fit of passion which approached madness, he had taken a switch and struck wildly at this dried hand riveted to the wall, and which had disappeared, no one knows how, at the very hour of the crime.

'He would go to bed very late and carefully lock himself in. He always kept weapons within reach. Often at night he would talk loudly, as though he were quarrelling with someone.

'That night, somehow, he had made no noise, and it was only on going to open the windows that the servant had found Sir John murdered. He suspected no one.

'I communicated what I knew of the dead man to the judges and public officials. Throughout the whole island a minute investigation was carried on. Nothing could be found out.

'One night, about three months after the crime, I had a terrible nightmare. I seemed to see the horrible hand running over my curtains and walls like an immense scorpion or spider. Three times I awoke, three times I went to sleep again; three times I saw the hideous object galloping round my room and moving its fingers like legs.

'The following day the hand was brought me, found in the cemetery, on the grave of Sir John Rowell, who had been buried there because we had been unable to find his family. The first finger was missing.

'Ladies, there is my story. I know nothing more.'

The women, deeply stirred, were pale and trembling. One of them exclaimed: 'But that is neither a climax nor an explanation! We will be unable to sleep unless you give us your opinion of what had occurred.'

The judge smiled severely: 'Oh! Ladies, I shall certainly spoil your terrible dreams. I simply believe that the legitimate owner of the hand was not dead, that he came to get it with his remaining one. But I don't know how. It was a kind of vendetta.'

One of the women murmured: 'No, it can't be that.'

And the judge, still smiling, said: 'Didn't I tell you that my explanation would not satisfy you?'

A supernatural story conveys a sense of the uncanny and inexplicable.

41

MONDAY OR TUESDAY

VIRGINIA WOOLF

Lazy and indifferent, shaking space easily from his wings, knowing his way, the heron passes over the church beneath the sky. White and distant, absorbed in itself, endlessly the sky covers and uncovers, moves and remains. A lake? Blot the shores of it out! A mountain? Oh, perfect—the sun gold on its slopes. Down that falls. Ferns then, or white feathers, for ever and ever.

Desiring truth, awaiting it, laboriously distilling a few words, forever desiring—(a cry starts to the left, another to the right. Wheels strike divergently. Omnibuses conglomerate in conflict) for ever desiring—(the clock asseverates with twelve distinct strokes that it is midday; light sheds gold scales; children swarm)—for ever desiring truth. Red is the dome; coins hang on the trees; smoke trails from the chimneys; bark, shout, cry 'Iron for sale'—and truth?

Radiating to a point men's feet and women's feet, black or gold-encrusted—(This foggy weather—Sugar? No, thank you—the commonwealth of the future)—the firelight darting and making the room red, save for the black figures and their bright eyes, while outside a van discharges, Miss Thingummy drinks tea at her desk, and plate-glass preserves fur coats.

Flaunted, leaf-light, drifting at corners, blown across the wheels, silver-splashed, home or not home, gathered, scattered, squandered in separate scales, swept up, down, torn, sunk, assembled—and truth?

Now to recollect by the fireside on the white square of marble. From ivory depths words rising shed their blackness, blossom and penetrate. Fallen the book; in the flame, in the smoke, in the momentary sparks—or now voyaging, the marble square pendant, minarets beneath and the Indian seas, while space rushes blue and stars glint—truth? or now, content with closeness?

Lazy and indifferent the heron returns; the sky veils her stars; then bares them.

∞

A creative collage of light and darkness, seeing and non-seeing!